The Grey Ghost:
The Jeweled Kiss Mysteries

By

Nicholas Cara

Copyright © 2017 Nicholas Cara
All rights reserved.
ISBN-13: 9798336093629

We are reaching the middle innings of the game but just picked up two very promising draft picks, Thomas and Amelia.
This book is dedicated to every swing at the ball, diving catch and tip of the hat you brighten all of our lives with every day.

CONTENTS

PART ONE: A VILLAINOUS CALLING CARD 1
PROLOGUE 1
CHAPTER ONE 5
CHAPTER TWO 10
CHAPTER THREE 17
CHAPTER FOUR 25
CHAPTER FIVE 33
CHAPTER SIX 40
CHAPTER SEVEN 44
CHAPTER EIGHT 49

PART TWO: GRAPPLING ON MULTIPLE FRONTS 55
CHAPTER NINE 57
CHAPTER TEN 65
CHAPTER ELEVEN 74
CHAPTER TWELVE 81

PART THREE: A JEWEL-ENCRUSTED SURPRISE 101
CHAPTER THIRTEEN 103
CHAPTER FOURTEEN 114
CHAPTER FIFTEEN 122
CHAPTER SIXTEEN 128
CHAPTER SEVENTEEN 135
CHAPTER EIGHTEEN 140
CHAPTER NINETEEN 145

PART FOUR: THE BONDS OF FAMILY 151
CHAPTER TWENTY 153
CHAPTER TWENTY-ONE 162
CHAPTER TWENTY-TWO 166
CHAPTER TWENTY-THREE 172
CHAPTER TWENTY-FOUR 181
CHAPTER TWENTY-FIVE 188
CHAPTER TWENTY-SIX 192
CHAPTER TWENTY-SEVEN 201
PART FIVE: ONLY A GHOST OF A CHANCE 209
CHAPTER TWENTY-EIGHT 211
CHAPTER TWENTY-NINE 218
CHAPTER THIRTY 225
CHAPTER THIRTY-ONE 231
CHAPTER THIRTY-TWO 239
CHAPTER THIRTY-THREE 245

Another special thanks to Mr. Dan Paloski,

editor aficionado, friend extraordinaire.

Thank you to my team of Ghost Readers

Austin Decker

Jolene Mastramico

Kimberly Mastramico

PART ONE: A VILLAINOUS CALLING CARD

PROLOGUE

The golden bracelet sparkled in the display case, twinkling as a star would in the night sky at the bearded face of Captain James Robinson. Scanning the case, the captain tried his best not to look as if one of the shiny bobbles would be his salvation, like those real stars were to sailing captains of old. He knew if he walked out of this store and back to his house without a gift for Gertrude on her birthday... again... then he might as well get comfortable on his office couch for the next couple of nights.

"Come on old man, focus," Robinson internally barked at himself. *"You blew it at Christmas so time to open that dusty wallet."*

"Can I help you Sir?" a gray bearded man sporting a buttoned down white shirt and vest asked out loud from behind the display.

Looking at the salesman, Robinson eyed the small pin attached to the tweed vest, read the name "Christopher - Store Manager" and figured the window shopping was over; it was time to lay his cards on the table. This guy was about his age and possibly married himself, so maybe he could relate to the corner Robinson had backed himself into.

"I hope you can... here's the deal..." Robinson started explaining the situation to the store manager. His hope for a deal disappeared in an instant as Christopher flashed a cat-like smile his way.

"Okay sir, let's see if we can find a follow-up act to this Christmas disaster. Here's my card, sir," Christopher replied handing the captain a white card with his name, position and the store's name before looking down at the case, the smile never leaving his downturned face.

"You know, Gertie isn't the flashiest gal. She usually likes to dress the occasion," Robinson stated, eyes widening as he noticed Christopher's hand start to pull some jewelry from the left side of the case containing items much higher in price than the bracelet he had originally been eyeing.

"Of course sir, however from what you said this gift isn't really about what she'd normally expect, is it? It's more of a second act to the story that *you* started at Christmas, if I may sir," Christopher began. "And sir, I've always found that the only way to jump start a successor to a… *good* story… is to come swinging out of the gate! Go BIG or go home I always say."

"Yeah…I bet you do…" Robinson grimaced, peering at the tiny price tag attached to the new bracelet's latch.

As Christopher started his well-practiced pitch of the real value of the bracelet, Robinson immediately started scanning the case again for the original bracelet he had been looking at earlier. He wasn't sure who the manager thought he was, but there was no way a police captain could afford Christopher's idea of a "second act." As the captain looked for the bracelet, he saw the reflection of an unusual pair entering the shop in the display glass. The leader, a finely dressed woman of about his size, strode confidently through the door as if she owned the very air that filled the establishment. Clad in outlandish sunglasses and an elaborate scarf covering her auburn hair, the dynamic diva seemed to be hiding her appearance while at the same time screaming out to the masses for attention.

Turning her head, the woman scanned the store beaming with a glowing smile, not so different from the one Robinson had witnessed on the store manager's face; a smile of someone knowing she had the upper hand. Making her way past the security guard sitting near the door, a larger man who seemed instantly smitten with her beauty, the woman traveled out of sight past a wall separating the jewelry department and the fine clothing section of the store. Shuffling in her wake was a small, older man struggling to carry a large wrapped parcel adorned with a fancy green bow.

Turning his attention back to his own troubles with Christopher and the continuously increasing sizes of bracelets now littered atop the counter, Robinson found himself thinking back to the woman and her small helper. The captain never claimed to understand the rich and their elaborate ways, yet something about the lady's smile unnerved him. Before he could shake the feeling and start calculating the number of packed lunches he would have to make himself to even attempt to pay off this gift, the captain heard someone from the back yell, *"Stop thief!" "Somebody stop her!"*

Turning his head back toward the door, Robinson saw the large security guard make a grab for the mysterious woman's small compatriot who had been making a break for the exit. As the guard tackled the older man, who was no longer burdened with the large package he had been carrying earlier, the security guard was suddenly grabbed from behind by the mysterious woman. Appearing faster than Robinson would've believed, the woman now clad in a long fur coat, struck effortlessly and threw the guard into the showcase near Robinson, sending both the bracelets on its counter and the store manager flailing to the ground in a hail of broken glass.

"Oh clumsy me," the fur clad thief purred with a giddy laugh.

Now within arm's reach of the dynamic woman, Robinson attempted to grab her shoulder, keeping himself prepared for what the trained fighter might have up her sleeve.

"Okay Miss, that will be enough of..." Robinson started but was cut off by his own shock. As his hand reached the mink fur of her stolen coat, it completely passed through it as if the coat and THE GIRL were made of air!

Taken aback, Robinson was dumbfounded as the girl slowly turned her head in his direction. Peering at him through her shaded glasses, the dynamo flashed a sinister smile, as if his surprise was the most amusing thing she'd see all day.

"My dear Captain, we just met," the thief sweetly said to Robinson. "And I'm not that kind of girl..."

Robinson never saw the backhand slap coming until it connected with his chin. Instead of the sharp sting the captain expected from such a blow,

Robinson was met with the impact one would expect from the right cross or left hook of a prized fighter. The attack sent him flying in a heap next to the store manager and security guard.

Trying to clear his head, the captain looked back at his attacker. As if daring one of the three men to test his luck again, she slowly reached down to pick up one of the store manager's scattered cards. Bringing the card up to her face, the thief quickly kissed the card with her now rosy red lips.

"Something to remember me by, big guy," she purred down at the captain.

Flinging the card at him, Robinson was startled as the plain stock card jammed itself into the wooden wall next to his head as if it had been a throwing knife. Looking back, he was equally shocked to find that the woman and her older helper had vanished from the shop. Peering at the wedged card next to his head, Robinson squinted at the lipstick mark left by the criminal. Instead of the red lipstick smear he would've expected to find on the card, Robinson was perplexed to find an imprint of two female lips made up incredibly of a multitude of small, shiny red jewels.

CHAPTER ONE

"Okay let's stand you up here, but take it... slowly," said the baritone voice, followed by the outstretched hand.

Joe Bevine looked at the offered palm of the older, wispy-haired Dr. Henry Segal. Bracing his opposite hand on the wooden armrest, Joe gripped Segal's arm and was mildly amused at the strength behind the family physician's grip. Joe had long ago conceded that most of his parent's generation really never got older; they just grew a few more wrinkles. With a quick push and heave from his old friend, Joe lifted himself from the seat and... nothing... absolutely nothing happened.

Looking around at the small gathering of spectators made up of his parents, Stanley and Vera Bevine, his best friend and partner on the Capstone police squad, Patsy Thomas, and of course his longtime girlfriend Kate Stone, Joe noticed the silent but beaming smiles directed his way. Smiling back, Joe looked at each of them and took notice of how different they all looked... how different everything in the house around him looked at eye level. Slowing lowering his gaze to the floor, which seemed so far away now, Joe shot another smile back at his crowd. The realization that Joe was standing completely on his own really started to hit home.

This wasn't an illusion or a wondrous dream, and the only magic involved could be based on one's opinion of Kate's amazing ingenuity. A year ago this simple action was beyond any fantasy he dared daydream about, but now Joe Bevine was a man of two legs again, even if one might be made of steel, wood, and springs.

"So far, so good. You didn't immediately fall on your bum," Dr. Segal said from behind him as he began to inspect Joe's lower left leg. "How's the pain near your knee?"

"Not bad, more sore than a pain, but a lot better than last time," Joe answered. "The strap around the stomach is pulling the most."

"Let me see that," Kate said, walking over and starting to lift Joe's shirt to inspect the leather strap. "Doc, can you please give me some of that blue padding?"

Loosening the strap to rewrap the padding around it, Kate started peppering Joe with her usual set of questions about the prosthetic that Joe had become accustomed to. "Is it holding the weight better near your upper torso or is it simply digging into you?"

"It's better, especially around the knee area..." Joe started to answer.

"Did you feel the joint stiffen as you stood up or was it...?"

"How about we let the boy try out the car before we start asking him how the engine works, my dear," Dr. Segal interrupted Kate as she finished strapping the rewrapped leather belt around Joe's waist.

Joe was happy the Doc had spoken up. He was dying just sitting there, waiting to try this new leg out. He was amazed by the advancements that Kate and her team at Capstone State University had made to the wooden peg leg the U.S. Army had sent him months ago. Having lost his leg directly under the left knee, Joe had been limited to fitting the simple peg leg to the bottom of his knee and then strapping the rest of the apparatus to his thigh. With no joint at his knee, Joe had been reduced to walking as a robotic man, his left leg a solid tree trunk that caused him excruciating pain at the bottom of his knee after only a few steps.

However, having a genius engineer and now the youngest Adjunct Professor at CSU as a girlfriend did come with a few perks. Seeing the flaw in the overall design, Kate took it upon herself to redesign the prosthetic for Joe. Her original design for the leg was such a step forward in the field, the military had recently started to partner with CSU's engineering department to fund her small team's research. With the war going on, Joe knew there were more men who could use something like this, but he was selfishly happy that Kate had built it for him and that he would be getting the first shot at it.

Working on the articulation for weeks, Kate and her team had crafted a proposed system of ball joints and springs allowing for his leg's full range of motion while still relieving the full pressure on the bottom of his knee. Kate's concept was a quarter body harness that distributed the force of every step throughout Joe's lower torso instead of centering it at the damaged area under his knee.

Like everything lately in Joe Bevine's life, the contraption looked straight out of a comic book or off the screen from a sci-fi serial; but through continued improvements by Kate and her team at CSU, it started working like a dream.

"Let's take this thing out for a spin," Joe said looking at his smiling girl.

Lifting his left foot slightly off the ground, Joe slowly moved it forward. After waiting for the artificial joints to follow along with the motion, he placed it solidly on the floor a few inches in front of him. Shifting his weight to the prosthetic, Joe cringed slightly as a small, sharp pain shot up his thigh. Ignoring it as best he could, he completed the step with his right foot. A small muffled cheer came from his mother, which caused a bark from the little brown-haired beagle Belle, who had wandered behind the family. Laughing at the little chaos, Joe took another step toward the group, again feeling the sharp pain in his thigh.

"Let's see my two step first," Joe said out loud, stopping Kate from coming over. He could tell that she hadn't been fooled at his attempt to mask the pain in his leg.

Taking a step to the right, Joe moved his left leg backward and to the side. Pivoting his left leg to turn around, he heard a small creak as the prosthetic leg's interior spin system bent as it was designed, allowing Joe to quickly turn in place.

"Sounds like you need some oil, Tin-Man," Patsy called out from behind him.

"When a man's an empty kettle, he should be on his mettle…" Joe hummed back.

"He needs more than just oil," Kate interrupted as she bent down in front of Joe to look at the engineered leg. "How bad is the pain when you put your weight on it? If you had to rate it from one to 10?"

"What did I tell you last time?" Joe asked.

"Last time you said it was a six, but I think you were lying tough guy," Kate answered.

"Okay, let's say it is a real six this time, more a sharp pain in the middle than overall pain, but not as bad as before," Joe admitted.

"Well, it's a step in the right direction," Kate offhandedly remarked.

"Kathryn," Stanley said, grabbing Belle by the collar to keep her from rushing at the two. "Terrible jokes are Patsy's area of expertise. You stick with the engineering."

The laughs from everyone slightly eased the tension in the room. They had all been disappointed when the leg hadn't worked perfectly. Kate had been toying with it for weeks trying to get the proper system of mechanisms integrated into the leg to allow for the correct mobility while still painlessly supporting Joe as it absorbed the weight and impact of walking. Today's test had been promising, but there was still a lot of work to do.

"Well, how about we don't wear the boy out too quickly," Dr. Segal advised.

"Actually Doc, I want to play around with this for a while, build a little callus on the bottom of the knee and toughen it up a little," Joe countered.

"Hon, I'm not sure if that's wise. Your leg will be…" Kate started to say before being cut off by Joe.

"Sweetie, I'll be fine," he said. "I just want to walk around the house a little. You know it's terribly mean to take the kid's toy away from him on Christmas right after he unwraps it."

"All right, well at least use this on your left side," Kate relented, handing him one of his crutches that had been propped up against the front door.

"It will relieve the pressure on your knee so you can walk around longer before it gets really tired."

"Okay warden,"

"Joseph, don't be hard headed and listen to Kate," Vera called out, walking away toward the kitchen. "She's the engineer and you're not."

Taking the crutch from Kate, Joe couldn't miss the "listen to your mother" smile on her face. The silent moment was interrupted by the clanging ring of the kitchen telephone. Joe's mother answered it.

"Hello..." Vera said listening for a second before she called out into the living room. "Here Patsy take this. It's the station."

Wondering why the station would be calling him at home on a Saturday morning, Joe, using both the crutch and new leg, started to make his way toward the kitchen as Patsy answered the phone.

"Hello?" Patsy said into the receiver. "Yeah, it's Thomas... I know but.... but... well why can't... all right, tell the Cap we're headed there now... okay bye"

As Joe entered the kitchen, Patsy answered the unasked question he knew his partner was thinking. "That was Judy. There was some big hub-bub over at Fulcher's Emporium last night that they want us to investigate."

"I thought the two of you were off today," Joe's father called out from the living room after overhearing Patsy.

"We are," Joe said. "Why are they calling us in, Patsy? Peck and Jones have the desk this morning. I even think Robinson was going to be putting some overtime in today since he took off early last night."

"That's the thing . . . the captain was a witness at the incident last night and is asking for us personally to come in," Patsy replied, walking toward the back kitchen door and plucking his bowler from the hat rack.

CHAPTER TWO

"I told you, I have no idea why the captain wanted us to come down here. Judy never spells anything out to anyone, especially me," Patsy answered, opening his door outside of Fulcher's Emporium. "It sounded like a simple smash and grab from all the chatter over the radio. Even Jones and Peck couldn't mess that up."

As the two walked toward the front door, Patsy could see the struggle Joe was having with his prosthetic. Even with the aid of one of his crutches, Joe was making every step look Herculean with the grimace on his face.

"Leg giving out on you already?" Patsy asked, concerned.

"It gets really sore after a while at the bottom of the knee," Joe replied through a clenched jaw. "But the new design is working better. I'm just going to have to get used to it."

"Well, Kate told you not to take that thing out of the house," Patsy replied, opening the door for his partner. "Right now your face looks like you are walking barefoot over broken glass."

"No, I thankfully remembered to wear my shoes," Joe countered while looking in the emporium. "Will you look at this place?"

As they entered, the sight before them was a chaotic mess. Two broken display cases lay strewn across the showroom floor surrounded by shards of broken glass and splinters of polished wood. However, all of the scattered valuables were untouched. The once immaculate room, adorned by a collection of what Joe assumed were reproduction paintings, was empty except for a police photographer recording the scene.

"Someone definitely thought they earned themselves a special little something," Patsy said, looking at the wrecked shop over the shoulder of the photographer, a blond female officer, as she lined up a shot of one of the destroyed display cases. "Don't get any ideas, Kennedy," Patsy jokingly whispered.

The female photographer slanted her gaze back at the larger man and replied curtly, "If I grabbed one of these bracelets, Thomas, you arresting me would be the closest to a second date you'll ever get."

Feigning a wounded look, Patsy turned his head to the loud voice calling out to them from the back room.

"Thomas, Bevine… about time you two decided to make an appearance," Robinson bellowed, coming into the front showroom. "Okay people, I need the room. Yes that means you too, Kennedy. You can finish those pictures after."

"See you around, Rose," Patsy smiled as Kennedy picked up her equipment and started for the door.

"In your dreams, Thomas," Kennedy replied as the outside door slammed shut.

"I take it Saturday didn't go well," Joe commented, limping up to his partner.

"I tell you Joseph, no girl, no matter how pretty, is worth all the fuss she made last Saturday when she found out where we were going," Patsy replied, rolling his eyes.

"Well I doubt Kate would've been that excited either if on our first date I wanted to take her to…" Joe started before getting cut off.

"May I interrupt you two for a second with a little police work, or do you need to talk about Thomas's nonexistent love life all day?" Robinson interjected.

"No problem captain, what's the story?" Patsy replied. "Judy gave us the cliff notes on the way here, sounded like a simple robbery."

"There was nothing simple about it. I'm not filing the official report on this robbery until I figure out if this is a bigger problem or simply me going out of my skull," Robinson replied, laying his hands on one of the remaining display cases. Lowering his eyes at the two officers as if to study their reactions to his news, Robinson took a long breath before continuing, "That's why I called you two here."

"Captain, what's going on?" Joe asked a little uneasy at the captain's stare.

"Out of all the boys on the squad, you two by far have had the most interaction with our fair city's little vigilante," Robinson stated, slowly measuring every word.

"The Grey Ghost..." Joe replied nodding, confirming Robinson's statement, but silently hating his choice of the word "vigilante."

"Yeah, of all the collars associated with this Ghost's activity you two have been either involved or extremely lucky to be around to be the arresting officers," Robinson continued. "And that doesn't even mention the craziness on the Trumbull last year."

Both Joe and Patsy stood silently waiting for the next shoe to drop. Neither was sure where this was going, but both worried where the line of bread crumbs Robinson was following could lead him.

"And mind you, I haven't pushed either of you on this because while the department's official policy is to bring in this 'person' on sight, I can't honestly forget who literally pulled my fat out of the fire last year. But things may have changed last night to a point where I can't keep quiet about things anymore," Robinson continued. "So I'm asking you a simple question and I need a straight answer here."

Joe audibly swallowed, fearing he had figured out the Grey Ghost's identity.

"From your interaction with the Grey Ghost, can either of you definitely state whether or not he is a man or a woman?" Robinson asked.

Both officers stood for a second staring at Robinson, then looking at each other as the absurdness of the question, at least to them, dawned on them.

"Cap…mercy me…ha-ha" Patsy answered first, as both tried desperately to stifle a laugh almost to the point of tears. "I think I can speak for the both of us to make a confident guess that the Grey Ghost is a fella."

"It's not a laughing matter, boys," Robinson bit back, annoyed at his officers' reaction. "I was seconds from putting out an APB for him, listing him as a suspect for both robbery and assault before I thought of calling in you two."

"Captain, from what we heard over the radio on the way here, a woman with a single older accomplice pulled this heist. What aren't you telling us?" Joe asked, confused as to why his captain would even think the Grey Ghost was involved. "How could the Grey Ghost be involved with her? He's always been on the level with us."

Robinson started to walk the two through the events of the robbery, elaborating beyond the radio chatter when he reached the mysterious thief's exit from the building. Joe was shocked nearly out of his shoes when Robinson explained his hand going directly through the female thief's shoulder.

"Captain, are you sure?" Joe asked, hoping there had been some sort of mistake. "I mean everything happened so fast; are you sure you simply didn't miss?"

"Yeah Captain, if this girl was that well trained maybe she's just extremely fast…" Patsy added, his voice almost a plea for an easier answer to this amazing situation, completely understanding the ramifications of this series of events if they were true.

"Thomas, my hand literally sat on her shoulder blade for a second or two before I understood what I was seeing," Robinson replied, quickly squashing the simplified explanation. "And if that doesn't convince you something wicked this way comes, this definitely will."

Walking to the back room where a display of fine mink furs was located, Robinson continued over to a side display closed off with a dark velvet curtain. Pulling back the curtain, Robinson revealed an exterior window display case full of mannequins adorned with high-priced fur coats. All of the displays faced the outside window visible from the street. Sticking out from the display was a large white box decorated with an outlandish green ribbon and bow.

"This was the large box the thief's older accomplice was struggling with as they entered the store," Robinson explained, "which makes this even more interesting…"

"Why Cap? Any idea what's inside?" Patsy asked, eyeing the large box.

"Why don't you open it up Thomas, and take a look?" Robinson simply replied.

Patsy shrugged and reached out to delicately grip the lid of the box when he was completely thrown as first his fingers and then his whole hand passed effortlessly through the box as if it wasn't there!

"Oh that's not good… really not good," Joe said, taking a step back from the sight, that even with his knowledge of the otherworldly powers of the Grey Ghost, was an impossible scene.

Curtis was having a terrible day. His supervisor was in one of those moods and had decided that pestering him repeatedly about sales from the moment he had clocked in was a brilliant way of increasing revenue. At the moment he was the sole warm body working the front of Rachel's Hat Boutique, and if his supervisor stayed in the back room working on paperwork until the end of his shift, he would simply count his lucky stars.

"I can't simply pull a girl out of one of these ugly things to buy his tripe," Curtis grumbled to himself as he cleaned a front shelf near the register. "He wants better sales. Well, get better merchandise. There is a reason these ugly things just collect dust."

Walking over to a side wall display, Curtis grabbed a white cloche off one of the display heads, gave it a quick dusting and flopped it back. "No matter how much he wants me to, I'm not going to sell one of these horrible, cheap pieces of trash if I don't have to," he emphatically added, repositioning the white cloche on the display.

"Well that's extraordinary news my dear young man," a voice sweetly purred from behind him.

The salesman quickly spun around, barely catching himself from falling backward. He had been certain he was alone in the showroom, but suddenly out of nowhere was the owner of the sweet voice standing before him. Peering through a pair of outlandish sunglasses, the striking, beautiful redhead smiled at him as she clutched her fur coat with both gloved hands. Curtis immediately knew this was the sale his boss was crying about. Everything about this woman screamed money. The fur coat had to cost more than he made in a month, and the scarf around her head had to be European from the intricate designs, maybe even French, which with the war going on was almost impossible to get nowadays which meant MONEY.

"Hello Miss, please excuse me, I didn't hear you...," Curtis started before noticing her companion, an elderly gentleman behind her holding a large, white box wrapped in a green bow.

"Must be on a shopping spree with Dad. How'd they both get through the door without ringing the bell?" Curtis thought.

"... or your friend come in," Curtis continued, "How may I help you?"

"Oh my dear, it's refreshing to hear a young man not corrupted by his supervisor's gluttony and greed, with things being as they are these days..." the woman said smiling at Curtis, lowering her head to peer at him over her glasses, emerald eyes flashing at him above the brown rims.

Curtis's face fell. The finely dressed woman had overheard him talking to himself and what he had said about the Boutique's lower class of merchandise. This had multiple ways of ending badly for him now if any of this ever got back to his supervisor.

"I... I was simply discussing with myself how the best thing for every customer is for them to...to..." he quickly stammered, trying to walk himself out of the hole he had dug for himself. Before he could finish, the woman laid a gloved finger smoothly over his mouth cutting him off.

"Shhh... My sweet thing, we'll keep this all between us... promise... I'm not here for those small trifles anyways," the woman said. "Let's say

I'm here for more of a statement piece, something that will REALLY catch a fella's eye. It will probably carry a price tag a little higher than those... *things*."

With that and a casual wave the woman turned toward the back case where the high class, high priced hats were locked under glass. Curtis's hopes started to rise as it started to seem that even with his foot firmly planted in his mouth this situation was still going to work out for him. Walking to the back case, he unlocked the door, all the while eyeing the green pearl inlaid wide brim. It was by far the most expensive piece in the store. If he could sell that today he would be on easy street with his supervisor for weeks.

"Miss, I can see you are looking for the best of the best. We both know that quality and workmanship of such pieces does come with a higher cost. However, I can see that you, my dear lady, have a fine eye for..." Curtis started his practiced pitch before being cut off again with another gloved finger to his lips.

"My dear..." the silky smooth voice cut in, her sparkling purple lipstick catching his eye. "I'm sorry, but it seems we might have started off on the wrong foot...you see... I didn't step into this store planning to *PAY* for anything..."

CHAPTER THREE

"Oh that's not good at all..." Joe mumbled to himself, watching Patsy fail repeatedly to take hold of the untouchable present.

Limping over to Patsy and the captain, Joe placed his hand on the display window's base, testing the carpeted wooden floor with his palm.

"Solid enough," Joe thought to himself, sliding his hand palm down along the base toward the box until, like Patsy's, his outstretched fingers slid directly through the box's side.

"So that's what it feels like," Joe mused, thinking of the times friends and foes had fallen through him in his adventures as the Grey Ghost.

Joe continued sliding his palm forward until his wrist came into contact with the package. At this, Joe looked up at Patsy catching his partner's eye, a quick raise of his eyebrow at the captain was all the communication his longtime partner needed.

"So Captain, you said that the older man with her was carrying this box when he came in?" Patsy asked, pulling Robinson's focus away from the display case.

As the two started going over the details again, Joe tried taking advantage of the opportunity. Joe continued sliding his hand, initially encountering no resistance until he suddenly felt his watch containing the sliver of the Spartan Cloak make a solid purchase on the cardboard exterior.

Pushing harder, Joe actually started to feel a heating sensation from the interaction.

"There's some sort of reaction when the two meet..." Joe thought, pulling his hand away from the box, trying to not push his luck with the captain being so close.

"Captain," Joe said, "Did the older perp wear gloves while carrying this?"

"Honestly, I don't remember any on him when he was trying to bolt for the door," Robinson replied. "But it's not like we would be able to lift prints off the thing; the powder would fall right through it. According to the clerk the older perp brought the package over, laid it carefully in front of this curtain, and pushed it under while he was conversing with the woman."

"Did he have a description of the older perp?" Patsy asked. "Anything about him that would explain how he was able to carry the impossible box here?"

"Just a height and guess on the types of clothes he was wearing," Robinson replied. "He was too distracted by the woman. She was definitely enough of a distraction."

"Better not let Mrs. Robinson hear you talk like that, Cap," Patsy chuckled.

"Thomas..." Captain Robinson started before his rebuke was cut off by Officer Jones running into the room.

"Captain!"

"What is it, Jones?" Robinson asked.

"A call just came in through the wire, sir," Jones started explaining. "A robbery was just reported at Rachel's Hat Boutique by two suspects matching the descriptions of the perps you reported encountering here."

"Rachel's? Isn't that just a few blocks up the street?" Joe asked.

"Nearly across town, they moved a few months back remember," Patsy answered, heading for the front door.

"I guess she needed a nice hat to match her new fur coat," Joe mumbled as the two detectives made their way to their cruiser.

"So there's no way you could do that?" Patsy asked, pulling the cruiser to the curb outside of Rachel's Hat Boutique.

"No bud, really, Kate and I have been trying for months to find the extent of what I can do with this sliver," Joe replied, shaking his right wrist. "I always have to be in contact with whatever I am trying to make intangible. Once I let go of the object, it becomes completely solid within a few seconds."

"So leaving a ghostly present like the one back there isn't possible unless the doll was still standing there touching it," Patsy muttered to himself. "And from the way the salesman, guard, and even the captain were talking about her, I'd think we'd notice."

"More than likely partner," Joe replied, opening the car door and hopping on his right leg to situate himself on his prosthetic and crutch. "The only thing I know for a fact is every time I think I'm starting to get a handle on this stuff I find out I'm usually wrong."

"So what happens if something you're 'ghosting' turns solid inside of something else?" Patsy asked as he walked around the car.

"Don't ask, it gets really messy," Joe replied, limping into the Boutique.

Joe's initial impression of the Boutique was far different from the scene they encountered at the Emporium. There weren't any broken cases, shattered glass littering the floor, or destruction of any kind. If someone wanted to label the earlier robbery as a "smash and grab," then this had been simply a "grab." Without the call to the precinct, Joe would've been hard pressed to even know that something was amiss in the store, except for the garishly large white box wrapped in a green bow sitting on the floor in the main foyer of the showroom.

"She just walked over, tried the hat on, smiled, and walked out," a store attendant at the counter explained to the patrolman taking his initial report.

"Just walked out, you say?" the patrolman asked, eyeing the salesman.

"She give you that before or after she walked out, buddy?"

Seeing the hardened gaze of the police officer, the salesman touched his left cheek and immediately recoiled from it as if his hand had been bitten. Rushing to one of the wall-mounted mirrors in the shop, the salesman cried out when he witnessed his reflection.

Joe limped over to the distraught man to see what all the fuss was about.

"What did she do to me?" the young man exclaimed, tearing up as he saw his own reflection.

Getting closer to the man, Joe was finally able to see what was causing his distress. There on his left cheek was a bright purple smear of lipstick. It was the kind of mark that a fella better have a good explanation for the Missus when he got home. In this case, however, the smear would need more explanation than that.

"Okay kid, hold still a second," Joe said, grabbing the young man's chin to stop him from moving so he could get a good look at the mark.

Joe realized his initial impression of the mark had been wrong. It wasn't a smear of lipstick at all, it was an imprint of a woman's lips in bright purple.

"Strange…" Joe said, rubbing his thumb over the panicking salesman's cheek. As he did, Joe noted the substantial, rocky texture of the imprint. Looking down at his thumb, Joe also saw a purple shine from the point where his thumb had touched the man's cheek.

"Hey Patsy, check this out!" Joe called over his shoulder to his partner. Turning his attention back to the salesman, Joe caught the young man's name from the tag on his shirt. "Curtis, did she give you this mark before or after she tried the hat on she stole?"

"After I gave her the green wide brim, she said she loved it. She leaned in and gave me a small peck on the cheek, that's all she did officer!" Curtis insisted.

"Well get a look at this Casanova," Patsy remarked, finally making it over to the two. "Is that shiny paint or something?"

"No Patsy, this is a large collection of small, dust-sized jewels," Joe replied rubbing between his finger and thumb the few small bits that had dislodged from Curtis's cheek. "They were perfectly organized and sized on this young man's face to resemble a pair of female lips."

"And how exactly did that collection get on this kid's cheek?" Patsy asked. "That would take hours to glue on."

"The young man says our mysterious thief gave him a peck on the cheek after he helped her find a new hat, isn't that right Curtis?" Joe replied returning his gaze to the salesman.

"Well that was some peck," Patsy scoffed.

"Officer Plattsmier," Joe called out to the patrolman. "George, call it in that we need Kennedy and her camera. I want pictures of this little jeweled kiss before we get it off his cheek," Joe said, pointing to the jeweled mark before adding to Curtis, "So don't rub that, its evidence."

"Evidence of what exactly?" Patsy asked as the two made their way back to the bowed box in the middle of the showroom.

"Evidence that this crazy dame likes to leave calling cards," Joe answered. "Remember what Robinson told us about the card she threw at his head as she left the first robbery? It's the same unexplainable jeweled kiss mark."

"Different color though. You would think this stupid gift box would be enough of a calling card for the lady," Patsy added, kicking at the box only to see his foot pass through the intangible piece of evidence.

"Wow, so what you're saying is this thief, a woman, left a magic box like this one at both scenes?" a feminine voice asked from behind the two detectives. "And a kiss mark like that one too, almost as a calling card... that's amazing!"

Turning around, the two detectives took notice of the voice's owner. Leaning against the corner of the store, almost invisible behind a showcase, was a short, black-haired woman scribbling feverously in a notebook. Her hair was pulled under a brown cabby hat, the brim blocking her face as the questions continued. "And what you're saying is that the thief, this jeweled kissing thief, is running rag-shot through the city's shopping district?"

"We are not saying anything of the sort... miss?" Joe interjected.

"Cordova...Miss Lynda Cordova of the Capstone Vindicator," the small dictation machine quickly answered, looking up at the detectives with a solid stare as she quickly walked forward offering her hand.

"A news hound huh?" Patsy asked, looking at the young woman. "Aren't you a little young to be writing the crime beat, lady?"

"Yes, yes I am," Lynda replied, shooting Patsy a defiant look. "Is there a problem with that detective...detective?"

"Thomas, miss. It's Patsy Thomas..." he answered. "I'm just used to Daycie or Hay hounding us for quotes."

"Mrs. Daycie is on a leave," Lynda said adding, "I will be taking her beat for the time being."

"Well that's great for you, but how about you wait outside like all the other hawks and stop disturbing our crime scene," Patsy said, pointing to the door.

"Officer, would you confirm or deny that the jeweled mark on that man's face is similar to the one reported earlier?" Lynda asked, quickly feeling her time on the scene coming to an end.

"We are not confirming or denying anything right now Miss," Joe replied. "Officer, please escort our star reporter outside, thank you."

"Do you think there is a connection between the stolen items? What of the stores?" Lynda continued peppering as Officer Plattsmier ushered her out the front door.

"You know what partner?" Patsy asked as he watched the young reporter fall behind the roped off line outside the store. "I think I'm in love."

"You would find that one interesting," Joe replied, shaking his head. "Back to the real reason we're here if you don't mind. I wish I had a few minutes alone with this thing."

"I don't think you are going to get any privacy with that crowd of newsies forming outside," Patsy commented, lowering his voice as he added, "Maybe you should stop by a little later tonight, if you know what I mean..."

"Yeah, I think I will," Joe smirked. "I just hope our kissing bandit doesn't decide she needs shoes or a matching purse before that."

The sharp steps of the visitor echoed off the marble floor of the furnished room. The steady pattern of the woman's heels following her from the moment she entered through a hidden side door as she approached the dimly lit desk adorning the middle of the shadowed office.

"I hear you have been making quite an impression on our fair little city my dear," a smooth voice greeted her, its owner sitting just outside of the desk lamp's illumination. "The Kissing Bandit? A bit showy in my opinion, but who am I to judge results..."

The visitor stood across from the desk, staring at the faceless voice. Her reaction to the silken statement was completely masked by the large sunglasses that still covered her face.

"Nothing to say my dear?" the faceless voice asked, an almost unnaturally white smile somehow visible through the shadows. "From the report I have, you seemed to be quite the chatty little girl during your outing. Why so shy now?"

"May I see them?" the simple question was the enigmatic woman's only response.

"May I see them....SIR?" the shadowed voice replied. "We are nothing without manners, are we not my dear?"

Silence once again enveloped the room, with the grandfather clock near the main entrance taking charge of the conversation, loudly ticking its reply. As the seconds of silence increased in number, the size of the bright smile behind the desk increased, widening before the woman's eyes until finally relenting. "May I see them....sir.......please."

"Well of course my dear, all you had to do was ask," the shadowed voice replied triumphantly, the smile never leaving his face.

The small sound that the woman recognized as the pressing of a hidden button on the oak desk prompted the opening of a side door to the office.

"My good man, please escort my guest to the security room. She wishes to see one of the monitors," the shadowed voice ordered the henchman entering the room.

"No...No...I...I meant I wanted to actually see them," the female bandit interjected, her cool resolve thrown into disarray at the orders.

"Then you should've been more articulate with your request," the shadowed voice laughed back, chuckling at the distressed look he now found on the woman's face. "Now go! I have got more important things to deal with than the pathetic likes of you right now. I have a whole city to run."

As the woman spun on her heels turning to go, the shadowed voice added, "My dear, do you not appreciate my gift?"

Never turning back, the female bandit, through gritted teeth, replied, "Why thank you Lord Minos, I... appreciate your generosity."

"You're welcome my sweet," Minos replied enjoying the moment of his superiority before adding to poke the flames. "Oh and in case I failed to mention it earlier, you are looking quite fetching this evening, that new fur suits you.... very beautiful indeed."

The compliment was met with a side look and a flinch from the female bandit as if something slimy had crawled on her back. Her stare never left the seated mayor and with a quick flick of her arms, she sent the fur falling from her shoulders onto the marble floor. Without another word the woman briskly walked out of the room, the sound of her heels on the marble mixed with Minos's laughter following her out.

CHAPTER FOUR

Officer Douglas Jones flipped the rusted key to the front door of Fulcher's into his front pocket and gave it a settling pat. As the rookie on the case and much to his chagrin, he had been given the "honor" of locking up the crime scene after the lab boys finished combing the place.

It was late and he was tired. Not only had it been a long day, it had been a long Saturday, the second in a row where he had been called in for the "rookie's double shift," or what his senior partner had dubbed "good learning experiences." Muttering to himself his opinion of these "good learning experiences," Jones never thought to look down the alley next to the empty store.

If he or any other passerby had noticed the macabre nature of the dimly lit alley along their way, they might have seen a lone shadow loitering apart from its brothers. Far down the paved alley it stood, aloof from the rest of the darkness, never moving, almost waiting, as if shadows themselves could make such rational decisions. Then, with a sudden motion, the shadow bounded across the dimly lit path, moving in between the flickers of light from the dying light bulb raised above the store's side door. And just as quickly as it had appeared, the moving darkness vanished as it reached the store's exterior brick wall, only to reappear on the interior wall of Fulcher's as the heroic form of the Grey Ghost!

Strolling through the wall as if it was an everyday occurrence, the ghostly guardian produced a compact yet powerful flashlight from his overcoat. Aiming the beam downward as to not betray his presence to anyone outside, the Grey Ghost scanned the empty showroom. The unseen eyes hidden by his Spartan mask and an unearthly cloud of white gas that comprised the form of his face quickly found the back room containing the curtained showcase that Captain Robinson had shown him and Patsy earlier.

Slowly pulling the satin curtain to the side, the Grey Ghost took stock of the untouchable large gift box, still in the same spot where the Kissing Thief had left it. Drawing the thin beam of light across the bottom of the mock present, the Grey Ghost studied the bottom edge of the box where it met with the showcase floor and amazingly found nothing out of place with the magical item. No trip wires or connections of any kind, just an innocent box sitting on the carpeted showcase floor, except the hero knew this box was in no way "innocent."

His hand now affected by the magic of the Spartan Cloak, the Grey Ghost reached for the bow entwined at the top of the white box and was able to grab a hold of the green ribbon. With a quick pull the knot came loose allowing the ribbon to fall from the top of the box to the showcase floor. The magical bow did not stop there. It continued falling directly through the floor only stopping because part of the ribbon was wedged between the carpet and the bottom of the box itself.

"Weird..." the grey guardian mumbled to himself noticing the ribbon's multiple levels of intangibility.

Reaching for the now unconstrained box lid, the Grey Ghost slowly lifted the lid as he trained his light on the opened seam. After close inspection and once he was confident there were no unwanted surprises awaiting him, the Grey Ghost completely removed the lid from the box.

Trying to place the lid on the floor, the Grey Ghost found it as uncooperative as its matching ribbon for it immediately started to pass directly through the floor as if it wasn't there.

"Oh for Pete's sake..." the hero grumbled to himself finding no

alternative other than holding the lid while he continued searching.

Throwing the cardboard lid under his arm, the ghostly sleuth finally looked inside the oversized gift box. There, as alien to its surroundings as a glass of water in the desert, was a short metallic cylinder. About the size of a small trashcan, the cylinder was perfectly smooth, betraying not a single opening, seam, or weld mark. It was so unnaturally smooth and unblemished, the Grey Ghost could even see his reflection peering back at him from the amazing mirrored surface. Reaching into the box, the hero cautiously gripped the metallic object and slowly tried to lift it out of the box only to find it impossible to move! Even with his enhanced strength, the cylinder, for no explainable reason, defied any attempt by the ghostly hero to budge it, almost laughing at the Grey Ghost's every exertion.

After a few minutes of almost comical frustration, the Grey Ghost conceded there was yet another otherworldly mystery sitting before him, this one literally gift wrapped for him.

"Well aren't we just the tricky little jewel thief..." the Grey Ghost said to himself.

Knowing his time of privacy was limited, the Grey Ghost decided not to push his luck any longer. Taking the lid from under his arm he started to place it back on the eerie gift box when something on the inside of the lid caught his eye. Focusing his light on the lid, the investigator was surprised to find a small message inscribed on the cardboard written in a flourished cursive hand.

"Near a great forest there lived a poor woodcutter..."

"A woodcutter?" the confused Grey Ghost repeated to himself.

Nicholas Cara

The Capstone City Vindicator

EARLY CITY EDITION

Est. 1869

Wednesday, February 11, 1942

JEWELED KISSING BANDIT STRIKES!

Numerous Local Businesses Vandalized During Daring Crime Spree

By: Lynda Cordova

Citizens were shocked yesterday during a daring series of robberies at both Fulcher's Emporium and Rachel's Hat Boutique in the downtown area. A hooded woman along with what has been reported as an elderly companion attacked both a security guard and others at Fulcher's to escape the scene with stolen merchandise. The attack has been reported by witnesses as supernatural in nature based on the woman's speed and strength. This same thief would later enter Rachel's and make off with a priceless pearl inlaid brimmed hat leaving the attendant stunned and fearing for

A MYSTERIOUS CALLING CARD LEFT AT THE SCENE OF THE

City Council Passes For Inaugural G. Celebration

By: Michael Hay

Thursday evening, the Caps council voted 10-3 to pass t the inaugural G.I. City Celeb The celebration, an idea c Editan, is to be a show of su our servicemen serving a Europe. Originally panned impractical use of city funds of war" by then City Chairman Vincent Rogers, the was never expected to pass thr city appropriations co However, after the unexpected of Chairman Rogers earlier thi in a tragic car accident, the found little opposition ... C

JEWELED KISSING BANDIT STRIKES!

Numerous Local Businesses Vandalized During Daring Crime Spree

By: Lynda Cordova

Citizens were shocked yesterday during a daring series of robberies at both Fulcher's Emporium and Rachel's Hat Boutique in the downtown area. A hooded woman along with what has been reported as an elderly companion attacked both a security guard and others at Fulcher's to escape the scene with stolen merchandise. The attack has been reported by witnesses as almost supernatural in nature based on the woman's speed and strength. This same thief would later enter Rachel's and make off with a priceless pearl inlaid brimmed hat leaving the attendant stunned and fearing for his life. This wonder in her satin tights besmirching our rights as a society of law and order left a calling card at both scenes in the form of a kiss mark made up of small jewels as well as brightly wrapped packages whose contents have not been released by police as of yet.

Numerous packages of the same design and signature of the Jeweled Kissing Bandit were also discovered and reported overnight across town, though Police are hesitant at this time connecting them to the mysterious female thief....Continued on A2

City Council Passes Funding For Inaugural G.I. City Celebration

By: Michael Hay

Thursday evening, the Capstone City council voted 10-3 to pass funding for the inaugural G.I. City Celebration.

The celebration, proposed by Mayor Editar, is to be a show of support for our servicemen serving abroad in Europe. Originally panned as "an impractical use of city funds at a time of war" by then City Council Chairman Vincent Rogers, the funding was never expected to pass through the city appropriations committee. However, after the unexpected passing of Chairman Rogers earlier this month in a tragic car accident, the funding found little opposition...

Continued on B5

"Will you listen to this stuff?" Patsy asked smacking the newspaper with his hand. "This wonder in her satin tights besmirching our rights... I mean really? Who writes like that?"

"Someone who definitely enjoys rhyming," Joe mumbled, taking a sip of his coffee. It had been a long and uneventful night, and early morning Mass did not help Joe's cause. Sitting there, he clung to the mug of caffeine as a drowning man would a life preserver. "So what is with the swell drawing of..I guess me?"

"Get this, on the next page she actually questions whether you are related to our mysterious thief. And remember, ever since they noticed you can't be photographed they've been having people at the paper actually draw what they think you look like," Patsy answered.

"This is definitely one of the better ones," Joe commented. "The skull under my mask and the eyes, wow that's an imagination?"

"You're not going to be able to save any cats from trees looking like that Mr. Hero," Patsy remarked looking at the sketch.

"Well it has promise..." Joe added.

"Anyways...who is this Cordova gal? You know me, I wasn't a huge fan of Daycie mind you. I never let her hear the end of it the time they misspelled SPECTER or put SPOILED instead of spoils in a few of your headlines but she at least didn't think she was Mother Goose!"

"Ha! I remember the Vindicator's editor Decker calling you at the station," Joe chuckled.

"What can I say? I appreciate proper grammar," Patsy shrugged. "And I'm not even sure if this gal understands the act of over-exaggeration! Here she says numerous cases of these magical gift boxes were delivered all over the... Numerous? Really? She acts like that crooked girl went on a real crime spree. I mean two shops in one day is gutsy but not...."

"Well she did act like Santie Claus a couple of more times yesterday before calling it a night," Joe interjected.

"What do you mean?" Patsy asked, surprised by his partner.

"Our little Mrs. Claus dropped off a few extra packages around town yesterday that we didn't know about," Joe answered in between yawns.

"And why was this little nugget of info kept from us before the press got it?" Patsy asked back.

"Because there wasn't any crime to report. She left them at the Mastramico Statue and the fountain at Paden Park," Joe shrugged. "If they weren't left in the open I doubt they would've even been noticed."

"And are those boxes ghosty too?" Kate asked, walking into the the living room from the den.

"From what I read," Patsy answered. "But I'm only guessing that Cordova got that right in her rhymes."

"Well I doubt our thief would go though all of the effort to do what she did on the boxes at Fulcher's and Rachel's to leave those sitting in the rain." Joe added.

"Were there any additional messages in the lids of those?" Patsy asked.

"Not sure. I haven't been able to make it over there since the precinct called about the drop offs earlier this morning," Joe answered before adding, "and if they are anything like the others, no one else is going to be able to lift those lids to see except me. She did leave her mark at both scenes though, a shiny bright blue kiss of gems on the cheek of the Mastramico Statue and then she decided to up the ante and went with diamonds at Paden Park on the bench next to the package. I'm surprised those were all still around by the time a patrol noticed them."

"Or after they noticed them..." Patsy added.

"I swear that cookie will apparently kiss anything," Kate remarked shaking her head.

"You might want to check those new boxes and see if our little narrative continues Joe," Patsy advised. "What was the message at the hat shop again? A wood cutter..."

"No, that was the first one at Fulcher's. The message at Rachel's was... *and his wife and two children...*" Joe answered.

"So near a forest there lived a poor woodcutter... and his wife and two children..." Patsy repeated out loud connecting the two messages before adding, "That randomly littered the place with stupid boxes and stole hats because they matched his old lady's eyes."

"It's no joke Patsy. This whole mystery has turned what I thought I knew about this thing on its ear," Joe said, tapping his watch. "All so this gal can leave shiny little kisses all over town."

"You got that part of it right hon," Kate said getting up. "From what you two know, she's been spread pretty much all over the city. Those four boxes, if that's all of them, are canvasing a good chunk of the metropolitan area. She does like to get around."

"Katie is right. These incidents are not centralized in one area; at all, even the two burglaries were a good run away from each other," Patsy said, continuing Kate's thought as she made her way back to the den to see if Joe's mother needed any help. Seeing Kate finally get out of ear shot, Patsy asked softly, "Speaking of shiny things and dames, buddy, when's the big day?"

"Well it was going to be yesterday before we got called into this mess, right after she showed off this little marvel," Joe whispered back, tapping his prosthetic leg. "Plan B is this Friday after work. I'm supposed to meet up with her at the University to see the upgrades to my kicker."

"That's going to eat at you all week," Patsy chuckled. "That little thing is going to burn a hole right through your pocket."

"Thanks, best man. Never would've thought of that without you," Joe groaned back.

"Well you won't have to wait at all, Joe, if you boys don't keep it down," Joe's father Stanley whispered peeking his head in the living room. "Some fancy secret agents you two are. I'm half deaf from the blast furnaces and I can hear you both as clear as day."

"They know?" Patsy asked looking back at Joe.

"You don't think he would even make it to the church in one piece if his mother found out about *that* after the fact, do you?" Stanley remarked.

"And buddy, with what we make saving the world, where do you think I got the ring?" Joe whispered back. "Little diamonds don't just appear out of thin air."

"You tell her that...." Patsy replied pointing to the newspaper.

CHAPTER FIVE

"Order up!" The call came out from the back counter of Ellie's Diner.

Hearing her order, Janet winked at her customer, a regular named Gary from the Mill, before grabbing the plate and then the coffee pot on her way over to table seven. Delivering the eggs and sausage, Janet topped off the customer's coffee and asked if he needed anything else before she pulled out her pad and walked over to the new walk-ins over at table nine.

"Morning sweetie, may I pour you a cup of joe or would you like juice, we've got fresh squeezed?" Janet asked, smiling at her new customers.

Peering down at her table, Janet was slightly surprised to be met with the beaming face of a finely dressed lady with large sunglasses smiling back at her.

"Cup of joe? Why what a simply *delicious* way to put that my dear lady," the shaded customer replied, nodding to her companion. "Why yes, I think we'd both like a cup of *JOE*."

"Okay sweetie, are you ready to order or do you need a minute?" Janet asked, filling the two mugs on the table. "Today's special has been getting some smiles all morning."

"Oh I think we are going to need a minute dear," the shaded woman replied, scanning the menu and smiling as a child would in a toy store. "Everything looks so scrumptious. May I ask you, what are, how do you put it here...*flap jacks?*"

"She did what?" Patsy asked Captain Robinson, not believing his ears.

Not appreciating the interruption, the captain shot a look the detective's way before he continued addressing the crowded morning roll call. The all too small room was jammed as usual since the department was still sharing the old courthouse with the City's Record's Department. The old station still lay in ruins next door, a burned out husk, and neither Joe nor Patsy could remember the last time they actually thought work was going to be done on its reconstruction.

"The thief our imaginative press has dubbed 'The Jeweled Kissing Bandit,' strolled into Ellie's earlier this morning with her elderly compatriot. Both ordered breakfast even ordering two additional plates to go, ate, paid for the meal, left a substantial tip next to another untouchable package along with her calling card on the check and left."

"So Cap," Joe asked, "This crazy gal has gone MIA all week since her little shopping spree over the weekend and suddenly decides Friday is the best time to go into a crowded diner like Ellie's and get breakfast?"

"The waitress, a Miss Janet Atwell, who reported the package after the two left, could not remember anything out of the ordinary about the woman, only the fact she really didn't know much about regular breakfast food," Robinson said. "She asked about plates such as flap jacks and eggs in a basket like she had never heard of them before."

"What about the elderly man with her?" a voice from the back of the room asked.

Joe turned around and was surprised to see officer Joel Bishop raising his hand. Joel, brother and partner of the still missing Officer James Bishop, whose participation with the events of the Trumbull Bridge attack last year had left a prisoner in their care dead, the old precinct in ruins, and the captain himself in the hospital, had been keeping his head down and mouth shut for weeks now. Even after the captain and a full review board cleared Joel of any possible connection to his brother's actions, it was impossible for the officer not to notice the slanted looks aimed his way, inasmuch as he had been trying to keep a low profile, at least until now.

"From Miss Atwell's statement, she was able to remember the woman's companion being there and what he ate. However, she was not able to recall anything of great detail about the man himself," Robinson replied. "Apparently Miss Atwell had read in the papers about the Jeweled Kissing Bandit's exploits over the weekend and connected the dots when she noticed the large gift box left on the table next to the dirty dishes and the kiss mark on the check next to the $10 tip the two left before disappearing."

"Ten dollar tip!" Patsy scoffed. "Now she's just rubbing our noses in this."

"Captain, did the waitress...?" Joe started asking before Robinson raised his hand stopping him.

"The reports are on your desks, Bevine and Thomas, so you two can go over how she liked her eggs later. Let's finish roll call first. Believe it or not this department has more to do than look into this woman's exploits," Robinson commented.

"Captain, shouldn't we be the ones following up on this?" an officer near the front of the room asked before standing up. It was Officer Bill Maggs, a veteran of 15 years on the force, though his gray hair and round midsection reflected the 12 years he enjoyed behind a desk over at booking. "Andy and I were the reporting officers at the diner so this should be our case. No disrespect to wheels and the leg man..."

"Hey Maggs, shut your yap before you end up needing one of these," Patsy warned smacking Joe's chair. No one was going to talk about his partner like that.

While appreciating his friend coming to his defense, Joe grabbed the back of Patsy's coat to stop the larger man from doing anything stupid. For the most part, everyone from Joe's family and friends to the captain and most of the precinct had been supportive of him since his return after being injured overseas. But of course there are always those guys. Even when Joe thought some of his less supportive brothers in blue had started to accept him back, especially after his involvement with stopping the attack on the Trumbull (or the little part of his involvement they could know about) the nicknames like "Wheels" and "Crutch" continued to be whispered behind his back as if he had lost his hearing along with his leg.

Joe's usual reaction to such nonsense was to ignore it. He didn't need their permission to breathe or to do his job, and they didn't deserve the satisfaction of seeing if their ignorance could rile him up. Patsy, as always, decided to take a different approach to it.

"Officers if I may...?" a smooth voice spoke up from behind everyone in the crowded room.

Noticing the surprised look on Captain Robinson's face, Joe turned his head to find the owner of the voice and noticed him just before he heard Robinson's greeting.

"Good morning your honor. How can we help you?"

There, standing in the back of the room in his tailored black suit was Capstone City's mayor, the honorable Daniel P. Editar. Smiling as if he was about to kiss a line of babies, the politician scratched his salt and pepper goatee as if wondering why everyone in the room was so surprised to see him.

"Oh there is nothing I need out of you James," the mayor answered, turning his eyes on Patsy and Joe. "I simply wanted to stop by and finally meet the infamous duo of Thomas and Bevine. The heroes of 'The Attack on the Trumbull' as our papers called it, AND now, from what my sources tell me, the investigating officers of our 'Kissing Bandit Thefts.' Oh my, the papers in our fair city do love to name everything."

"It's a pleasure your honor," Patsy spoke up, offering his hand as he purposely brushed past the now simmering Maggs.

Patsy and Joe had both seen the elected official before. For a while they bragged around the precinct about saving the politician's neck, but neither had ever officially met the man.

"A true pleasure, officer," Editar replied, taking Patsy's hand in a light-hearted grip. "You have no idea how I've been watching you and your partner's exploits over the past year. No idea... I'll sleep very soundly knowing you two are on the case of this felonious female and her partner."

"We'll get her your honor. She and her old man will be behind bars before they know what hits them," Patsy replied, puffing his chest and taking in every bit of the politician's adulation.

"Oh, I'm not just talking about the woman and the elderly gentleman, officer," the mayor continued. "Bringing in those two will more than likely do very little to stem the tide of this recent crime wave if we don't find a way to apprehend the ringleader of it all, the Grey Ghost."

"I'm sorry your honor, the Grey Ghost?" Joe chimed in, taken aback by the mention of his alter ego. "Your honor, we don't have any evidence supporting the involvement of the Grey Ghost in..."

"Of course you do, officer," the mayor cut in, extending his hand to Joe. "And may I add, Officer Bevine, what an inspiration you are to the entire city. Coming to back work in the trenches every single day, protecting our fair city even with such a disability, a true inspiration."

"Thank you sir, but I don't see why we are..." Joe continued, reaching out to take Editar's hand.

As soon as his hand touched the politician's palm, Joe felt the floor fall from underneath him or to be more precise the wheelchair where he was sitting. Before he knew what hit him, Joe felt his backside crash into the ground directly underneath his chair. Noticing what had really happened, Joe immediately pushed the wheelchair backward making it look as if he had simply slipped forward out of the chair. Looking up, Joe was slightly hopeful his ruse would work since he noticed that when he fell he had inadvertently pulled Editar face first into Patsy next to him.

"Your honor are you okay? I'm so sorry" Joe cried out to the politician trying to pull himself away from the much larger Patsy. *"I hope he didn't notice..."*

"No, no I'm fine. You might want to be a little more careful you mis..." Mayor Editar barked roughly, pushing himself away from Patsy before catching himself and smiling. "I mean, no, I'm fine officer, no worries... Believe it or not you have to be made of stronger stuff than most people might believe to survive the world of politics."

Turning quickly from Joe, the mayor looked back at Captain Robinson who had made his way over to the three during the commotion. "I trust Captain, you will be making every effort to apprehend both this vigilante and his apparent two cohorts post haste. We have allowed this ruffian too much leeway in our fair city, and we can see now where that has left us. Our fair city will no longer stand for this 'Grey Ghost' haunting our population."

"Yes your honor," Robinson replied ushering the politician out of the room. "We will get down to the bottom of this quickly, you have my word. Officers dismissed."

Joe pulled Patsy aside as the other members of the department filed out of the conference room. "Patsy, what is Editar talking about with our friend?" Joe asked whispering. "Why does everyone keep connecting this kissing dame and me... I mean the Grey Ghost at all?"

"I overheard Maggs laughing about it while you were getting all weak in the knees about meeting the mayor," Patsy answered looking around for any stragglers in the room. "And what was up with that anyways? When did you start becoming a teenage girl around his honor?"

"I'm not sure what happened, but let's just say I'm glad the new station doesn't have a basement," Joe answered looking over at the floor.

"According to what I overheard, that crazy gal at Ellie's didn't just leave her lip mark," Patsy stated heading out of the conference room, Joe wheeling in tow. Making his way down the hallway, Patsy turned into the pen heading for his and Joe's desks. As Robinson had mentioned, there were two copies of the Ellie's Diner report on their desks waiting. "Let's see if that good for nothing was full of hot air like usual," Patsy said opening the folder. As soon as he found what he was looking for, Patsy's jaw fell to the floor. Handing the report to Joe, all he could say was, "that little minx..."

Still not understanding what his partner meant, Joe started scanning the contents of the folder until he got to a photograph taken of the diner bill. There in the photograph, sitting next to a fresh $10 note, was the check with the jeweled thief's kiss mark. Joe couldn't tell what color the gems were from the black and white photo. But also adorning the kiss mark and the check was a note to the waitress, a note written in a feminine cursive hand that Joe knew was slowly tightening a noose around his neck.

"Get something nice for yourself, from me and the Grey Ghost -TJK.

CHAPTER SIX

The fine mist of ocean water started to pepper Marcus Benford's face on the deck of the Heqet. It was nothing the ship's captain wasn't used to, but the repetitive waves crashing into his ship's side as it was roped off to this makeshift pier were starting to make him uneasy. Looking over to the port side, the larger black man eyed the rocky coast of Dagger Island almost daring his vessel closer as it drifted back and forth along the small pier.

"Hey Washington, how much longer, brother? This surf isn't being too polite up here!" Marcus called into the open hold.

Sticking his head out from the hatch, the ship's first mate James "Washington" Benford gave his captain and brother a slanted look.

"If these two would let me help them stow this junk faster, we could get the blazes out of here, but it's all hands off," Washington yelled back trying to be heard over the surf.

Marcus couldn't stifle a laugh seeing the top of his brother's head popping out of the hold like a gopher peeking out of his den. Even after sinking their money into the modified hold of the Steelcraft Tug, James, who cleared a good five inches taller than his brother, still had to bend down to get anywhere on the boat and hated every second below deck.

"See if you can hurry our customers up down there, Washington," Marcus said, pointing to the side. "The old girl may be stronger than most, but hitting those rocks, if this rinky-dink pier gives way, won't be good for anyone."

Turning his head to where his brother was pointing, Washington's face was smashed by another wave crashing over the side of the Heqet, smacking the forward deck. Dropping his head back in the hold, James bent down to make his way aft, calling out to the two men strapping a small collection of crates to the hull.

"Gentlemen, we need to get all of these on board and stowed. This surf isn't making Dagger Island a friendly port of call. So the faster we get on our way the…" James called out before being interrupted by one of the men.

"We will go when we say we will go, boy," barked a tiny man, with an almost unhealthy skinny frame and a pencil mustache. James had caught his partner calling him by the name Otto. "If you and your captain can't take a little rough ride every now and then, maybe the sea isn't for either of you."

"Yeah maybe the two of them…" his plump partner started laughing.

"Shut up, Horst. You're no better than these two useless fools," Otto snapped before turning his attention back to James. "Boy, your job is to get these artifacts to the city, not to keep yapping, so how about you leave the real work to the professionals."

This was not the first insult these two, especially Otto, had thrown either Marcus' or James' way since this job had started. Ignorance didn't always have an explanation attached to it, but in this instance it didn't make a lick of common sense as the two brothers had bitten their tongues while literally towering over their two customers. James again bit back his reply, but he knew his patience was hitting its limits. Money was tight and so far the fishing aspect of this vessel they had bought secondhand hadn't struck gold. They had been lucky finding this job, easy route, easy money, and if it hadn't been for the two stooges being nasty from the moment they stepped on board, it would've been smooth sailing.

"Horst, get the remaining crates on the dock," Otto barked pulling at one of the belts crossing a few of the crates already loaded. "I'll finish strapping these down and then we can be on our way before our tall green-gilled friend here and his brother throw up over the side.

"You know friend, if you'll let me give you a hand here we can get these stowed faster," James gritted through his clenched teeth as he reached out for one of the small crates on the ground. "I know where all of the tie downs are on this boat like the back of my…"

"Don't touch that!" Otto yelled actually swinging his arm to smack away James's hand from the small crate. "Don't ever touch any of these. What's wrong with you boy, you don't understand English, you lanky good for nothing dunce?"

Seeing red at the final straw, James clenched his fist and was about to take a step toward the small man when he heard his brother call out to him over the sound of blood rushing through his ears.

"Washington! Hey, I need a hand top side!"

Staring down a moment at the smug man in front of him, James didn't reply. The smug look returned his way was too much to walk away from…

"Washington!'

James grimaced as he turned away from the ignorant man and called back out of the hold to Marcus.

"Aye Captain, I'm on my way! You *fine gentlemen* call if you need any help down here."

"The day I need help from the likes of you two will be the day I eat my hat *boy*," Otto sneered to James's back.

Making his way back to the deck before he had to hear another comment from his unfriendly customer, James found his brother in the wheelhouse looking over the instruments.

"So what's up?" James asked. "You sounded like it was important."

"Huh, oh yeah… I need you to NOT beat the tar out of that skinny pig and his merry man down there," said Marcus, shaking his head and smiling. "I could hear that peach all the way up here, and let's just say… I know you"

"Just tell me one thing brother…tell me the money is worth all of this," James sighed wiping his brow with his knit hat. "You know I signed on with you for fishing, not taking insults from pea brains on our own ship."

"The money is worth it," Marcus replied. "And don't worry, once we get above water again with the payment from this little excursion we'll get back to mackerel and tuna. I don't love being a carrier pigeon for this little dig any more than as you."

"That's what we're moving, rocks and bones?" James asked.

"Something like that," Marcus answered shrugging. "That's what the stooge that hired us told me, and it makes sense, I mean what else could be on Dagger Island worth moving?"

"Well, those guys are acting like those crates are full of gold down there," James replied throwing his thumb in the direction of the hold.

"That's science nerds for you," Marcus shrugged. "And that guy probably would be a pain if those crates were full of sand. But hey, a few more boxes left and then the Heqet will be on her way back to Capstone."

"You know I still hate that name," James smirked. "I mean why did you have to name the boat after a frog?"

"It's an Egyptian goddess," Marcus replied. "How could you not like the name of an Egyptian goddess?"

"An Egyptian goddess with the head of a FROG!" James laughed. "And you know full well you just named it after that doll you met overseas. You really didn't care what her name meant."

"Well brother, I can tell you one thing," Marcus whistled, thinking back to the girl James mentioned. "That girl definitely did not have the head of a frog… nor the legs of one."

CHAPTER SEVEN

"For the love of all that is good and holy, he may have been broken in half!" the announcer screamed from the side table as the young man's body clad in a worn Matador costume crashed into the mat.

Standing over the beaten contender, the massive form of King Lawless screamed a triumphant roar of victory over the fallen Matador before placing his foot on the man's chest. Appearing from where he had been hiding in the corner of the ring, a striped-shirt official slid next to the unconscious wrestler and mercilessly slapped the mat three times, ending the bout.

"And there you have it, ladies and gentlemen. Your winner by pin fall and still undefeated, the GREEEAT KING LAAWLESS!" the announcer bellowed, watching paramedics or more accurately white clad stagehands help the beaten Matador to the back locker room.

"I bet you, Joseph, that guy is seriously rethinking careers right now," Patsy laughed, throwing a handful of popcorn in his mouth from the large paper sack in his hand. "That job as a butcher or lawyer that his momma probably wanted for him is probably looking pretty inviting after a Samoan Drop from the second rope!"

"I can't believe you talked me into this," Joe groaned, stealing some popcorn from his partner. "With all the plans, and I mean PLANS buddy, that I had for tonight, being here with you next to the stockyards wasn't even on the list."

"Cheer up pal," Patsy smiled. "It's not like Katie said no. I mean, I think we all know what the girl's going to say once you finally get down on one knee."

"Which was supposed to be, I don't know, about two hours ago," Joe chimed in, looking at his watch.

"Well what can you do bud?" Patsy garbled through another handful of popcorn. "I mean when the Dean of the school and the mayor himself call you to a meeting, even at this hour, you probably want to be there."

"I waited in that lab staring at that silly grad student for over an hour with this ring burning a hole in my pocket," Joe grumbled. "I had it all planned out, after she showed me the work they've done on the new leg model, we were going to head up to the Math Department's roof and…"

"Wow, slow down there Casanova. The roof of the Math Department, why I do declare…you romantic little thing you," Patsy joked as he fanned himself like a southern debutante on a warm summer's day.

"It's where we had our first kiss, you ugly southern dumpling," Joe laughed at his friend's impression. "Remember way back when the university had that large replica of the prototype Hornet Rocket on display? Back then, Kate was really interested in the capsule or something at the top. So I talked to the security guard Willy, a buddy of my pops, and he swings me a key to the rooftop that was right next to the display. Kate was thrilled, and let's just say that night went well because, you know here we are. I checked earlier with Willy and lo and behold, I got my hands around the keys again for tonight. Man, it would've been perfect!"

"Well you'll just have another fun story to tell your kids, like the time she stood you up on Valentine's Day. Come on over here youngins and let me tell you about how your good old Dad almost proposed to your Mom," Patsy chuckled before adding. "Hey, at least we got to use these tickets to the fights. I threw some good money down for these."

"Why in the world did you think Kennedy would want to go to the stockyards to see a wrestling match?" Joe said shaking his head. "I mean I know you're a little out of practice with the ladies, but you couldn't believe for a second a girl like Miss Saks Fifth Avenue would like this kind of stuff, do you?"

"I tell you Joseph, the right girl would and one day I'm going to find her, believe me," Patsy replied. "Hey look, here's your chance to win some of that dough back you spent on fixing up your Mom's ring."

"Ladies and gentleman, boys and girls of all ages," the ring announcer now standing in the center of the canvased ring bellowed into a small microphone, his arms spread wide to draw the audience's attention. "It is time for the infamous 'Money on the Clock Challenge!' Entering the ring, weighing a whopping three hundred and thirty seven pounds, hailing from the rough riding city of Detroit, Michigan, the master of the cauliflower ear, and reigning Northeast Regional Champion, MONDDES THE CRUSHER!"

The small area of seats near the back locker room erupted in a chorus of boos and hisses as the champion entered from the backroom. Standing nearly seven feet, the monster-sized wrestler stomped along the entranceway to the ring. A large purple cloak the size of a full blanket was draped over his back making the huge man appear even larger. Literally stepping over the ropes surrounding the squared ring with a single swing of his tree trunk leg, the wrestler stared out at the booing audience before snarling at them.

"No, that's okay, I think I'll earn my money the safe way buddy," Joe replied, taking in the massive hulk stalking the ring, who now looked more bear-like than human. "You know, dealing with con artists and thieves, possibly a few killers for good measure."

"Probably a good call," Patsy chuckled. "Remember what happened to the last guy who thought he could make his fortune?"

"They had to start having the poor bums sign waivers after that one," Joe whistled before noticing the awaiting challenger standing near the ring. "Oh you got to be kidding me. That's the poor kid they roped into this? He couldn't weigh more than a buck-ten if you soaked him to the bone."

"Five hundred clams if you can last five minutes in the ring buys a lot of courage I guess," Patsy shrugged.

"Yeah well the dime you get to telephone the docs after trying and getting your face rearranged never seems worth the trouble," Joe shook his head as the smaller man started to, very tentatively, climb into the ring.

"Well come on bud, what do you think? You think you could, if you headed up there, take the champ?" Patsy ribbed Joe. "That kind of money would make for a nice honeymoon."

"You mean me or *me me*?" Joe asked, raising his eyebrows.

"Hey, whatever would get you back home in one piece," Patsy shrugged. "I actually think Monddes is larger than the big mook on the bridge."

"He might be," Joe replied remembering the killer Vega all those months ago as he looked over the roaring champion in the ring. "But I don't think it's the right time for the Grey Ghost to make his in-ring debut just yet. With the pressure the mayor has been putting on the captain this week about my crime wave, you might have to arrest me."

"I don't know about you, but I think the station has seen the honorable mayor one too many times this week," Patsy scoffed, puffing his cheeks in exasperation. "You'd think it was an election year or something."

"You're telling me, buddy. Or are you forgetting who is part of the reason I'm here with you and not on the Math Department's roof?" Joe nodded his head in agreement before looking back at the ring. "Hey where did the little guy go?"

"I guess the little fella wised up..." Patsy answered, also noticing the now empty ringside. "Hey, maybe they got the little guy a tag team partner; somebody new is coming down the entranceway. Wow, they're getting smaller as we speak."

Following Patsy's direction, Joe noticed two new entrants. Both cloaked individuals walked methodically down toward the ring. The cloaks were what hit Joe first, their color, cut and intriguing design were familiar, way too familiar.

"Patsy..." Joe started.

"I see them," Patsy interrupted. "Apparently those two also shop at the same place that Wiggy and Vega did last year when they decided to interrupt the mayor's press conference."

As Patsy finished his thought, one of the hooded "challengers" threw the garment to the ground in a flourish of showmanship. To everyone's surprise, there standing in the middle of the squared circle was a finely garbed beauty. Flowing red hair pulled behind her head in a tight bun and face covered by a set of large sunglasses, the woman gave the crowd a welcoming smile as she grabbed the microphone away from the announcer and cheered.

"Capstone City, it is such a pleasure to finally introduce myself to you all! Your papers call me 'The Jeweled Kissing Bandit.' Wow, I must say that is quite a mouthful. How about you simply call me, since we are now such good friends, THE JEWELED KISS? It will save so much time with all the fun we are going to have!"

"Did she just name herself?" Joe asked taken aback by the scene.

"Bet you wish you had at least told the papers to spell the word GRAY correctly now, don't ya?" Patsy joked.

CHAPTER EIGHT

"What is this? A woman? Bring me a real challenger!" Monddes scoffed at the unmasked beauty before yelling to the crowd. "Bring Monddes a worthy opponent and he will celebrate his glorious victory with this red-headed pretty thing afterward!"

At the champion's bellow, the shaded beauty turned to look at him, almost as if she had not really noticed the behemoth before that comment.

"That was rude darling. How about after this *pretty thing* is done turning you inside out *I* take you out for a meal? Possibly one fitting the caliber of a man, or should I say a beast that you seem to want to act like," the red-headed beauty smiled. "I hear the children's meal at Carmen's comes with a toy. Would you like that little man?"

The laughter from the small crowd infuriated the brutish champion. With a quick slap of his arm, he threw the ring announcer, who was standing in between the monster and the mocking woman, out of the way. Reaching a large paw of a hand out to seize the woman, Monddes never knew what hit him as a woman's heeled pump connected with his large jaw flooring him. The crowd at first sat in stunned silence before breaking into a loud cheer at the wrestler's fall. Monddes became so incensed at his humiliation that he jumped up and charged the dynamite female. The attack, so senseless and barbaric, would have crushed even the strongest grappler, let alone a woman of such small stature standing before the brute.

But amazingly, in what only could be explained as the impossible happening before the shocked crowd's eyes, the crazed champion was suddenly stopped in his tracks as the mysterious female effortlessly grabbed him by the throat. Waving her index finger in front of the champion's face as a mother would scold a small child, the shaded woman threw the large wrestler into the ropes surrounding the ring with a simple lurch of her arm. As the wrestler bounced off the three cords, he rebounded directly toward her only to be met with an extended arm clotheslining the man.

"Now apologize, you ape," the super strengthened Amazon huffed at the stunned Monddes. Noticing a patch of red hair had sprung loose from her bun, the woman incredibly turned her back on the downed champion.

"Do you have any idea how hard it is to get this just right?" the Jeweled Kiss complained, annoyed that the World Champion had caused her to look disheveled in front of the crowd.

As the woman tended to her hair, the 300 plus pound man, apparently not learning from his earlier mistakes, once again tried to rush the beauty from behind. As he reached the distracted female, Monddes murderously smiled realizing she had allowed him to get too close for her to have any chance of escape. That smile quickly vanished as he passed directly through the woman, still with her back to him, as if she was made of air! Disoriented from the lack of any contact with the woman, the champion let his momentum carry him through the ring ropes sending him crashing head first into the concrete floor.

After repairing her bun, the amazing thief glanced down at the fallen wrestler and smiled. "You know what dear, I actually am not that hungry right now. How about a rain check on the meal?"

The crowd, thinking this was part of the show, ate up every bit of the action. They cheered and clapped for the mysterious Amazon as if she was the grandest champion ever to lace up a pair of boots. The cheering soon subsided when a few of them noticed the amazing woman's still-hooded companion remove a brightly wrapped package from underneath his cloak and place it in the middle of the ring.

"That looks like one of the wrapped packages I read about in the papers!" someone yelled.

"They're not foolin' around!" echoed another. "That's the real Jeweled Kissing Bandit!"

"Didn't I tell them not… say not even five minutes ago… to not call me that?" the mysterious female asked her hooded companion shaking her head. "The people in this country…"

Back in their seats, Patsy stood up searching for a clear path to the ring through the now standing crowd. "Looks like the floor show is over. I'll let you take her highness over there. I'll take care of our messenger boy."

"I guess I get to make my big in-ring debut tonight after all," Joe replied.

Hearing the now familiar sound of a watch face rotating against its metal housing, Patsy turned back to where his partner had just been sitting to find that he was already gone.

Back in the ring, the beautiful victor stood soaking in the crowd's reaction, the mix of fear and excitement in their voices was music to her ears. Only when she noticed that her companion had finished his job did the boastful thief decide it was time to address her new fans.

"It's been a blast my darlings," the Jeweled Kiss smiled as she bent over the placed package, touching the top lid with one of her gloved hands. Closing her eyes as if in a silent prayer, the thief's brightly colored lips moved without sound. After a few seconds, the woman's eyes popped open and her bright smile once again appeared beaming for the crowd before she continued. "But like another good time with a beautiful woman I read about once, the clock is striking midnight! And I must be away before you all turn into pumpkins, so ta-ta!"

Turning to take her leave, the Jeweled Kiss was just about to bend under the ropes of the ring when she was stopped by the loud cry of a rough voice snarling behind at her.

"WOMAN!" the snarl spilt out. "Woman, where are you going? Your dance with Monddes is not over! Get back here and take your medicine you wretched creature!"

Glancing behind her, the Jeweled Kiss sighed in disgust when she found the massive form of the wrestler back in the ring limping toward her. A massive black ring had started forming over his right eye, but the crazed man continued across the ring at her.

"Oh come now..." the Jeweled Kiss frowned. "I know brains are not really a strong requirement for your line of work, but even a dumb animal like you can see you're outmatched here. Don't let your deflated ego add to the number of bruises you leave with you imbecile."

"Me? Ha! Woman, you will know your place!" Monddes yelled making his way closer. "This is my ring and you will leave it when I say so!"

"Now darling you are just being rude on purpose." The Jeweled Kiss stood her ground in front of the monster of a man. "I guess a...ahem... man like you only understands a good backhand. Oh well spare the rod and such..."

Taking a step toward the monster of a man, the Jeweled Kiss snapped a right cross at the large man's jaw. As the punch sailed at Monddes with the same invisible speed as her earlier attacks, the Jeweled Kiss's mouth fell open in surprise as the wrestler amazingly reached out and grabbed her fist mid-flight in his bear-like hand. The two combatants stared at each other in silence, the shock of the tables being proverbially turned on her.

"I apologize for the 'woman' remarks," the giant man calmly spoke, his voice completely different than that of the brutish animal that had roared seconds ago. ***"I simply couldn't let you leave so early..."***

Glancing up at her fist encased in the steel-trap grip of the wrestler, the Jeweled Kiss noticed a large amount of commotion behind him. Outside of the ring, on the floor, fans and a few medics were helping a large man off the ground. As a fan moved to the right of the helpless man, the beautiful thief recognized him... it was Monddes! Looking up at the man gripping her hand and back to his apparent double on the ground, the

Jeweled Kiss's eyes widened even more as she realized who was really with her in the ring.

Noticing the jig was up, Monddes smiled at the shocked woman before his face, chest, and midsection started to dissolve in a cascading reaction leading to his extremities. As the reaction reached the hand holding her fist, the bare, giant-like paw suddenly became a black gloved hand. Looking up at the face of the man now in front of her, the Jeweled Kiss shook her head and coyly smirked at the heroic form of the Grey Ghost!

"I figured it was time we met... darling..."

Nicholas Cara

PART TWO: GRAPPLING ON MULTIPLE FRONTS

Nicholas Cara

CHAPTER NINE

Gripping the controls, Marcus felt the floor under him shift sharply starboard. So far the trip wasn't any more pleasant than his passengers since being "allowed" to take off from the make-shift pier on Dagger Island. The sea was surprising him at every turn on this trip back, no matter which direction he took the Heqet. If he turned into the waves, he was hit portside, if he tried to turn against them, the Heqet was again board-sided and so on.

What smacked him hardest was the fact he knew this rough trip was all on his head. He had been far too eager to jump at the job, blinded by the payout. He never properly mapped out the area before he took his brother and boat to that forsaken island. The guy back at Capstone had said takeoff or don't. Maybe Marcus should've thought for a moment before setting off or why no one else had jumped at the job as fast as he did.

"Huh, man this is quickly not becoming worth the trouble!" James yelled from behind him in the wheelhouse over the roaring ocean.

"Yeah, we're in this for a pound now, Washington," Marcus yelled back. "Why don't you head below and see how mister personality and his little buddy are doing?"

"Forget those two," James scoffed. "If that pig calls me 'boy' one more time with that smirk of his, I swear I'm sending him and his little friend over the side flank."

"Getting a little thinned skinned there, little brother," Marcus chuckled. "Guys like that are a dime a dozen. You look a little different and you're not worth their time until they need you, then suddenly you're important. You would've lost your mind with some of the jokers I had to deal with back overseas. When you're the only remaining expert around, any regime will take you along, no matter what color your skin was, but it didn't mean they liked having you around."

"I still don't know how you made it back from over there, fighting with that squad you told me about. I'm surprised one of them didn't put a knife in your back," James frowned. "I thought you were half dead when they shipped you back last year."

"There were a few good eggs in that bunch brother," Marcus nodded. "I came back half dead, but if not for one guy I would've left the other half over in Germany too, and Joe definitely took it for…"

"CRASH!"

"Ah crud. Washington, that sounded like it was near the engine room," Marcus yelled while checking his gauges. "Head down there and make sure there isn't any damage or this is going to be a really short trip."

Hopping out of the wheelhouse into the rain-like ocean spray, James made his way to the front hatch. Throwing it open and quickly climbing down, James closed the door to seal the deck below from the ocean water. Taking the small staircase in two wide steps, the tall man ducked slightly as he made his way to the middle engine room. Before he even made it there, James could see in the dim lighting what caused the crash. There in front of the metal engine room door was Horst hefting away one of the small crates where it had slid across the hold. Looking at the crumbling crate in the man's hands along with the others still scattered on the floor, James noticed a few more of the wooden crates had lost the fight against the metal door.

"Let me give you a hand with those," James said, bending even lower to take the crate from the small man. "These come loose in this merry-go-round?"

"Don't touch that boy!" Otto's voice rang out from behind him. "What's that moron of a captain up there think he's doing anyways? He's going to kill us all with his incompetence at that wheel. I guess I shouldn't have expected better from a couple of..."

"THE CAPTAIN is doing the best he can with the weather up there buddy," James barked, interrupting the ignorant ramble. "How'd these get loose anyways? I thought you had them tied off?"

"Don't go blaming me boy," Otto yelled back. "Now get your hands off that crate and let us take care of our equipment. Who knows what you and yours might do with..."

"I don't care a bit for your rocks and dirt pal," James again interrupted, not having it from Otto. "You and your friend can eat the whole lot for all I care. Just don't let it damage our ship or none of us are making it back to Capstone."

"Quite a mouth on you," Otto growled, reaching for one of the crates. "If we weren't in the middle of the ocean on this piece-meal boat of yours, I'd cure you of that real quick."

"Oh would you now?" James said standing up to the squat man. "Please bud, finish that thought, I dare you!"

As James took a step toward the bag of hot air, the crate in Otto's hands crumbled as the man recoiled, surprised that the larger man came toward him. As one of the crate's sides fell away, the straw-packing material inside dropped along with it.

Peering at the exposed contents, James looked back at Otto furiously. "That doesn't look like a pile of rocks and bones from any expedition. What are you having us take into the city, little man?"

"Well there you go, boy," Otto smiled deviously. "Curiosity always kills the cat and now we are going to have to cure that mouth of yours earlier than planned."

Focused on the mysterious cargo in Otto's hands, James never noticed the man's slight nod to Horst. The squat man, still standing behind James at the engine room's door, slowly stalked toward the two pulling a small knife from his belt.

The slap rang in the Grey Ghost's ear as the Jeweled Kiss's palm sharply found purchase across his helmeted face. Looking back at the thief, the ghostly guardian found the striking woman frowning at him as if disappointed.

"And… what… may I ask was that for?" the hero curtly asked, his face stinging, even while invisible under the helmet's face-shield.

"That? Oh that was for absolutely ruining our introduction darling," the coy villain pouted. "I mean, I had such plans for when we finally got to be face-to-face and you had to spoil it all by tricking me in front of all these people."

"Sorry to spoil your fun…"

"Oh are you? I seriously doubt that big fella, but if only you knew…" The woman's eyes sparkled at him as she spun her head over to her elderly companion, who was kneeling on the mat next to the wrapped box, desperately trying to keep his face hidden from view.

"Old timer," the Jeweled Kiss nodded to the man. "How about you give us some privacy? As they say, three's a crowd."

At her command the small accomplice bolted through the ropes and started a mad dash away, much too fast paced for such a seemingly old man.

"Oh no you don't, get back here pops!" the Grey Ghost heard Patsy bellow as he noticed his partner emerging from the crowd, chasing after the rabbiting perp. Losing sight of him as he sprinted around the back curtain, the hero turned his attention back to the high-heeled vixen in front of him.

"Lady, you've been quite a busy bee," the Grey Ghost mused. ***"You know the police probably have a laundry list of questions for you that would reach the bottom of the Scar."***

"I do not doubt it," the Jeweled Kiss smiled back. "But let's leave the flat foots out of this for now, my ghostly friend. What about you, my dashing hero? Any little question marks floating around that marvelously macabre helmet of yours?"

"One or two... but I'll get my answers in time," the Grey Ghost answered.

"Nothing rattling around up there you just NEED to know?" the Jeweled Kiss asked almost pouting. "I mean speak up, my tall and gray friend. It's not like we have all night here, as... fun... as that could be. But it's getting late, and all the little girls here need to get home for their fairytales before bed."

"I hope I'm not stopping you from being somewhere important," the Grey Ghost countered, pulling at her still trapped arm. ***"But like I said, the authorities would like a word. To be honest I'd appreciate it if we could be... civil... about this. I'd hate to have to drag you out of here."***

"Drag me? Really? Kicking and screaming the whole way?" the Jeweled Kiss deviously smiled. "Such a brute! I'll forgive you this one time for such a beastly thought because I sadly think you've fallen into the same trap all men of your ilk just can't seem to avoid. You boys always think simply getting a lady's hand is the easy part."

And with that, the Jeweled Kiss turned and started to walk away from the ghostly guardian. Still feeling the woman's arm tightly gripped in his left hand, the hero looked down and was surprised to see the form of the woman's entire arm, from finger tips to shoulder, still there!

"It's keeping it... THAT's the real challenge..." the amazingly still two-handed Jeweled Kiss finished while winking back at him. As she did, the unattached arm gripped in the hero's hand instantly dissolved as if it was made of air!

"How'd she do that?" the Grey Ghost thought to himself, amazed at the unknown and uncanny abilities the thief possessed.

Stepping forward, the hero extended his arm to clamp down on the leaving thief's shoulder.

"Please don't make this more diff...*"

But before the ghostly avenger could even finish his sentence, he felt weightlessness as the Jeweled Kiss struck with cat-like speed. Grabbing his outreached arm, the thief expertly pivoted and using the hero's own momentum against him flung him hard into the ring's corner pole.

"Now don't get grabby," the Jeweled Kiss reprimanded, looking down at the stunned hero. "I was just starting to like you, you know. I mean look at us; two cloaked figures of the night, a guy like you and a girl like me strolling through town scaring the pants off of people…"

"I'm already spoken for…" the Grey Ghost grumbled, righting himself from the corner. Straightening himself and ignoring the drunken laughter from the crowd around him, the Grey Ghost started cautiously approaching the mysterious thief.

"Lucky girl. I didn't see a ring on that ghostly hand of yo…"

"I'm not going to get into a slugging match with a woman, but I've got to take you in," the Grey Ghost said, cutting off the playful banter. *"So please don't make this more difficult than it needs to be."*

As before with the slap, he never saw the attack coming as a straight kick hit him solidly in the solar plexus knocking all of the air out of him. Struggling to remain upright, the Grey Ghost was barely able to dodge two jabs directly aimed at his face. Swinging his legs outward, the hero attempted to sweep the legs from under the thief, however, she again proved too fast as she sidestepped his counter.

"I see two things happening right now, cowboy," the Jeweled Kiss smiled as she expertly danced in the middle of the ring. "You're either going to have to break that rule about fighting girls or you're going to have your backside handed to you in front of all of these people."

"What makes you think those are my only options?" the ghostly avenger retorted, removing his long coat.

Gripping it in his left hand the hero propelled off of the ring's middle rope launching himself toward the thief. As the thief expectedly side stepped the lunge, the Grey Ghost twisted his body allowing him to drape the gray coat over the area where the Jeweled Kiss had retreated. Concentrating the power of the Spartan Cloak through his coat, the Grey Ghost changed the coat's density and form into a weighted net. Before she was able to dodge the trap, the Jeweled Kiss found herself hopelessly entwined in the magical netting.

Struggling for a few moments, the Jeweled Kiss yelled in frustration at being caught off guard by the hero. Relenting, the thief stopped pulling at the netting and started to mockingly clap at her capture all the time staring daggers at him through the netting.

"Well aren't you just full of surprises…" the Jeweled Kiss remarked still clapping.

"As long as I keep the netting in flux you're not going to be able to simply pass through it lady," the Grey Ghost explained, seeing the confusion on the face of the female thief as she tried to use her own power to pass through the netting. ***"You're not the only one who has been practicing a few parlor tricks lately…"***

"Don't hurt your arm patting yourself on the back too hard there cowboy," the Jeweled Kiss shrugged. "I mean, high marks all around for ingenuity and this has been a blast, but I really must be going."

"And how, may I ask, are you planning on doing that?" the Grey Ghost confidently asked.

"Poor boy, you really must start to think in all dimensions, but you'll learn," the Jeweled Kiss smiled. "But so you're not bored, how about I give you some friends to play with?"

Reaching her arm through one of the holes in the netting, the Jeweled Kiss was suddenly gripping a large stack of $100 bills.

"Oh boys, how about we up the ante on that $500 purse tall, dark and ugly had earlier?" the female bellowed to the crowd. "How about $5,000 cold hard cash for the first fella to land a punch on my boyfriend here!"

"Oh come on, there isn't anyone that stupid here that would…" the Grey Ghost scoffed before a bottle pinged off of his shoulder.

Looking back at the crowd, he was astonished to find nearly half of them advancing toward the ring.

"I guess I gave these guys way too much credit," the hero thought, seeing the murderous looks from the crowd squarely focused on him.

"Follow the bread crumbs cowboy…"

Hearing the Jeweled Kiss's voice, the Grey Ghost looked at the captured thief barely catching a glance of her blowing a kiss in his direction as she phased through the ring floor and out of sight!

"Oh come on..." the Grey Ghost thought, now understanding the thief's comment about dimensions.

Turning his head back to the yelling crowd, the haunted hero dodged to the right as a left hook sailed past him from the first hopeful moneymaker. Tripping the attacker as he went by, the Grey Ghost ended any thoughts of the man making a payday off of him with a sharp chop to the back of the neck. Looking to the outside of the ring, the ghostly avenger estimated at least a dozen crazed fans coming for him and the stack of bills the Jeweled Kiss had left in the middle of the ring. Only then did he notice that all of his avenues of exiting the ring had been cut off. He was completely surrounded.

CHAPTER TEN

Outside of the stockyards, the roar of the crowd slowly began to recede as a shadowy form made its way from the craziness. Flowing over the side crates outlining the edge of the pier as if it was a liquid living darkness, the shadow cast by no owner encompassed every board and nail of the containers as it made its journey to the last crate in the row. Standing by the last crate, Patsy impatiently rocked back and forth scanning the pier seemingly unaware of the unearthly form headed in his direction. Looking left and right, the detective finally gave the shadow a side-eyed glance as it reared up behind him.

"The coast is clear bub, so get your spooky behind out here. There's a lot we have to talk about," Patsy told the shadow.

At the officer's signal the shadow stepped forward until it pulled itself away from its two-dimensional plane gaining corporeal form as its leg stepped solidly on the pier next to Patsy. Soon the rest of the shadow pulled itself away from the crate until the fully three-dimensional form of the Grey Ghost stood leaning against it. Holding himself up with one arm, the hero nodded to his partner through labored breaths trying to slow his breathing, his coat tattered and stained from the attack back inside of the ring.

"You decide to play in the mud while I was waiting for you?" Patsy asked, taking stock of the hero's appearance. "You look terrible..."

"I had to... let off some steam..." the Grey Ghost answered looking at his stained jacket arm. "Hold on a second."

Closing his unseen eyes, the Grey Ghost focused on his form, allowing the power of the Spartan Cloak to envelope him and manipulate the very fibers of his outfit. In an instant, the hero became an unfocused cloud for a second before suddenly regaining sharpness, his clothes and appearance now mended and clean. The tears and mud were magically gone as if the clothes had been taken fresh from the rack.

"Neat trick," Patsy smirked, looking over his friend.

"Saves a ton of time on laundry day," the ghostly guardian chuckled through labored breaths to his partner. ***"Coast still clear?"***

Looking back to the still deserted pier, Patsy nodded the all clear before adding, "But hurry up, that place is going to be clearing out soon."

Reaching into his jacket the Grey Ghost produced a playing card with a hand-drawn image of a chair on it. Throwing the card on the ground in front of him, the Patsy smiled in amazement the card become cloud-like and unfocused, much like the gray hero moments earlier. Where a normal playing card should've landed as a solid, instead a fully-formed wheelchair multiple sizes larger than the card bounced against the wooden pier floor. Moving in front of the chair the Grey Ghost sat down, expertly releasing the side brakes as Patsy casually walked behind him pushing the chair along. In a practiced motion, the hero's hand reached for the timepiece adoring his arm and with a muted click of the watch's crown, the heroic form of the Grey Ghost vanished replaced with the smaller one-legged persona of Joseph Bevine.

"I sure hope you had better luck than I did," Joe said to his partner. "Where's the old man? Already at the car?"

"It's a long story," Patsy huffed shaking his head.

"What do you mean?" Joe asked, knowing something was wrong from the way Patsy was acting.

"I'll tell you in the car. It's starting to get crowded," Patsy answered, noticing people starting to exit from the stockyard area. Pointing to Joe's face, Patsy added, "We're going to need to get that beauty mark off of you before we head into town anyways. You don't want Katie to see what kind of night you've been having."

Reaching up to his right cheek, Joe felt what his friend was referring to, mumbling to himself, "No way..."

As they made it to the cruiser Joe twisted the side mirror to confirm his suspicion. There in the mirror glittering on his cheek was the outline of two lip marks made up of sparkling green gems.

"Green is definitely not your color, Joseph," Patsy added after collecting Joe's chair from him. "Is that why you took so long?"

"She blew a kiss in my direction..." Joe offhandedly reported, thinking back to the moment the Jeweled Kiss made her exit. "But how in the blazes did it get through my mask or on me at all? I mean she just... blew... a... kiss."

"Well here, scrape the evidence off in this," Patsy offered a white handkerchief. "We are going to have enough to explain to Katie when we see her. Do you think she's done with that baloney with the mayor by now?"

"Probably, but why would we drag Kate into all of this?" Joe asked as Patsy settled into the cruiser's driver seat, turning on the ignition.

"Because Joseph, she would literally murder both of us if we didn't after what we witnessed tonight," Patsy answered before adding, "Well at least what I think I saw, or ah darn it I don't know. I mean it's just not possible..."

Hitting the wheel in disgust before he put the cruiser into gear, Patsy gunned the engine, fishtailing the car in the direction of the high-rise lights of Capstone City.

"All I can tell you buddy, is you and Katie might have to adjust the guest list to your big day once you get around to asking her the big question."

"What?" Joe started to ask.

"That is unless we have to throw her old man's dead or undead behind in the slammer first..." Patsy cut him off, starting to explain what happened to him after he ran off back at the ring.

"Yep that's him," Patsy said, eyeing the small black and white photograph in his hand. "This a pretty recent pic, Katie?"

"As recent as it can be, Patsy," Kate replied with a shrug. "It's not like Dad has been taking a lot of shots lately. What's going on guys? Why would you two come all the way over here just to ask about an old picture of Dad?"

Sitting back in his chair, Joe looked over to his partner, silently wishing he would keep his trap zipped about the real reason they had jumped across town to City Hall to find Kate after her meeting with the Dean and the mayor. However, looking at his partner he knew that wasn't going to happen here. Under Kate's gaze, Patsy was sweating like a perp back at the station and the engineer was too smart to not know something was up. Joe knew keeping her out of this wasn't going to be easy as soon as Patsy told him the whole story back in the car. Not once since his passing last year was it safe to mention her father in an unfavorable light if Kate had anything to say about it, and if Patsy was right about what he saw back at the wrestling match, Joe knew someone was going to be in her crosshairs pretty quickly.

"Well Katie," Patsy stammered slightly. "Earlier this evening I thought I... I mean after the wrestling match I took off after a fella that..."

"Patsy, please stop," Kate interjected before turning and walking over to Joe. "Honey, I've been awake since 5:00 a.m. this morning. I haven't eaten and I'm really annoyed that I've been added to this affair of the mayor's because I have no idea why they need an engineer for this fiasco except that she'll be looking pretty standing next to him. So please just lay this out for me quickly, because if it has anything to do with Dad I want to know about it and I want to know now."

"Patsy thought he saw someone tonight that was pretending to be

Professor Stone," Joe said, knowing flowering anything for his girl wasn't best right now. "We didn't know if we had a photo of him at the house and I remembered you always carried one in your purse so we came over here to have him get a good look at it while it was fresh in his mind."

"What? Why would anyone pretend to be Dad?" Kate asked, completely confused. "You said you were at the wrestling match. Why would anyone want to act like Dad near a wrestling match?"

"We don't know, honey," Joe answered trying to calm her down. "But trust me, Patsy and I are going to find out."

"You mean Patsy, you and I are going to find out right?" Kate asked sharply looking at Joe, almost daring him to try and correct her.

"Kate, unless you're going to start walking the beat every afternoon with us there really isn't much you can do right now," Joe cautiously replied. "This man who is impersonating your Dad is connected to the thefts going on all over town and you know we are more lost than anything on those."

"We'll see, so you're saying you went to the stockyards to watch wrestling and this bandit just showed up?" Kate asked, moving on from the conversation. "Was she there to steal the purse or ticket sales?"

"No," Joe replied thinking back to the events of the night. "It felt more like she wanted the audience this time. She was really putting on a show up there for the crowd. A lot different than at any of her smash and grabs; she was in and out of those before most people even knew what was going on."

Going over the action at the wrestling ring for Kate, Joe paused at the part where the Jeweled Kiss's elderly companion sprinted from the ring.

"For one thing, I doubt that he's really an older man at all," Joe added, looking at Patsy. "The way he bolted from the ring was just too fast. I almost thought you wouldn't be able to catch up to him."

"For a second I thought I was going to lose him right after he made it into the locker rooms, but the mook ran out of gas like an old junker," Patsy replied. "One minute he's a track star and the next he was limping around and huffing like he was going to fall over."

"A limp?" Kate asked. "What leg was he limping on?"

"The right, I think," Patsy answered, noticing the corners of Kate's eyes slightly narrowing at the information. "When I grabbed him I got a quick look at his face and for a second I swear he had a gaunt, skinny face but when I turned him around, there was your old man staring back at me like Marley's ghost himself."

"Well chains or not, it couldn't have been him," Kate spat.

"No, there's no way," Patsy nodded. "But Katie, I'm telling you, whoever is acting like him did his homework. I mean it was the spitting image of the man, even his voice."

"He talked to you?" Joe asked.

"Just for a second," Patsy replied. "Like I told you in the car, I had a hold of him and was walking him back to the ring when I saw her hand reach through the side wall of the locker room and grab his jacket."

"The Jeweled Kiss?" Kate asked.

"Yeah, that crazy self-naming dame reached right through the wall and pulled him through me!" Patsy finished.

"That must've been right after she left me in the middle of that scrum in the ring," Joe connected. "But you said he talked to you?"

"That's just another looney toon part to this, bud," Patsy answered. "As soon as the mook sees that dame's hand grab hold of him, he looks back at me and I swear, with the most sincere look I've ever seen on a face says, 'I'm sorry my boy.'"

"I'm sorry my boy..." Kate repeated softly, every single word almost a memory of her father. The impersonator had not only taken his face and voice but his mannerisms.

"Well the easy explanation is this doppelgänger is associated with our Jeweled Kiss. Much like the boxes, she's figured out a way to manipulate her friend's appearance from afar, possibly for a limited time..."

"Okay, but Joe, why Dad?" Kate injected. "I mean you were at a wrestling match. Dad never had anything to do with stuff like that!"

"I don't know... maybe she thought it would throw Patsy, but that doesn't make sense..." Joe quickly answered cutting off his own thought. "How would she know we were going to be there tonight to have thought of that?"

"We didn't even know we were going to be there tonight!" Patsy added before noticing the strange, distant look on Joe's face. "Hey bud, what's up? You look like you were the one who saw the ghost tonight."

"Joe, what is it?" Kate asked, noticing the look on her love's face as well.

"Ahh nothing... just... Kate are you done here? Can we drive you home?" Joe stammered before catching himself.

"Yes, I'm done here. Let me grab my stuff and we can head out," Kate replied, studying Joe's face as if expecting him to add something else to what he had said.

As Kate left the room, Patsy walked to his partner's chair and whispered, "You've got that look on your face. What's going on?"

"What look?"

"You always get the same look when you're trying to hide something important," Patsy answered. "Don't clam up on me, partner. What's the deal?"

Minutes later on street level, Kate was tired of waiting on an explanation. This topic was too personal to her now to be left in the dark. Waiting for Joe to close the passenger door to the police cruiser, she made her move. Reaching forward, she snatched the keys from the ignition and dropped them to the floor in the backseat.

"We are not going anywhere until you spill on what you were trying to hide from me up there," Kate decreed as she sat back in her rear seat.

"Hon, what are you talking about?" Joe asked.

"Don't give me that," Kate replied. "You got that look on your face up there just before you wanted me to get my things so we could leave. I gave you all the way down to the car to fess up and now I'm tired of waiting."

"Patsy!" Joe yelled, looking over at his partner.

"Don't look at me, bud. You really thought she couldn't read you like a dime novel? I tell you Joseph, you're just a bad poker player," Patsy said, shaking his head.

Looking back at his girl, Joe weighed his options before giving in and starting, "First off, I don't have a look."

"Yes you do," both Patsy and Kate replied.

"And second..." Joe continued, frowning. "I only tried to keep this from you because I'm worried it might either confuse you or upset you more..."

"Fat chance of that at this point," Kate scoffed, rolling her eyes.

"It just... it occurred to me when we were going over the night's events that we missed something about the order in which they happened," Joe started, looking back at Kate. "We are assuming that for whatever reason, this Jeweled Kiss is disguising her partner to look like your Dad, or at least she did tonight. We know from the gift boxes all over town that she's somehow able to disguise or manipulate objects and apparently people without being in contact with them for a long time, unlike me."

"So what part of that would bother me more than I already am?" Kate asked. "I already knew this gal had a large bag of magic tricks. Does she have more we don't know about?"

"Again, it's the order that things happened," Joe continued. What bothered me was when Patsy mentioned the perp in the ring having dark hair. You see, the Jeweled Kiss was busy in the ring with me the whole time until she ran off and grabbed her partner from Patsy. And from what it sounded like when Patsy grabbed the perp, the guy didn't start to look like your father until he was farther away from the Jeweled Kiss."

"So what does that mean?" Kate asked, not understanding Joe's implication.

"I don't know for sure... AND... I hope I'm dead wrong here but..." Joe started, trying to choose his next words carefully. "It occurred to me that if the Jeweled Kiss was busy with me in the ring when Patsy grabbed her partner in the back, she couldn't have changed him into your father. If he started looking like your dad when he got farther away from the ring, it might not have been him being disguised... it might have been that...his disguise was wearing off."

CHAPTER ELEVEN

"Ah, Mrs. Renae must have finally gotten the grinder working again. I swear if I was tortured with another cup of that instant slop she gave me yesterday..." Editar thought cheerfully to himself as he walked down the dimly lit hallway. Sipping his morning coffee, the mayor was in a cheery mood, even this early. His plans for the G.I. celebration had been checked last evening by some of the brightest minds the city had to offer and all was going according to plan on all fronts with the exception of a small detail that he planned to rectify without delay.

Gracefully strolling along the shadows of the hallway, the enigmatic politician took every step along the corridor as precisely as a dancer performing a practiced routine. Stopping halfway down the hall, Editar took another sip from his steaming cup and thought to himself.

"Needs just a little more cream..."

A quick turn of a marked key through its tumblers along with a sharp push against what surprisingly heavy door and the hallway was bathed in the light from the room's lone window discreetly covered with steel bars.

There, sitting on the small cot was the disheveled, but still quite alive Professor Harold Stone. Editar could see from the daggers being sent in his direction that the professor wasn't happy to see him, but when was he ever?

"Good morning, Professor!" the politician smiled. "I trust you slept well?"

"Like you would care you piece of..." Stone spat back.

"Professor! Manners please!" Editar smiled coolly, interrupting the older man. "Is that any way to start off a day? I mean honestly, to awake with such thoughts in that brilliant head of yours, I'm going to start to think you are not enjoying our little chats."

"Waking up every morning as your guest is no way to start a morning," the professor retorted.

"Well my friend, life is a series of ups and down, tos and fros as they say. We are all here to simply ride the waves," Editar chided back.

"First off, I'm not your friend nor that of your Nazi Führer you goose stepping..." Professor Stone replied, struggling to stand up from the cot.

"My dear man, do I look like someone who would... how do you put it 'goose step'?" Editar asked enjoying the sight of Stone struggling to stand. "No, no, my days of parading around for the party are long past me now. As you can attest to, we can't all stay young forever."

"I usually respond to such comments from my friends with some anecdote about being young at heart but..." Stone shot back as he finally made it to his feet leaning heavily against the small table next to the bed. "But as we've already stated, you are not any friend of mine and I'm not completely certain that black rotten lump beating inside of your chest can be considered a heart."

"How droll..." Editar frowned, masking his annoyance by taking another sip of coffee. "Well, MY FRIEND, as enjoyable as this has been I must get to the real reason I came to visit you this morning."

"And that would be?" the professor questioned.

"Well, I was looking over my agents' report of last night's activities..." Editar started.

"We did what you asked..." the professor mumbled shamefully.

"Now don't interrupt!" Editar cut him off. "Yes, from what I hear, you and our little, what's she going by? Ah yes, our little Jeweled Kiss were successful, however there was the small fact about your actions after the delivery of the package. It seems while our little lady was toying around with that ghostly hero, you allowed yourself to get caught by the authorities."

"He caught up with me once I got further away from her," Stone explained, pointing to his right leg. "Once her influence starts to fade my knee starts to act up again and I didn't have my cane."

"That's just disappointing... to lose a leg race with a one-legged man is just an absolute disappointment," Editar tsked, shaking his head. "Did you recognize the officer? Was he someone you used to know?"

Looking at the man standing in front of him, the professor slightly confused by the one-legged statement, regrouped and calmly lied. The professor saw no reason to throw Patsy's name in the mind of such a devious man. "No, I never saw that officer before. He must have been new."

"Really? Never? That's a little surprising..." Editar said, leaning against the open door frame suddenly lost in thought before continuing, "BUT... the part of your bumbling that really gets me is, if you were so far outside of our lady's influence then this officer saw you... the real you... What, may I ask, is the first rule I told you and our lady before I sent you out on your little errand?"

"But I got away..." the professor said, it now dawning on him where this conversation was starting to proceed.

"The first rule was do not be seen," Editar continued, ignoring the older man. "It wasn't avoid being caught, or avoid being taken to jail, or even talk your way out of being sent to the Russian Gulag, which I guess if you follow rule one is all implied but the first rule is TO NOT BE SEEN!" Editar barked, all playfulness in his voice now gone.

The professor could tell from the look in the man's eyes that the playful banter was over. The villain's facade had been thrown aside to reveal his true nature, a presence whose name was whispered in shadows as Lord Minos.

"And as we all know professor... rules must be followed... order must be maintained for if not, where would we be?" Minos sadly smiled. "And as any young child knows when rules are broken there are... consequences..."

"No! Please!" Stone cried out, reaching for the villain.

Batting his reach away with a wave of his unused hand, Minos reached behind his jacket and produced a small, black walkie-talkie. Pressing the machine's lone button, Minos spoke into the radio.

"Put the boy on..."

"*Yes Lord Minos*," a gruff voice replied through the walkie.

A few moments later a weaker, exhausted-sounding voice came over the radio.

"*Yes?*"

"Ah my dear boy," Minos smiled, looking directly at Professor Stone wanting him to soak in every word he was about to say. "I'm sorry to tell you that you will not be dining on the extra rations that you were promised this evening. You see young man, as I've told you before, I like to follow what they call the 'carrot and the stick' mindset. I reward my associates when they succeed and well... don't... when they fail. Sadly our dear professor here broke the rules last night and well that... well I think you understand what that means by now, don't you?"

"*No! Please not that again... Please! Professor!*" the voice pleaded from the walkie.

"Stop! Please, it was my mistake. Take it out on me and leave the boy alone!" Professor Stone pleaded with his captor only to be sent falling to the floor with a strong backhand from the villain.

"Professor, why in the world do you think we've kept the boy alive this long?" Minos chuckled. "A man of your caliber wouldn't simply cooperate if his neck was the only one on the line, and if I let the boy slide after last night's gaffe, you might start to think of me as a man not of my word... and we can't have that can we?"

"*Please not again...*"

"I am truly sorry my young man, but it is out of my hands," Minos replied into the walkie. "We are all but players in the game, Ralph? Ralph are you there?"

"*Yes Lord Minos...*" the gruff voice returned over the walkie.

"A lesson must be learned," Minos stated over the walkie.

"*Yes sir,*" Ralph replied.

"Well then…" Minos casually replied looking at Stone the entire time.

"*No! Please! No! Professor Help! Please!*"

Roger's cries were interrupted as Minos cut off the small walkie, allowing each plea from the student to echo in the cramped cell around the professor.

"I'll get you for this you, monster," Professor Stone yelled from the floor to the villain. "If it is the last thing I do, I'll make you pay for this!"

"I truly think you believe that old man, but you won't be the first to make that mistake," Minos smiled. "Remember, all it takes is for you to start following the rules of this game. I truthfully hope you come around soon. Our young friend there has been through so many of your failures and I truly believe he's starting to resent you."

"Blast you and your game!" the professor roared, nearly choking in his own fury.

His point made, Minos receded into the dark hallway, closing the door behind him. With the sound of the key quickly turning, the world was again quiet in the small room. Slowly pulling himself up from the floor and onto the bed, the elder adventurer felt his anger at his captors building inside of him. Exploding in a rage, the professor grabbed the side table and with every last bit of strength, threw it into the room's large door. The wooden table crashed, raining shards down on the carpeted floor. Looking at where the table had impacted the door, any brief hope of the door buckling after such an attack was quickly dashed as the professor noticed the now exposed solid steel reinforcement where the wood had splintered. Throwing his head in his hands, the professor relented into grief, beaten by the villainous man.

"Roger my boy… I'm so sorry…" the professor moaned as tears began to form for the tormented student.

On the other side of the large door Minos stood in the darkness enjoying the sounds of the professor's dismay. Smiling to himself, the villain waved his hand through the air as if he was listening to a piece of music rising and crashing as the anguish echoed softly through the hallway. Slowly he danced his way back from his captive's room through the darkened hallway. Engrossed in the sick perversion, the villain almost didn't notice exactly where he was until he was on top of the hidden doorway exiting the darkened hall. Stopping short, he accidentally spilled the remains of his morning coffee on his suit coat and furnished carpet.

"Blast!" Minos cursed, hissing at himself. "Well you clown, this is why we can't have nice things."

Minos opened the secret door made to look exactly like the neighboring wall and suddenly transformed himself back into the persona of Daniel P. Editar, Mayor of Capstone City. He brushed the small droplets of beverage from his suit coat and entered the main hallway of his office in City Hall.

"Ralph! Come clean this up before it stains the carpeting," Editar ordered as a finely dressed stocky man appeared from a side office and began walking in step with him. "The taxpayers spent a sizable penny on this imported rug. We wouldn't want it to go to waste."

"Yes sir," the assistant replied crinkling his lip at the menial task. "Did everything go well, sir?"

"Of course it did, Ralph," Editar chuckled. "Congratulate Mr. Tookings on a job well done. I do believe we finally may have motivated our guest for the future."

"Excellent, I will pass this along," Ralph nodded.

"Oh and Ralph, last night I was able to have Rosán's plans for the celebration checked," Editar added, entering his private office. "Please inform the good doctor that his plans were acceptable and then have him moved to site B. I'd rather not risk leaving him around now that he isn't needed."

"Are we done with the doctor, sir?" Ralph asked.

"Did I say we were *done* with him, Ralph?" Editar said, stopping in his tracks to look at his assistant. "I said I simply would like him moved to site B. We will need him to start working on the facade as soon as possible."

"Yes sir, I will look into possibly using the same passage Otto had reported procuring…" Ralph started.

"Ralph, do I look like I care how you do it?" Editar snapped. "Just get it done!"

"Yes sir!" Ralph quickly replied, exiting the office.

Watching as his assistant hastily walked away, Editar unconsciously went to take another sip from his mug only to be reminded its contents were spilled in the hallway. Disappointed, the politician placed the mug on his desk and walked over to his personal calendar. Flipping to the day's date, he quickly scanned his morning meeting, which had been hand written in by his secretary, Mrs. Renae.

"She scheduled Ms. Craig and the Women's Auxiliary this early in the morning?" Editar thought, frowning as he eyed the first appointment. *"And they call me a monster…"*

CHAPTER TWELVE

"Joe, will you tell me what in the blazes we are doing here?" Patsy asked, glancing at his watch as he clamored out of the cruiser. "We were supposed to be downtown 10 minutes ago working the mayor's G.I. shindig with the rest of the precinct."

"I told you Patsy, I needed to check this note Judy took down for me last night," Joe replied, pushing himself up from the passenger seat.

Balancing on his good leg and cane, Joe finally found purchase, engaging his full weight on the brace of his new prosthetic left leg. The new leg Kate and her team had modified was better with physical movement. However, Joe hated the fact he still had to act like a newborn trying to get his balance as he walked on it with his cane.

"And this couldn't wait until later?" Patsy asked, coming up beside him. "The captain will have our badges if we are not there during the celebration."

"It doesn't start for another 20 minutes, partner," Joe replied, glancing at his watch as they started making their way from the small, graveled parking lot near the docks. The wooden pier had a different look to it in the daytime, Joe thought. It was less dark and mysterious with a slight whiff of ocean water, and more run down and trashed, simply reeking of dead fish.

Watching every step carefully on the broken boards, Joe slowly made his way next to Patsy along the pier, making sure not to get his leg or cane caught in one of the loose boards.

"We just need to check out this note quickly, Patsy and then we can jet off downtown with plenty of time to spare," Joe smiled, trying to mask the exertion the walk was demanding from him.

"Will you at least explain to me who this mook is that got you all in a tizzy?" Patsy asked, pulling his coat closer around him. "Jeez, it's getting cold out here. Who kicked Jack Frost in the pants?"

"He's an old Army buddy of mine," Joe answered, shaking his head at his large friend's bellyaching.

"Yeah you said that, an old Army buddy," Patsy eyed his partner. "But if I'm going to get chewed out by the captain for being late, I'd really like to tell him we dropped everything and rushed out here for something more than an old Army buddy."

Reaching into his coat pocket, Joe produced the handwritten note he found from Judy on his work desk earlier.

"Bevine - Call for you - EARLY - all he would say was - dock A8 ASAP Q.P. Blind Ben."

The man who called earlier, if it is him, went through a lot with me over there buddy," Joe gritted as he slowly tapped his left leg. "He saved my life after this..."

The balloons just wouldn't stay still around the large stage that had been erected in front of the doors to City Hall. Grimacing at the flailing inflatables constantly slapping across his podium, Mayor Editar finally shook his head and whispered to one of the closest junior volunteers.

"How about you take those and pass them out to some of the children in the audience?"

"All of them?" the young man said, surprised to even be noticed by the mayor let alone spoken to.

"No, how about just the ones near the podium," Editar smiled back, pointing to center stage. "Mother Nature seems to be content in bludgeoning me with those, and that might be just the slightest bit distracting when I stand there for my speech."

"Yes, your honor," the young man agreed, looking at the podium. "I'll get right on that. My mother always said you can't control the weather."

"Speak for yourself..." Editar silently chuckled thinking back to Rosán's failed plan last year.

Looking out from the main foyer of the old City Hall building, Editar watched the young man make his way through the crowd, pleased with the large turnout. It was important the city invested itself in these "celebrations" if his plan was to succeed.

"Tell any of these sheep something is for their precious boys overseas and they would show up for anything," the villainous politician thought to himself, looking at the unlit yellow orb sitting on the makeshift stage. The yellowed glass bauble, roughly two feet in diameter, sat straddled by two large cables on each side atop a carpeted table, the overcast morning sky reflecting back at Editar in its unique mirror finish.

"One thing I will miss about this country is how predictable these Americans can be..." Editar darkly thought as he scanned the crowd before noticing the time on one of the numerous public street clocks. "Fifteen more minutes and then all of the fun begins..."

"Okay, I get it partner, but we've got to get hustling or the Cap…" Patsy started.

"PING!"

The shot ricocheted off the board a few feet in front of them sending a volley of splintered wood in the air. Diving to his right, Patsy grabbed Joe rolling with him behind a small stack of crates trying to find cover.

"Argh!' Joe cried out in pain as his prosthetic leg ended up being pinned under his partner.

"You hit?" Patsy asked, looking back at his friend, his service pistol already drawn.

"No, but get off me!" Joe yelled back, his thigh now throbbing. "This used to be easier..."

"We must be getting old," Patsy quipped, looking back in the direction of the shooter. "Capstone Police, drop the rifle and come out with your hands where we can see them!'

"No chance!" Joe heard the man call back. Quickly peering over the crates, he could only see the barrel of a rifle perched out of a window aimed in their direction. The shooter was somewhere in that docked wheelhouse, but Joe couldn't get a bead on him.

"Hey pal, we're here to see an old friend of mine," Joe called out. "What's with the warm welcome?"

"Yeah, an old friend," the shooter called back. "Neither of you look like this friend we're waiting for. One too many sets of shoes out there!"

"Let's say I got better!" Joe called back, understanding the comment. The shooter had been expecting a one-legged man. There wasn't any way he could've known about Kate's prosthetic.

"We don't have time for this," Joe said. "Just keep your head down. I'm going out there to talk to this guy."

"You nuts?" Patsy replied, looking back at his partner. "He's got us pinned down everywhere to Sunday. I can't even get a look at him."

"I didn't say I was just going to stand up, walk out there and say hi," Joe said, pointing to his watch.

"Ladies and gentlemen!" Editar started, spreading his hands out in front of him in a welcoming gesture. "Thank you so very much for coming out to what I believe will be an extraordinary day for our fair city."

The large crowd assembled in front of the hastily constructed platform burst into applause. All of them, including the young children in attendance, waved small United States flags that had been passed out earlier by the mayor's staff.

"This is the first of two celebrations honoring our fighting men overseas who are bravely, and with no thoughts of their own safety, defending our rights and liberties. Because of them the Germans and their lot are learning they should've never messed with the USA!" Editar continued, the crowd eating out of his hands, their cheering deafening.

"My dear mother once told me the story of a soldier and his girl during the Civil War," Editar started as the crowd slowly simmered down. "When that brave man went off to fight, his girl promised she would leave a candle burning for him every night so that he could find his way home one day. And that, my good people, is what I intend our great city to do for our brave boys overseas."

Leaving the podium, the mayor crossed the platform to where the Police Commissioner, the Head of the City Council, and other elected officials had been sitting for the event. In front of them sat a large yellow plastic orb, slackened support chains with thick electric cord entwined along their links hanging off of each side.

"Let this beacon of light, which will be strung between the expanse of the two Seaman Towers, shine as a welcoming sign for our brave boys to follow home!" Editar yelled to the crowd, having moved away from the microphone. Motioning to his men on the sides of each tower, the mayor reached his hand inside a small panel on the orb flipping a discreet switch that brilliantly illuminated the object.

The crowd erupted as the lit orb slowly started to rise skyward from the podium. The chains on each pole of the orb feathered out to a long series of pulleys and winches attached to the outside of the Seaman Towers now being controlled by the mayor's assistants. The orb continued to rise higher and higher to the excitement of the assembled crowd until it rested in between the expanse of the towers near the 47th floor, the lines fully taut on each side. Suspended in midair, the orb sat as an otherworldly sun illuminating the crowd underneath and the surrounding buildings.

"I would be amiss if I didn't thank everyone who had a hand in the planning of our City's G.I. Celebration, such as..." the mayor said as he started announcing the names of the City Council and other officials. "And of course, none of this would've been possible without the help of the Mechanical Engineering Department of our own Capstone University, especially department head Doctor James Waldon and the newest member of the faculty, Miss Kathryn Stone!"

Both Doctor Waldon and Kate quickly raised their hands to acknowledge the scattering of applause from the crowd.

"Apparently the Doctor Stone part of my name wasn't put on his cue cards," Kate thought to herself, annoyed.

Looking at his watch, Editar smiled to himself before finishing his wrap up.

"Showtime..."

"Once again, I'd like to thank all of you, the amazing citizens of Capstone City for coming out."

"BAM! BAM!"

Two gunshots echoed in the plaza, unexpectedly cutting off the mayor's finish. Screams rang out as Editar fell to the podium clutching his right arm. There standing above him, seemingly out of nowhere, was the Jeweled Kiss. Next to her loomed a large man clad in a gray trench coat and brimmed hat, his face completely covered by a black silk stocking, but his intentions known by the smoking revolver in his right hand.

"I'm so sorry to crash the festivities, Mr. Mayor," the Jeweled Kiss smiled as she looked down at the injured man. "But it would seem that our invitation was lost in the mail."

"Okay big fella, let's not get trigger happy!" Joe yelled, slowly rising from his cover. "I'm leaving my weapon here and coming out."

"Keep your hands where I can see them!" the shooter's voice rang out over the small dock. "How about your pudgy friend there?"

"Hey!" Patsy barked in return.

"Let's just say I'm more trusting than he is, especially when someone is taking pot shots at us," Joe answered, taking a careful step toward the boat. "Okay pal, I came out here to meet an old Army buddy of mine."

"Maybe that's me? What do you think of that, paaal? Remember those good old days fighting for Uncle Sam?" the shooter quipped back.

"Now friend, I'm sort of doubting that. You see, this buddy wouldn't be able to see his hand in front of his face let alone take the wings off the flies buzzing around all of the dead fish over there with that pea-shooter, so how about you clue me in as to what's up with the warm welcome here," Joe replied, taking another step toward the boat. He could make out the name "Heqet" painted on the hull.

"Joooooooeeeee!" another voice rang out from the shooter's direction. Suddenly, a large man jumped out from the wheelhouse, landing a few feet in front of Joe. "Is that really you? How are you dancing over here Bengy?"

"Bengy, no one has called me that in a long time Marcus," Joe replied to the boat captain, happy to see him but still wary of the concealed shooter. "Let's say they call me Pegleg Bengy nowadays . . . How about you? Where's your seeing eye dog?"

"Hahaha!" the large man laughed almost doubling over. "You know me Bengy. I've always been more of a cat person. Washington! Come on down man. You're probably making my friends here nervous."

"Is that him?" the shooter yelled out.

"No, it's his Aunt Petunia. Get down here, man. This guy's okay," Marcus yelled, looking back in the shooter's direction.

As he did, Joe watched a tall man, Marcus's brother James, somehow unfold himself from the wheelhouse. Patsy cautiously made his way to them as well.

"Give me that!" Patsy barked grabbing James' rifle from his hands.

"Hey!"

"Old buddy or not, taking a few potshots at me usually will get you a black eye or a night at the station so start counting your lucky stars I'm in a rush today pal," Patsy replied to James, quickly unloading the rifle. "If you mind your manners maybe you'll get this back after class."

As the interchange between Patsy and James continued, Joe discretely flipped a knob on the decoder watch on his right hand. Unbeknownst to anyone besides him and Patsy, Joe had secretly been under the influence of the magical powers of the Spartan Cloak the entire time he had ventured toward the boat and its unseen shooter. Not wanting the sight of the Grey Ghost to escalate things, Joe had decided to stay out of costume but stay solid as a stiff breeze in case Marcus's friend had gotten trigger happy. He silently thanked his stars that Marcus hadn't rushed out and tried to hug his old army buddy since that would have made things interesting.

"So Marcus, what's with the welcome?" Joe asked finally interrupting the two before the situation fell apart again. "I'm hoping you don't welcome everyone like that."

"I might have to start," James grunted, finally relenting.

"Never mind him," Marcus cut in his tone serious again. "We've got ourselves into a bit of trouble here Joe. I'm sorry to say you and your friend here aren't the first visitors we've had wearing blue since we docked and called your office."

"How about you two start filling us in here," Patsy demanded, still suspicious of the two. "We're already late for something and I'm only one cup of brew in this morning."

The quartet went below deck on the Heqet near the converted hold and engine room. Greeting them were two men, both bound hand and foot, one a short squat man, the other a lanky, almost unhealthy looking man sporting a thin mustache and a large black eye on his right side. Marcus started to fill them in, telling the group their names were Horst and Otto, respectively.

"So I come down here and this joker has a knife pulled on Washington from behind."

"Who's Washington?" Patsy asked confused.

"That's me," James answered. "It's an old nickname."

"So I grab him and these two put up a fight, nothing we couldn't handle, but then I noticed something on this one's arm that told me we were in the deep end here," Marcus said pointing to Otto's ripped shirt.

Grabbing the thin man as he tried to yell through his gag, Marcus moved the remains of the tatters on the man's right arm revealing a dark tattoo. The inked mark was a full circle of red bordered by a thick ring of white, the lone exception to its crimson interior being a reversed letter L angled toward the man's back.

"Is that really what I think it is?" Joe asked, staring at the mark.

"I'm afraid so buddy. For a while I thought this was the last thing I was ever going to lay these baby browns on again," Marcus nodded back.

Nicholas Cara

Every time Joe thought back to that moment, the scene would play out in front of him like a foggy dream. The sounds of that forest surrounded him as before, each footstep by the squad in the loose morning snow, another eerie march in the wrong direction. Even the smell returned to him, a brisk, early air with a distinct grit to it, one that Joe never was able to describe even to himself except as the smell of the land's innocence being lost. No matter how much powder covered the war-torn plains, the death underneath always rose through. Yet the players in the memory are always out of focus to him, just ghosts in the shadows calling out their lines except for the memory of his younger self and Marcus in the foreground. Invading the memory, more in his imagination than in the retelling of the actual events, was the skeletal face of the reaper himself, stalking their every move in that other worldly forest.

"Benford! Double-check that bunker at 2 o'clock!" Sergeant Burns calls from the rear.

"Dogs gone through here already, sir?" Marcus calls back. "I can't make out any tracks in this new snow."

The squad had two K-9 units assigned to them, experts in sniffing out traps and tripwires, which the Germans in this area had littered the ground with before retreating behind the ridge two clicks back.

"Yeah, they cleared that area already," Burns replies quickly.

Seconds drift by in the haze before Joe watches Henry with one of the red heelers, the larger one named Jojo, come up behind the Sergeant.

"Sir, we haven't gone anywhere near that area yet," Henry reports to Burns, Jojo barking loudly next to him pulling at the leash.

"Keep the mutt quiet, Henry!" Burns curtly replies. "Benford is a big boy. He can take care of himself."

Thinking back to this moment almost physically hurts Joe because scream as he might at the memory of Marcus, the large man never stops approaching the abandoned bunker. Every time in Joe's memory, no matter how much he wishes it would change, the small sound of the pin being pulled by a tripwire can somehow be heard as loud as a gunshot and is just as sinister as the laughter from the ghostly form of death close behind them.

"Grenade!" Marcus calls back, warning his fellow troops.

"Fall back! Fall back! Get down!" Joe could hear Burns cry out, diving for cover.

And then Joe watches the memory of his younger self sprinting toward his friend Marcus, trying to outpace the reaching hand of death's specter. The reaper's laughter grows louder and louder as it approaches the large man. Those precious seconds last an eternity as the action slows before him, every movement a choreographed motion that no matter how much he wished, was forever written in stone.

As the gruesome play continues before him, Joe watches the memory of himself connect with Marcus's midsection, pushing the large man away from the explosive just as it ignites. The reaching hand of death, no matter what Joe screams out to the ghostly memory, always remains undeterred, missing the large man but in his place taking hold of Joe's left leg. The skeletal face of the reaper laughs while looking down at the leg in his hand as it hovers over his memory's crippled body, not what it wanted but a pound of flesh in any regard.

There, on the bunker door behind that cackling specter, is where Joe remembered seeing the image, a red circle encompassed by a white border surrounding a simple, yet almost sinister-looking mark, an angled inverted letter L....

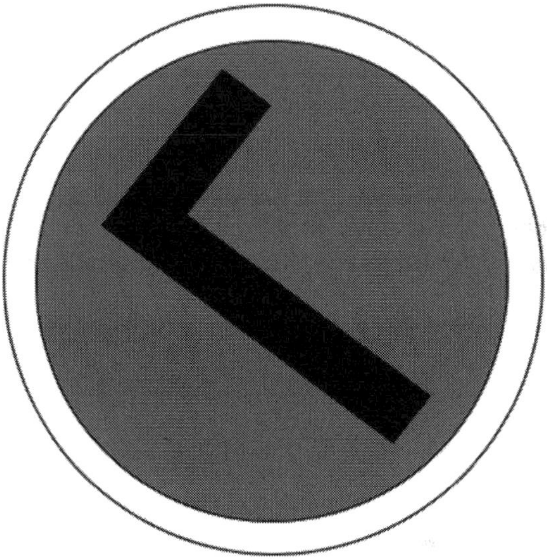

"I'll never forgive Burns for telling us he had already scouted that area. Lazy sack of trash," Joe mumbled.

"He was more telling *ME* Bengy. That guy didn't like my colorful disposition and it wouldn't have cost him a wink of shut eye if I'd been blown to Kingdom Come," Marcus said. "I've always been sorry you got mixed up with all of that. After I hit my head, the swelling shut the lights off until weeks after the Army had discharged my blind behind stateside."

Pointing to the tattoo and then his own head, Marcus added, "This was the last thing I saw before you hit me Bengy, and it was burned in here for weeks. I'll never forget it."

"I remember it buddy," Joe said, peering at the symbol. "It was the last thing I saw too before I woke up next to you in the hospital."

"I'll never know how to repay you Bengy," Marcus replied, thinking back to those days lying next to Joe never really knowing if either was going to make it. "I mean man, you lost your leg saving me. I liked the rest of those boys in our squad well enough but none of those guys would've noticed I was gone if my backside was blown away."

"Well we probably could have gotten clear if you weren't built like a brick wall," Joe smirked. "How'd your vision come back? The doctors kept saying the swelling in your head was permanent."

"Oh those guys... remember that one started to call me 'Blind Ben'?" Marcus shook his head. "Those docs wouldn't know a cold from a gunshot. I got back stateside and I tell you, a month to the day I wake up one morning and suddenly I'm seeing my ugly mug in the mirror. Why did the swelling go down? Don't know, don't care, but I can tell you the last thing I ever thought I would see was this thing."

Slapping the marked arm of the bound Otto, the captive yelled back at the captain through his gag.

"I bet that was all nice and pretty," James cut in, laughing at the muffled curses.

"So what you're telling us is that these guys are Nazis?" Patsy interjected. "I mean we have Nazis in Capstone now?"

"You might have a bigger problem," Marcus sighed. "Like we said, you two weren't the first company we had this morning."

Walking over to the engine room, Marcus reached out and opened the door, revealing another bound and gagged man. Joe was worried for his friend as soon as he noticed the man's garb.

"Joseph..." Patsy started, noticing the man as well.

Sitting on a crate, the third prisoner was dressed in the blues of a Capstone City police uniform. Before Marcus could start to explain himself, Patsy grabbed the bound man.

"Who is this joker?" Patsy asked, picking the man up off of the crate to stare him in the eye. "Where'd ya get the tin badge, you mook, a Cracker Jack box?"

"You sure he's not one of ours Patsy?" Joe asked his friend surprised by his quick reaction.

"Joseph, I know every beat cop on the force and I can tell you this bum never got invited to the Christmas party," Patsy replied, grabbing the rag in the man's mouth. "Speak up buddy. What's with the trick-or-treat act?"

The fake officer coughed as the rag was removed from his mouth. "My name is Russel Parks, check my badge. You two know how much trouble you are in for assaulting an officer..."

"Get off it pal!" Patsy cut him off, shaking the man. "First thing, I know Rusty and unless you dyed those red curls and grew a good foot taller you ain't him, so cut it out!"

Grabbing the badge pinned to the man's front shirt, Patsy read the name, finding it was Parks's badge. "I swear you mook, if you hurt Rusty to get this I'll leave you at the bottom of this pier!"

"If it makes you feel more fisherman like, check out the ink on his arm," James piped in from the back.

Both Joe and Patsy searched the bound man's arms, and there on his right arm, just as James had insinuated, was the tattoo of an angled letter L encircled by white and red colors.

"So boys, fill us in on what happened to mister academy wannabe here," Joe said, looking back at the two shipmates.

"We made port with these two stored down here after the ruckus," Marcus said, throwing his thumb at Otto and Horst. "I sent James to a payphone near the restaurant to call your precinct."

"Yeah, so I talked to some lady named Jody or something," James continued.

"Judy..." Patsy corrected.

"Yeah Judy," James said. "So I told her the whole deal and the woman tells me she'll have someone out as soon as she can. So we sit here waiting and then this guy shows up. We take him down here explaining everything and suddenly he pulls his piece on us and starts untying skinny over there."

"He starts to get all chummy with the fella," James continued, trying to explain their actions. "He said stuff like you're lucky I got here first, if he hears about this...he definitely wasn't acting like any cop I've seen before."

"He couldn't keep an eye on both of us while he was trying to get his buddy free, so we got the jump on him," Marcus finished in disgust. "Look Bengy, I knew we were in a heap of trouble either way here. Either we attack a cop on my boat, which never ends well, or these nuts here are so connected that they have someone on the police force intercepting our call. So I called back and left another message I knew only you'd understand."

"The second time you called was it Judy again?" Joe asked.

"It was her again," James replied. "That's why I left the message like I did for you."

"Well good news big guy," Patsy added, pushing the bound imposter. "Besides trying to win a stuffed bear by shooting cans off my shoulders back on the pier earlier, you didn't attack any cops today. This guy is as blue as my Aunt Kelly."

"Bad news is somehow this guy got a hold of your call to our station," Joe commented. "What were the polite twins here having you transport from... what was the name of the island you mentioned earlier?"

"Dagger Island, it's about three hours off the coast," Marcus answered. "When we were hired, they said the cargo was going to be bones and rocks from some dig over there. But when one of their crates cracked open, this thing fell out."

Marcus reached over to a tarp near the two captives. Pulling it away the captain revealed the splintered remains of the crate Marcus had mentioned. Joe and Patsy couldn't believe what was sitting in middle of the broken wooden box... a small, silver cylinder casting their dumbfounded reflections back at them. It was the exact same type of cylinder the Grey Ghost had found inside of the wrapped packages left all over Capstone City by the Jeweled Kiss.

"Well, what do you know?" Patsy whistled, reaching out to poke the cylinder. Finding purchase on the mirrored surface, Patsy added, "It seems that the lady of the lake hasn't worked her voodoo on this yet..."

"I can make out a seam on this one," Joe said examining the cylinder. "Grab the bottom Patsy. Let's see if we can take a look under the hood on this one."

As Patsy gripped the sides of the cylinder, Joe produced a small pocket knife and started wedging the blade in the seam. As he did both Otto and Horst started yelling through their gags at them and jumping up and down crazily.

"What's got into those two?" Patsy asked, looking over at the bound men.

Ignoring them, Joe continued working the blade into the seam until he was finally able to slightly lift the lid of the cylinder. Slowly working it up, Joe carefully checked for any connections between the parts of the cylinder before lifting the lid away from the base. The captives' unease at this was disconcerting. Placing the lid on the swaying deck boards of the hold, Joe replaced the small knife with a small flashlight from within his coat. Illuminating the inside of the cylinder, both Joe and Marcus felt a cold shiver run down their spines as they recognized the mysterious contents from their work in the Army.

"Get those off of my boat Bengy," Marcus softly spoke, almost terrified to speak any louder.

"Partner, what's the big deal about this junk?" Patsy asked, not understanding. "It looks like moldy bread dough."

"You don't want to try to bake with this stuff, Patsy," Joe sullenly answered. "Marcus and I saw this kind of stuff working with the Brits over there. Remember that almond smell, Marcus?"

"Yeah I'll never forget it," Marcus whispered. "They called it 'Exploif Plastique'... French name I think. Wire a charge into a brick of this stuff and you can take out a Panzer Tank. But Joe, look at this stuff, remember those rumors of the green dough those Germans were working on?"

"Yeah I remember, what were they calling it again?" Joe quietly asked noticing the green hue of the contents.

"Der grüne Freund... the green friend," Marcus answered. "I never saw this stuff in action, but there were rumors that they had somehow tripled the explosive power. But I remember hearing they could never keep it stable enough for use."

"Whoa, so if this is that stuff, this amount of it..." Patsy started, estimating the amount of the yellowish green putty in the cylinder.

"This one cylinder has enough kick in it to level a city block if not more..." Joe finished shaking his head. "And there is no reason to think that the others all over Capstone are any different."

Patsy slammed the cruiser's rear door in the face of Otto. The goon's threats were slightly muffled outside the car to the officer, but Patsy still got the point. From the moment Joe and Patsy had removed the gags from the two captives' mouths, neither had decided to exercise their right to remain silent. Now cuffed, the two would-be mutineers and the fake Officer Parks had continuously cursed out both Joe and Patsy from the bottom of the Heqet's hold to the cruiser.

"Should've left the rags in their mouths..." Patsy thought to himself knowing the drive to the station was going to be a long one with the three of them in the back.

"Joseph, are you sure we should leave the ship's cargo here?" Patsy called over to the other side of the cruiser. "I mean if those babies are as dangerous as you say..."

"Like I told Marcus, I don't see how we can get them into town with just us and the car, Patsy. I mean there were at least 15 crates in there," Joe replied, slapping the back door on his side hoping to settle their collars down. "And as much as I would like to pile them up on the three village people in the back here, Marcus said he'd find somewhere safe to stow them until we get back with some help. I'm not completely sold on taking them back to town anyways. From what I saw those things were wired and set to go like this one and probably all of its friends throughout the city."

Hopping into the passenger seat, Joe placed the cylinder they examined on the Heqet onto his lap. Just the sight of the explosive in the car started to settle the ruckus in the backseat.

"You sure it's okay to drive that one back?" Patsy said, nervously eying the cylinder.

"We need to get this one back to the station to show the captain what we are dealing with," Joe answered. "Marcus was part of the demolition team back in our unit. The one thing that big guy understands is disconnecting wires. If he said this one is okay to take then that's good enough for me."

"That vast knowledge didn't help him too much during the war from what you've told me," Patsy countered.

"Marcus wasn't usually the one who stepped on wrong spots," Joe answered. "Trust me, there were plenty of bums in my unit that owed their lives to him. And if we had a sergeant worth two beans over there, neither Marcus nor I would've ever been near that thing."

"Calling all cars... ** calling all cars... be advised ** crowd control needed in the vicinity of Phillips and Steeve...** ambulances are on scene... ** Reports of multiple injuries..."

"What's all the hub-bub?" Patsy asked picking up the microphone to the car's two-way radio. "Central this is Car 21, we are inbound with a full backseat. What's all the chatter about?"

"All cars are to report to the downtown district as soon as possible. Multiple reports, ** the mayor has already been transported to Capstone City General. **

Warrants have been issued for one female assailant known as the Jeweled Kiss, and her cohort known as the Grey Ghost, *** descriptions have been varying from the scene **

"Oh crud, buddy. Someone went after the mayor again…" Patsy said, listening to the descriptions. "It must have been during the big celebration. Oh man, the captain is going to have our heads."

"Apparently for some reason they believe the Grey Ghost did…" Joe replied, shaking his head. He knew that vixen, the Jeweled Kiss, was crafty but he never would've guessed she'd take it this far.

Joe started to tell Patsy to gun it back to town when he was interrupted with the follow-up report, one that cut both officers to their very core.

"***Be advised ** most injuries reported considered minor *** except one female, Caucasian, red hair, age estimated in early twenties… ** transported to CCG *** a Dr. Kathryn Stone of Capstone University *** latest reports from CCG are listing her condition as*** serious…***"

PART THREE: A JEWEL-ENCRUSTED SURPRISE

CHAPTER THIRTEEN

This was the perfect moment…

A clear blue sky, not a cloud in sight, and the sun perfectly framing Paden Park. Kate's head rested against his shoulder as they claimed the entire bench underneath the Mastramico Statue just watching the world go by. And as the sun warmed his face in the afternoon light and a slight breeze from nowhere lofted a patch of Kate's red hair in front of his view, Joe knew this was the perfect moment for what he wanted to do.

"Kate…?" Joe said softly, worried she might've dozed off relaxing next to him.

"Hmmm?" was her only reply as she continued resting next to him.

Shifting his shoulder slightly, Joe could tell Kate was amused, sitting up and stretching as if she had just woken up. "Did I make your shoulder fall asleep?"

Waiting for her to look at him, Joe started to carefully choose his words. He had rehearsed this moment over and over again in his head and wasn't about to rush through it now.

"You know I was thinking…" Joe started. "We have been through quite a lot lately…"

"That, my love, should be considered as understatement of the year…" Kate beamed back at him.

"True, true… and through all of it you've always been there for me

Kate," Joe continued, patting his left pant leg which hid the marvelous prosthetic underneath. "I mean I can literally say you've helped me stand back up when I've continued to fall time and time again."

"What kind of girlfriend would I be if I didn't build you a custom state of the art piece of machinery?" Kate chuckled. "I mean you knew when you met me that I hated working in the kitchen, so I have to pull my weight somehow."

"Oh sure you know all the girls are doing that nowadays…" Joe smiled. "And that got me thinking… you know we've been together for quite a while now, and know each other pretty well…"

"Yes…?" Kate asked her eyes raised.

"I guess there is a time that a fella should understand where his priorities really are in this world and…" Joe tried to continue, stumbling with his words now.

"Joseph, are you trying to say what I think you are trying to say?" Kate asked, her face glowing with anticipation.

"Well… oh blast it… what is it you always say? The straightest way through something?" Joe said, using Kate's saying of a straight line to convince himself to just go for it and stop bumbling around. Words were never his strong suit anyways.

Shifting his weight off the bench to lower his right knee to the ground, Joe used his left arm to correctly position his prosthetic in front of himself to keep his balance. Amazingly, Kate had not built it for such an occasion. Taking a long breath to steady himself, Joe looked up at Kate, who returned the look his way, one full of love and nervous anticipation. It only strengthened his resolve that he was doing the right thing. Why either of them would be nervous, Joe couldn't really say. They had been dating for years now, longer than most couples usually stay together without tying the knot.

Joe thought back to what his grandpa had told him years ago before he passed, that a man shouldn't date a girl for years on end if he wasn't willing to marry her. Joe had known almost the moment he met her that without a doubt there was no other girl on planet Earth for him than Kathryn Stone.

She was one in a million and if he was honest with himself, all of the nerves he was feeling right now were probably based on the fact he didn't think he deserved her. But kneeling there, the thought of his grandpa made Joe smile. Good old grandpa had told him a couple in love that decided to stay together for three or more years was pretty much married already. According to that, Kate had unknowingly married him years ago, the war tearing them apart for a year notwithstanding. Thinking of it that way helped Joe's nerves, if only slightly.

"Kate, you know a life with me isn't going to be easy…" Joe started again staring in the eyes of his hopeful fiancé. "I mean, you more than anyone understand what kind of life I'm leading now…"

Kate returned his look, never saying a word.

"But if you think you can handle that…and well me…" Joe continued, his confidence building as he went.

Joe reached into his pocket and produced a small black box. Opening it toward himself, he pulled the small golden ring from the setting and held it up for Kate to see. There was his mother's ring she had passed down to him. At the top was a solitaire diamond shining in the afternoon sunlight standing atop a series of stones on each side. Along the right side of the ring were three small diamonds signifying the three owners of the ring as it had been passed down through the Bevine family. First his grandmother, then Vera his mother and now Kate. Adorning the other side of the band were three birthstones. Starting with his grandmother's, a sapphire, then an emerald for his mother and ending with a peridot for Kate's birth month.

Looking at the ring and then back to Kate who was smiling almost tearfully at him, Joe asked, "Kathryn Stone, will you make me the luckiest man alive and marry me?"

"No…" Kate replied, her smile never wavering.

Shaking his head, Joe knew he must have heard Kate wrong. "Wait, did you…?"

"I said NO!" Kate emphatically cut him off as if he was being foolish. "Of course I can't marry you Joseph… I would've but…You couldn't save me…"

"But Kate…I didn't mean…" Joe started.

"After all I've done for you. After all the time I was faithful to you when you were away. I even accepted how you are now when you got back and you couldn't save me…" Kate continued, not acting like she could hear him.

"Oh and buddy there were so many guys knocking on our Katie's door when you were off playing hero," Patsy said, suddenly walking into view next to Kate.

"Patsy where did you come from?" Joe asked his friend.

"We thought poor Patsy was going to have to beat them off with a broom for you son," Joe's father added, appearing out from behind Patsy. "Looking at you now though, I don't know if he was doing poor Kate any favors."

"Why couldn't you save her, son?" Joe's mother added as she suddenly next to him.

"Mom and Dad…Please…I wasn't there…I didn't know…" Joe started, trying to explain, not understanding where the three had come from. Looking up at the group, Joe saw the calm blue sky behind them now erupting into dark clouds. Thunder and lightning started echoing and flashing from the unbelievable storm silhouetting Joe's family in front of him.

"I mean Nick-Nack, I never would've given you that ring for this girl if I knew what a failure you are," Joe's mom added. "You couldn't save her and now look at you. You can't even hold the ring for her."

At that Joe saw the ring passing through his fingers as if he was made of air. Reaching out for it, the ring continued to fall, his hand always passing through as if it was made of smoke until finally the golden heirloom bounced off the concrete sidewalk. As it did, Joe could see another flash of lightning reflect off the top diamond and one of the birthstones break off the side, landing on the sidewalk under the bouncing ring. Somehow the ring continued to bounce on the sidewalk as if it had a mind of its own. Joe couldn't believe his eyes as gem after gem continued to break off of the band. The number of gems falling off didn't stop at the three adorning the ring, as if a dam of gems had burst and dozens and then hundreds of gems started pouring out of the ring, piling between Joe and the others. Joe still couldn't believe his eyes as the pile in front of him blocked his view of Kate, Patsy, and his parents.

"You couldn't save me…" Kate continued to say, her voice now almost an echo in the raging storm swirling around them.

"Kate, I'm sorry, please…" Joe yelled, trying to be heard over the storm and sound of gems flowing outward in front of him. Joe tried to stand but couldn't. His prosthetic leg was now gone. Trying again, Joe lost his balance and landed in a heap on the gems in front of him. Crawling with his hands, Joe tried to push his way through the tidal wave of sparkling stones flowing around him. Looking for Kate and his family, Joe saw them walking away from him!

"Please help me!" Joe cried out to his loved ones, unsuccessfully trying to swim through the world of glittering stones now filling his every view. "Kate, Patsy, mom, dad…don't leave me!"

"You couldn't save me…" Kate's voice still echoed around him. "You couldn't save me…"

"No! I'm sorry," Joe yelled as the gems started to overcome him, swallowing him from below.

Seeing this, Joe dived to get away from the sea of gems, crawling and scratching at any surface he could get his hands on in a desperate attempt to save his own life from the sure death the sea of gems threatened if it overcame him. Seeing a small break in the avalanche of gems, Joe, now buried hip deep in glittering stones, was caught off guard as a gloved hand sprang from the gems and grabbed his outstretched arm. Pull as he might, Joe wasn't able to release himself from the vise-like grip of the gloved hand. The owner of the hand slowly rose from the pool of gems like a monster rising from the murky depths. Staring back at Joe, whose hand was still clenched by the mysterious man's grip, was the armored face of the Grey Ghost!

"You couldn't save her…" the hero rumbled to Joe.

"No, it wasn't my fault!" Joe yelled back. "You did this!"

"You couldn't save her..." the Grey Ghost repeated.

"Stop it!" Joe yelled back at the Ghostly Guardian.

"You couldn't save her..." the Grey Ghost repeated.

"I SAID STOP IT!" Joe roared, kicking off his leg and lunging at his alter ego. "WE FAILED HER! WE FAILED ALL OF THEM!"

"Did you ever expect anything else?" the Grey Ghost repeated.

"STOP IT!" Joe screamed, grappling with the hero as the gems continued flowing, now raining down upon them. The avalanche of jewels continued burying the two combatants as Joe and the Grey Ghost locked themselves in mortal combat.

Joe, his vision fading as the gems overcame them, lost his grip on the Grey Ghost. As the last point of light started to fall away from him he could still hear the hero's voice echoing in the distance somewhere.

"You couldn't save her..."

"No!" Joe yelled out, crashing onto the tiled floor of the hospital room, the small wooden chair where he had been snoozing now empty. Joe took a few moments to collect himself after awaking from the nightmare. Looking around he found the room devoid of vistors, with only the muffled noise of doctors and nurses making their rounds outside. They had recommended Patsy and Joe head home to rest but both detectives refused. Until he walked out of this room with its occupant, he wasn't leaving.

And that's where the nightmare continued even as he brushed the sleep from his eyes. Using the small chair to right himself, Joe looked at the patient lying asleep in the room's center bed. There, undisturbed by Joe's cry and crash, lay Kate, her right arm heavily bandaged in a sling and her head wrapped in gauze. Kate had sustained a deep cut on her head after falling from the stage at the G.I. Celebration. She had apparently, according to the morning paper next to him, been pushed from the stage by the Grey Ghost.

Nicholas Cara

CITY G.I. CELEBRATION ATTACKED!

Onlookers Horrified as City Officials Wounded in Spray of Gunfire.

By: Lynda Cordova

Chaos ensued at the inaugural G.I. City Celebration as masked compatriots identified by the mayor's office as the vigilante known as the Grey Ghost and the thief known as the Jeweled Kiss attacked the main stage. Minutes after the start of the celebration, the crowd was shocked with the sounds of gunfire near the elected officials chairing the event. Witnesses reported that Mayor Daniel Editar, speaking at the time to the crowd, was wounded by the assailants in his arm during the initial attack. As the main stage and the collected crowd erupted in chaos, onlookers were then stunned as the Grey Ghost, at one time thought to be a conveyer of truth and justice, maliciously continued his attack throwing a Ms. Kathryn Stone, an organizer of the event, from the stage to the street below. After the assault on Ms. Stone, the attackers were witnessed fleeing from the scene using the crowd to mask their escape. Reports from the mayor's representatives list the mayor in stable condition at this time. Doctors at Capstone General declined to comment on Ms. Stone's status at the time of this report; however sources inside the hospital have listed her condition as serious to critical from the injuries she received during the fall from the stage. ... *Continued on A2*

Police Captain Questions Initial Reports of Attacker's Identification

By: Michael Hay

Numerous witnesses at the City G.I. Celebration have been reported on record identifying the main stage attackers as the vigilante known as the Grey Ghost and the thief known as the Jeweled Kiss; however Police Captain James Robinson is hesitant to assign blame so quickly.

"I was present at the attack and all I saw was a man in a coat. Other than someone saying the name out loud there was no reason to assume the shooter was the Grey Ghost," Captain Robinson stated at a press conference hours later.

When asked about his hesitance in identifying the shooters, the police captain said, "Our job is not to guess the facts we need and I'm calling on the citizens of Capstone to please come forward with any information that could help in our investigation. I'm not saying anything at this time except that the full power of this department will not rest until the perpetrators of such a terrible act are brought to justice."

Continued on A3

"So sleeping beauty still resting?" Patsy whispered from the doorway, two paper cups steaming in his hands.

"Yeah, she hasn't stirred even with me making enough racket around here," Joe answered, dropping the paper on the side table.

"I talked to the docs out there when I was calling the station and they don't see a reason she won't wake up soon. The bump on her head might not have been that bad," Patsy said, passing one of the cups of coffee to Joe. The two detectives had almost thrown their prisoners and explosive evidence at Robinson back at the station hours ago before they had made a beeline to the hospital. So Patsy had wanted to call the station to really fill the captain in with the details.

"You couldn't save her…"

"It was bad enough," Joe said, shaking his head, trying to get the whispers of his nightmare out of his mind.

"Well if she had to hit anything, her head was best for her to knock." Patsy halfheartedly chuckled, tapping his own head. "Katie was always hard headed."

Joe knew Patsy was trying to cover his own worry with silly remarks so he let him go on. That was Patsy, the graver the situation, the worse the jokes got. Letting his friend continue, Joe sat in silence looking at his sleeping love.

"You couldn't save her…"

The whispers of his dream kept echoing over and over again in his head. Almost standing in frustration, Joe was cut off by a voice coming from the hallway.

"Oh don't tell me about your rules young lady. I don't care a hill of beans…"

"Vera…"

"Don't Vera me, Stanley. We're the only family that poor girl has left and if this lady…"

Peering into the hallway, Joe made eye contact with the voice. His mother started making a beeline toward the room while his father, a few steps behind, tried talking to the nurse that Vera had just brushed past.

"Joseph, how is she?" his mother asked quietly as she walked in.

"Same…" Joe replied, using his cane to stand, offering the chair to his mom. "We're just waiting for her to wake up."

Instead of sitting, Vera made her way to Kate's bedside. "Those monsters! Look what they did to our poor Kate."

"How's she doing?" Stanley asked, as he made his way into the room, the night nurse apparently placated.

"Resting… oh look at her poor arm…" Vera answered him, looking over at the two detectives. "Why in land's sake did it take you two so long to call us?"

"Sorry Mom, I just wasn't thinking clearly…" Joe apologized, thinking back to the hours he had just sat there in a haze before he even thought about calling his parents.

"Well, either way, we're here now so you two can get a change of clothes or something. You look terrible son," Stanley piped in.

"Dad, I can't leave until she wakes up," Joe countered, looking at his father.

"Yeah, there's nowhere we need to be right now," Patsy agreed.

"Now listen you two," Vera said, picking up the discarded newspaper. "The monsters that did this to poor Kate are still out there. They even tried to kill the mayor for Pete's sake, and you two aren't doing anyone any good sitting here, especially not when the blasted *Vindicator* is reporting utter nonsense about it. The Grey Ghost pushed her indeed."

"Mom I really…" Joe started, wondering why his mother would immediately think the headline was wrong.

"Joseph," Vera cut him off with his full name as she ripped the newspaper in two throwing it in the trash bin. "The doctors told us downstairs that she could wake up at any moment and when she does we will get in touch with you at the station. Your father already called off from the Mill so he'll be here with me. At most you'll be minutes away doing SOMETHING while we wait for Kate to wake up instead of being here silently driving yourself mad."

"I guess but…"

"No buts son, you heard her," Stanley added. "We'll let you two know as soon as she wakes up, I promise. I'll run all the way over there if I have to."

Relenting, Joe looked at Patsy who shrugged back, not having anything to add. "All right but the minute she twitches…"

"You'll hear from me, I promise you," his mother replied.

Making his way to Kate's bedside, Joe noticed his leg in the prosthetic was getting really sore. It dawned on him that this was the longest he had ever worn the contraption since he usually took it off as soon as he got home.

"Something I'll have to tell you when you wake up," Joe thought, looking down at Kate.

"Okay, you heard her. The foreman is kicking us out but you don't go anywhere until we get back, okay?" Joe said to Kate, kissing her on the head.

Taking a last look at Kate, Joe steeled himself and began walking toward Patsy who was by the door. He knew his parents were right but it didn't make leaving there any easier.

"Come on Patsy, let's go find this imposter Grey Ghost," Joe said, looking at his partner.

Nodding, Patsy popped his bowler on his head asking, "You still have all of those notes we made on the miss shiny jewelry? She's really our only lead right now."

"They are back at the house," Joe answered, stepping out of the room.

"Joe, if you are talking about all of those Hansel and Gretel papers that were on the dining room table, I moved them to the mantle," Joe's mother said from behind them.

"The what?" Joe stopped, looking back at his Mom.

"The side mantle by the coffee pot. I mean you left them all over the table and I didn't want them to get…" Vera started to answer before Joe cut in.

"No, no, mom," Joe stopped her before asking. "What did you just call them?

CHAPTER FOURTEEN

Flipping over the closed sign on the front window, Kimberly squinted as a stray sunbeam in the morning glare flashed in her eyes. The brunette was exhausted; her sister-in-law Christa's idea of a girls night out was more than she had planned last night and the early shift at the library wasn't helping.

"Some of us have to wake up early in the morning to get to work..." Kimberly thought to herself, yawning as she slowly walked from the small entranceway to the center of the library.

Making her way to the information desk, Kimberly fell back in her chair. Looking around the large main room with its dark maple bookcases standing at attention surrounding the circular desk, Kimberly was enjoying the silence of the empty library.

"If you could only stay like this for a few hours... Really who needs a book that badly to come out this early...?" Kimberly thought, resting her head back.

"SLAM!"

The jarring sound of the front door she had just unlocked being flung open startled her as it echoed in the large main room.

"Really?" Kimberly thought irritated, hearing someone running down the entrance hall toward her desk. "Hey kid, no running in the library!"

Kimberly was surprised when the runner made his way around the entranceway corner into the main room. It definitely wasn't some kid. The bull in the china shop was a large man who was so out of breath she thought he was going to pass out by the time he made it to the information desk.

"Hi... *huff*" the man said, barely able to get out a complete sentence, his face red as a beet under his bowler. "I... *puff* need a copy of... Brims... *huff* Tales..."

"Tales?" Kimberly looked at the man. "Is the author's last name Brims sir?"

"No, no Brim's Fairytales," the man replied, catching in his breath.

"Sir, do you mean *Grimm's Fairy Tales*?" Kimberly asked, annoyed with the spectacle in front of her.

"Yeah, that's the one..." the man replied nodding.

"Well sir, we should have a copy of it if it hasn't been checked out," Kimberly replied. "You of course can use our card catalog in the room to your right to find where Jacob's and Wilhelm's Fairy Tales are shelved. It uses the DDs as you would expect..."

"DDs?" the large man asked confused as he looked in the direction of the catalogs.

"The Dewey Decimal system, sir," Kimberly answered, not appreciating being cut off. "They must've gone over that system when you were issued your library card."

Reaching in his coat the large man produced a wallet. Flipping it over the man slapped the wallet on the desk in front of her. It included a golden police shield and an identification card with the man's picture and the name "Officer Patsy Thomas" along with other information.

"Miss, I don't mean to be rude, but I made the silly mistake of thinking I could run over here from the station and I'm in a hurry," Patsy said, looking the librarian in the eyes. "I don't know who Dewey is and this is the only library card I have, so please just show me where the silly book is."

"What took you so long?" Joe asked, looking over at Patsy as he entered the office.

Red faced and sweating profusely, Patsy looked back at his friend daring him to say another word. The office in the middle of the old city hall still being used as a makeshift police department was hard enough to find. Add on the four block run from the library and the usually jolly detective wasn't in the mood. Slapping the leather-bound book on the lone table, the sweating man finally spoke up.

"The blasted librarian made me sign up for a library card!"

"Really?" Joe stifled a laugh. "You try that, 'My badge is my blah blah' line again?"

"Go ahead, laugh it up funny boy," Patsy barked back. "Next time it's your turn to run across town to get whatever and I'll sit here spinning in my chair."

"I wasn't just sitting around," Joe said, rolling his wheelchair to the table to pick up the book. His prosthetic leg was leaning against the far wall now. Wearing it all night as he sat vigil in Kate's room had done a number to his knee and thigh so much so he decided to revert to the wheelchair.

"Perfect..." Joe mumbled to himself as he started flipping through the fairy tales.

"So what were you doing here while I was learning the Dewey Decimal system?" Patsy asked, looking at the city map pinned to the wall with a circle of push pins scattered almost uniformly around the city.

"You had to learn the Dewey Decimal...? Never mind," Joe started to ask before deciding against it. "I've been trying to see a pattern in where the Kiss has been striking and leaving those boxes. Kate made a good point when she said that the Kiss was spreading out all over town. But the more she struck, the more you can see a perimeter of hits."

"Is there anything to the order she's been going?" Patsy asked, looking at the circle of incidents. "Is she actually going along a circular path? Maybe we could predict where she's going next from this."

"Looking at the dates of the attacks they don't follow the circle she's making around the city," Joe answered looking, down at his notes before pointing back to the city map full of push pins. "See, these four down here actually were after the initial attack at Fulcher's. The incidents make up what looks like a pattern but the order isn't there."

"Well it doesn't matter where or when she's been dropping off those things. If those are all like the one we found on your friend's boat, she can blow the whole city to Kingdom Come and back with the spread she's left out there," Patsy commented, counting up the pins.

"I know the captain has teams out there trying to work with a few of the most isolated gift boxes, but like the rest the teams can't even touch them," Joe added. "I'm the only one that can even make contact with them, but even I can't get through that metal casing for some reason."

"Any relation to where she actually did something like at Fulcher's or Rachel's against where she just dropped boxes off?" Patsy asked.

"Thought of that too, but for as much noise as she has been making with the attacks, she has almost doubled those in number with her drop offs," Joe said, pointing to the pins that were simple drops. "There really doesn't seem to be anything between the two except to spread the perimeter around town. I'm hoping the connection mom pointed out might shed some light on this."

Flipping through the copy of *Grimm's Fairy Tales*, Joe quickly found the story of *Hansel and Gretel*. Reading a few pages, Joe angled the book toward Patsy.

"See, mom was right, listen to this... 'Near a great forest there lived a poor woodcutter'... It's the first sentence of the story."

Scanning along the story, Joe continued to point out the passages that the Jeweled Kiss had left inscribed on the inside lid of each gift box. "I'm surprised I didn't remember these earlier. Mom used to read this stuff to me all the time when I was younger."

"Chalk one up for your mother's steel trap memory," Patsy commented. "But big deal, so the Kiss likes fairy tales. How does that little nugget of knowledge help us? Is she leaving us a trail of breadcrumbs?"

"Possibly, remember what she said at the docks before she left? *Follow the breadcrumbs cowboy*...I thought she was still hamming it up but maybe she was trying to clue us into something," Joe commented.

"Specifically, clue the Grey Ghost into something because remember, she only left these passages inside the lids of those boxes, a place only you could get to," Patsy added before asking. "But why?"

"I don't... wait! Patsy... maybe it's not bread crumbs, maybe... maybe that statement and the passages in the lids were all just to get this story in our hands..." Joe theorized while pointing to a section of the book he had just skimmed. "Because if we follow along with these two kids here it's not breadcrumbs that we should be looking for... it's flints."

"Flints?" Patsy asked confused.

"Yeah, look here in the beginning of the story," Joe said, flipping back to the first section. "Everyone remembers Hansel leaving breadcrumbs, BUT the first time they were led into the forest, Hansel left flints as a trail for them to follow back home."

"What is a flint?" Patsy asked.

"In the story Hansel uses reflective stones that shine in the moonlight as a trail back home. They call them flints in the story," Joe added, running his finger across the text of the tale.

"Okay, so what?" Patsy asked.

"Think about it, flints... reflective rocks..." Joe said, trying to make his point. "The story says that the flints sat in the front of their house glistening like pieces of silver."

"Glistening in the light... like a *jewel*," Patsy said nodding now getting what Joe was hinting at.

"Exactly!" Joe replied, slapping his hands. "Where are those reports?"

Rooting through the boxes they had brought in earlier, Joe found the files he was looking for.

"Patsy, mark these on the map for me as I read them off," Joe said, pointing to the city map. "We'll start at the first incident at Fulcher's. That one had dark red jewels, and then Rachel's was purple. Someone wrote 'amethysts' down here."

As Joe went through the order of the incidents where the Jeweled Kiss either struck or left her mysterious boxes, Patsy marked the map with what kind of jewel the thief left at the scene. Looking at the finished map, both Joe and Patsy nodded to each other seeing the same thing.

"She left the same color jewels in the same vicinities even though they weren't in order...so what does that mean?" Patsy asked frowning.

"All of the rubies are grouped together even though the three events are more than a week apart..." Joe thought, shaking his head. *"So are the diamonds, the opals, the emeralds, etc., all in a circular pattern around the city. What is she doing? Is she trying to lead us somewhere like in the fairy tale? And if she is, are we headed home or to the witch's oven?"*

"How many?" Lord Minos hissed at the shadowy form standing by the doorway.

"The entire shipment, which was the entire remaining stock of cake," Mr. Tookings answered, walking from the shadows and entering the room.

"Blast it," Minos spat, slamming his fist onto the top of his marble desk, nearly knocking over his half-full wine glass. Wincing in pain at the impact, the evil man reached for his upper arm wrapped in a heavy gauze from the earlier gunshot wound. "Next time Mr. Tookings, when I tell you to graze something make an effort to 'graze' it! The doctors told me you nearly took my arm off!"

"Once again Lord Minos, my apologies..." Mr. Tookings replied, slightly bowing his head.

"Or did you think it was your opportunity to rise in the Hookened's ranks?" Minos scoffed. "Is that it, Tookings? Did you see your chance to grab at the brass ring? Did you think for a moment before you pulled that trigger what it would be like to be the one sitting in the chair?"

"No sir, not once I swear!" Tookings stammered.

"Pity Tookings, I can respect a man who has ambition," Minos snickered. "Heavy is the head that wears the crown my good man. And I promise you, in case you ever do become a man of ambition, you just don't have the spine to hold it up."

And with that Minos squeezed the stem of the wine glass that had been on his desk until the thin glass pole snapped like a twig causing the remaining red drink to the fall across the desk. Looking at the ruined glassware and spilled wine, Tookings understood his employer's implication.

"Back to your earlier news," Minos moved on. "What are you doing about this missing shipment?"

"We have not been able to contact either Horst or Otto while they are in custody. With our mole in the department being outed before their arrest at the docks, it has spooked the police department and caused them to put Horst and Otto under a 24/7 watch," Tookings reported.

"No one at site B knew this crew Otto hired to transport the shipment?" Minos asked.

"No. Otto simply said that he had secured passage with a crew from a neighborhood tavern," Tookings replied.

"Idiot..." Minos hissed. "Keep at it, but step lightly Mr. Tookings. Right now the plans can still proceed with the explosives our operative has already placed around the city. And none of my plans has ever nor will ever from this moment onward require Otto or Horst seeing the light of another day."

"Do you mean...?" Tookings wanted to clarify Minos's meaning.

"No, not yet..." Minos cut in, raising a hand to silence the man. "However, if you ever hear a whisper of either of them becoming a problem while in custody, do not hesitate to cut ties immediately."

Standing, Minos casually walked to an adjacent doorway hidden in the office's side wall. With Tookings in tow, the crooked mastermind traveled a dimly lit corridor until he reached the one lighted window in the hall. Peering inside, Minos examined the occupants of the room with a studious eye.

"Has her condition changed?" Mr. Tookings asked.

"I do not recall when I've become the one who has to answer anything to you Mr. Tookings…" Minos shot back, looking at his assistant who out of habit had stayed at least an arm's reach down the dark hall. "But yes, her condition has improved considerably over time."

Looking through the window, Minos observed the private nurse inside writing something on a clipboard. With the window being a one way mirror, he wasn't sure if the nurse knew she was being observed. Either way, the nurse understood the severity of the injury to the sleeping patient lying on the bed and the importance her recovery meant to their plans. The politician had *stressed* that to her before leaving the patient in her care.

"From the reports I've received, the arrhythmia subsided as soon as you got her away from the square. The shock to her system is what has her lying there," Minos added, looking at the Jeweled Kiss's monitors steadily beeping next to her bedside. "Until our jeweled thief awakens we may need additional help to make sure our plans remain on schedule. I believe it is time to welcome our friend home."

"It will be done, Lord Minos," Mr. Tookings nodded.

Turning from the lit window, Minos started up the corridor, his words echoing eerily back at his assisitant.

"Tookings, have my car pulled around front. It's time I visit my petite savior that you put in the hospital. I am very curious to find out how she knew about the chink in the armor of our little Jeweled Kiss."

CHAPTER FIFTEEN

"So what are we missing here?" Patsy asked staring at the map. "Am I seeing a pattern here or am I crazy?"

"I don't know…" Joe mumbled, wheeling closer to the wall. "The Jeweled Kiss's attacks circled the entire city multiple times, but does the fact that she left the same jewels at the scene of multiple attacks in the same vicinity mean anything?"

"Or is it nothing at all and her just being cute?" Patsy wondered out loud. "We are making an assumption the jewels mean something because of the story she left you inside of the box lids."

"And we don't know why she even left those…" Joe sighed. "We are trying to put a jigsaw puzzle together here not even knowing if it's really a puzzle at all."

"I can almost taste it partner. There has to be something here," Patsy slapped his hands. "There's too much of… something… to be just nothing."

"Either way Patsy, we aren't getting anywhere just sitting here. We've been staring at this map and going over this fairytale backward and forward for hours now," Joe relented, hearing his stomach growl. It was dawning on him it had been more than 24 hours since either of them had a bite to eat. "How about we pop back over to the hospital and check in on Kate and

The Grey Ghost: The Jeweled Kiss Mysteries

then grab a late lunch?"

"Okay, but I'm not going to enjoy it," Patsy mumbled, starting for the door. "Mysteries kill my appetite."

"We might want to get you on more mysteries then, big guy," Joe quipped at his partner.

"Hardy har har," Patsy mockingly laughed, grabbing Joe's black overcoat from the coat rack and tossing it at him.

Catching Joe unaware, the coat engulfed his face. As Joe removed the coat from his head, he and Patsy both noticed a small, black box fly out of one of the jacket's inside pockets. The small box arced in the air away from Joe, landing on the long table in the middle of the room. As it struck, the lid popped open, sending the small ring inside bouncing along the table's surface.

It was Joe's mother's ring. As it bounced on the table top, Joe caught a glimpse of the light catching the main diamond and colorful gems along the side of the engagement ring.

"Ah dang it," Patsy cursed, seeing the ring finally stop. "Did I ding it Joe?"

"The gems... Grandma's... Mom's... and Kate's....birthstones," Joe thought to himself, wheeling over to pick up the ring.

"No... it's fine," Joe replied to his partner as he examined the gems on the side of the ring. *"A sapphire, an emerald, and a peridot..."*

Looking back to the map on the wall, it finally occurred to him what they were missing.

"They're birthstones!"

"What?" Patsy asked, confused by Joe's exclamation.

"The jewels the Kiss is leaving, they are birthstones!" Joe answered rolling over to the map and pointing to the top. "Look at the top of the map. That one was a grouping of dark red jewels right?"

"Yeah, dark red..." Patsy replied, checking the report.

"Aren't both of these locations almost on top of each other? Joe asked. When he saw his friend nod he knew he was onto something. "Dark red are garnets for January. If she was going in a clockwise pattern, I bet these to the right were light purple."

"Yep, at both scenes. I still remember the kid at the hat shop freaking out about the bright purple kiss mark she left on his cheek," Patsy confirmed.

"That's amethyst for February," Joe added. "And I bet these here were either light blue or aquamarine for March."

"Well what do you know," Patsy said, confirming the next set. "When did you become so interested in birthstones?"

"Remember I had to have Kate's added to the engagement ring," Joe answered. "And trust me partner, having this little stone added wasn't cheap so I made sure I knew what I was talking about before I ponied up all of the dimes and nickels I had."

As Patsy and Joe continued to go over the map in a clockwise pattern, the birthstones continued to match the suspected pattern perfectly. Next came April with diamonds, followed by emeralds for May before they ran into a bump in the jewel encrusted road. The next set of jewels left by the thief were not June's birthstone, but rubies for July. This was followed by peridots for the month of August. Deciding to finish off the calendar year, the detectives were rewarded by finding the pattern intact, continuing until the circle reached back around to the top and ended with the month of December's birthstone next to where they had started with January.

"That nut in the skirt made our city into a decorative calendar," Patsy said, looking at his partner when they finished with the reports. "Just so she could blow it sky high?"

"But she left out the month of June," Joe said, pointing to the area between the attacks that had occurred with July and August birthstones. "This area should've had pearls left behind, but this five to six block area didn't have any sightings of the Jeweled Kiss."

"Do you think we just missed the boxes there?" Patsy asked.

"Not likely," Joe said. "She pretty much made sure that someone found them even if she didn't make a grand appearance at all of the other spots."

"So she purposely avoided that area entirely," Patsy added, circling the area on the map with his finger.

"What's there Patsy?" Joe asked, looking over to his partner. "I don't really remember ever hitting that side of town lately."

"Well, there's a good reason for that partner," Patsy answered. "Before you left for the service that whole plot of land was the old Barnes and Groot Mill property. Nothing more than a storage yard for steel and pig iron before they transported it down to the Scar."

"They stored it all the way up here? I thought the shipping lanes took that stuff directly down to the mills in the Scar," Joe asked.

"I think this was the stuff transported in by train; the depot is right over here," Patsy said while pointing a few blocks to the right. "They used to have a system to lower the materials down into the Scar here and here, but I remember they had to sell those plots to the city for some reason. The mayor made a huge pitch in the papers a while back before you got home about turning the area into an economic development or something. I think they started last year building a few mom and pop shops there."

"Do you know any of the stores that are there now?" Joe asked.

"There aren't many. Bishop and Henrys might know more about them since that's their beat. I think there is a hardware store named Motts or something and a bakery next to that somewhere."

"We said we were hungry so let's go satisfy our sweet tooth," Joe said placing the engagement ring into the box and back into his coat. "There's a reason the Jeweled Kiss skipped this part of town and I bet it's not because they make her favorite chocolate éclairs."

"Well your honor, it was such a nice gesture for you to visit," Stanley said smiling as the two shook hands just outside Kate's hospital room.

"Oh...Stanley it was the least I could do," Editar returned the smile after he remembered Joe's father's name. "I'm only sorry to find Ms. Stone still in such a state. I wanted to personally thank her for what she did at the rally. Dare I say I might not be here if not for her bravery distracting the Grey Ghost and his companion."

"So it WAS the Grey Ghost at the rally?" Vera asked, coming out into the hallway. "From what I've been hearing no one really knows what our city's hero looks like. How can everyone be so sure?"

"My dear, the only thing I can tell you for certain is that it was the thief known as the Jeweled Kiss at the rally," the politician confirmed, trying to use his charm on Vera. "And from what my sources have been collecting on that brazen woman, she has been nothing but forthcoming about her relationship with the vigilante known as the Grey Ghost, so it stands to reason that..."

"It stands to reason that the civil minded people of this city would want to give a hero such as the Grey Ghost the benefit of the doubt after all he's done for this city before they start to assume anything," Vera cut him off. "You know what they always tell children about assuming, don't you Mr. Mayor?"

The politician shot a glare at the woman before he caught himself and suddenly returned the charming smile back to his face, Vera's scrupulous stare never flinching from his reaction.

"How could I ever argue with such good old-fashioned logic like that?" Editar replied, biting back his fury at the lack of respect the woman was showing him. "Well I should be going. I doubt Ms. Stone would want my face to be the first she sees if she awakens."

"When she awakens," Vera immediately corrected.

"Of course," Editar replied, slightly bowing at his mistake in words.

"Please Mr. Mayor, let me walk you to the elevator," Stanley offered, ushering the politician away from the room. "And thank you so much again for stopping by."

"No, thank you Stanley," the mayor replied, starting along the hallway with Stanley. It did not go unnoticed by Vera that he did not say goodbye to her. "And please let my office know if there is any change in Ms. Stone's condition."

"Of course, we will..." Stanley nodded, walking farther away with the mayor from the hospital room.

"I don't trust that smooth talking snake for a minute," Vera thought to herself, watching the two disappear down the hallway. *"To think poor Kate is lying here in that bed after risking her life to save that man, and here he is acting the hero..."*

Vera was so engrossed thinking about their elected visitor she never noticed the subtle movement at the bedroom window back in Kate's hospital room. Without a sound, the wooden sliding window moved upward revealing the hooded face of the Jeweled Kiss in the afternoon shadows. Effortlessly, the thief snaked her way through the window, never catching Vera's eye as she waited for Stanley's return only a few feet away in the hallway. Softly landing next to the bed, the dangerous thief stood staring at the still unconscious Kate, her now frowning emerald lips glistening through the room's shadows as she reached down.

CHAPTER SIXTEEN

"Well isn't this a picture worth showing dear old mother," Patsy bellowed, swinging through the front door of the bakery a little over an hour later.

As the detectives entered, they were met with surprised looks from the two customers sitting at the counter bar and the lone worker in the white apron behind the register. Joe could feel the shock radiate from the one customer closest to them, a rough looking bearded man who spun around so fast to see them he almost fell off his stool.

"Hiya fellas!" Patsy smiled, smacking his stomach as he took in the faces of both customers before turning to the bakery's employee. "So what's good around this joint? I'm starving!"

"Ah...they got..." the bearded customer stammered before the worker cut him off.

"You should try the cream puff mister," the worker recommended. "They are fresh this morning."

"Cream puff?" Joe laughed, raising his voice slightly as he limped over to the counter next to his partner, once again balancing with his cane and Kate's amazing prosthetic leg. "Now how good is this puff of yours? Because I would put money on Carla's over on 5th as some of the best desserts in town."

"So why don't you head over there then? These are my dear old mother's recipes," the worker rumbled, surprising Joe.

"So here we must have the employee of the month..." Joe thought, still smiling broadly at the man.

"Joseph, where are your manners? They're his dear old mother's recipes..." Patsy smiled at his partner. "You'll have to excuse my friend here. What kind of person walks into such a nice place like this and starts talking about the competition? I'll try a cream puff and a hot cup of coffee to wash it down."

"Alright, one special coming up..." the worker announced, walking off.

As Patsy waited for his confection, Joe limped the few steps from the front counter to the bar where the other two customers were seated. A hushed conversation between the two patrons quickly stopped as he approached.

"You boys come here often?" Joe asked, smiling as the two purposely avoided making eye contact with him. He put a friendly hand on the closest customer's shoulder. "It seems like a nice place..."

"It's okay..." the man with the beard grumbled, flinching from his touch.

"Yeah, I bet a place like this on this side of town has seen all sorts of colorful characters walk in those doors," Joe remarked, purposely overselling it as he reached and grabbed a handful of grapes from a large bowl of fruit sitting in front of the bald-headed, larger of the two customers.

"Wouldn't know..." the other customer, a thinner man with curly black hair, commented, never looking at Joe. "A smart man knows when to keep his eyes on his own business."

"I bet a smart man does," Joe replied, never losing the broad smile as he looked directly at the bald man before making his way back to the worker who had returned with Patsy's dessert. "You know what I love about this place the most? We were walking up Berwyn Street here and when I saw that sign, I went to my friend Patsy here... Patsy you see that place? The one across from Koz Funeral Home? Buddy, that's a place with a name that has a story behind it. I mean 'Martensii's', that's a name with meaning!"

"It's just a name," the worker replied, confused at Joe's excitement. "My pop opened the place 20 years or so ago and named it after our last name. It's not that big of a deal..."

"You said 20 years?" Joe repeated, looking over at Patsy who was taking a bite out of the cream puff. Joe noticed the grimace on his partner's face as he tasted the dessert.

"Well, what's the origin of Martensii?" Joe asked, pushing the issue. "Is it Sicilian? I mean it's got to be Italian, right?"

"What does it matter; it's just a name," the worker replied.

"Really, just a name? Well I bet you'll get a kick out of this," Joe continued, boastfully ignoring the look the worker returned to him that indicated the opposite. "You see, I walk into this jewelry store over in the 'burbs a little bit ago and there is this cute girl behind the counter waiting for me. A real doll this one. You see, I'm trying to get my girl something to get myself out of the doghouse. You know those girls always are mad about something."

"Yeah I guess," the worker shrugged.

"So I start talking to this doll, and I tell you she's a pretty little thing. Christy...no...no... Christa, yeah, that was her name," Joe continued.

"And you wondered why you were in the doghouse in the first place?" Patsy added laughing, throwing a napkin over the remaining three-fourths of the cream puff when the worker wasn't looking.

"Oh you know her bud, like I said, always mad about something," Joe laughed before continuing. "So I get talking to this Christa about a nice pair of earrings, really nice ones, and you know what they say, 'Nice doesn't come cheap!' I mean let's just say, buddy, I could've bought a couple of cream puffs for those little things."

"Okay...so what?" the worker replied, visibly bored with Joe's story or just Joe in general.

"So I ask, why so much?" Joe continued, leaning closer to the counter. "And you know what she tells me? She looked right at me and said it's because it's hard to find Martensiis lately because of the war. Martensiis, no kidding! You see pal, Martensiis are oysters over there near the Japanese Islands! Who would have known? And what I had in my hands were a pair of genuine Martensii cultured PEARL earrings! Joe paused there, letting the words hang in the room as he studied the man in front him.

"Well... that was an interesting story, wasn't it boys?" the worker replied, looking over to the two bar customers who had never looked up from their cups.

"In the end those would've cost me an arm and a leg so I figured, hey I already lost this one over there and there's no good reason to give the Japanese the other, so I told that girl of mine to hit the bricks!" Joe laughed, patting his prosthetic leg while shooting a glance at Patsy. "That story just popped in my head when we walked by here! I mean what are the chances my buddy and I get off work, head across town to this dump of an area, and just happen to see the name Martensii?"

"Yeah... what are the chances?" the worker slowly replied after hearing Joe's last sentence, quickly glancing downward.

"What you should be wondering is, do you think you can reach that shotgun under the counter before my partner pulls his trigger? I see it in the reflection on the metal cabinet behind you," Joe replied, throwing a thumb over to Patsy, his voice deepening from the happy-go-lucky storyteller it had been seconds ago. "Sloppy pal, real sloppy..."

"You forget there is more than one of us in here copper," the heavy man at the bar said, jumping down from his stool behind Patsy. Patsy didn't even turn to face the man instead leaving his service revolver trained on the worker. Seeing this the customer smiled as he reached inside his jacket pocket, producing a... banana...

"What?" he exclaimed.

"Well, it is good of you to offer such a balanced healthy snack, but I bet you're looking for this, weren't you big fella?" Joe asked, producing a small caliber handgun along with his police badge.

The other customer was equally shocked when he reached into his jacket and found a handful of grapes instead of his gun, which was safely in Joe's other coat pocket. Neither of them had thought a handicapped man with a cane could pull such a fast one on them, and that arrogance had been Joe Bevine's opening.

"Capstone City Police, but you already knew that right buddy?" Patsy announced, moving behind the counter toward the worker, his revolver never lowering. "Let's keep those hands where I can see them."

"And you two, drop the fruit, hands flat on the table," Joe ordered the would be assailants. "Koin, Despotorich, did you really not think we wouldn't recognize either of you even if you crawled into those coffee mugs? Both of you have at least two warrants out for your arrest from that Brown's Drug Store job you pulled a few months back!"

"I told you we should've iced these turkeys as soon as they came in," the bearded customer Koin grumbled at his bar companion.

"Koin, we had you dead to rights before you even knew we were here," Patsy said, exasperated as he placed the worker in cuffs. "I mean why would you just sit there on those stools right next to a huge window like this? We saw you almost a block away."

"And what about me?" the cuffed worker asked Patsy. "There aren't any laws against a man having a shotgun to protect himself."

"Attempted murder after you tried to end me with that terrible cream puff," Patsy replied, sticking his tongue out as if he was gagging. "But I will have to settle with taking you down to the station for skipping your parole Campbell. What? Did you really think I wouldn't remember you either?"

"Hey, those really were my mother's!" the worker barked.

"Oh just shut it!' Patsy replied. "First you're going to try to pull a heater on us and then you're going to try to make me feel guilty about what I said about your mother's cooking?"

"Watch these three while I sweep the back room," Joe added, rolling his eyes at the two. "I doubt these three were up here just to guard his mom's recipes."

With his cane, Joe pushed aside the red curtain partitioning the front room from the back of the store. Drawing his service weapon in a fluid, practiced motion, he stepped in, checking every angle of the room. Besides a few racks of pastries, the room was empty save for a single door along the far wall. As Joe came to the solid, wooden door, he placed his ear against it and could hear numerous men talking to one another from behind it. Taking a single step back, Joe slowly tested the door handle only to find it locked.

"Why try to pound a nail in with your right hand when you're holding a hammer in your left?" the detective mumbled one of his father's sayings as he started to reach for his watch.

With a few twists and a soft clicking sound of the small, metal door inside of the backing of the watch, Joe Bevine disappeared and was replaced by the heroic form of the Grey Ghost!

"So let's see what's behind door number two..." the Grey Ghost thought to himself as he went to walk through the solid door. But as he neared the door a strange dizzying sensation overcame him, pausing his advance. Stumbling back to the far wall, the weakened Grey Ghost looked at the door, puzzled by what had happened.

"What was that?" the hero thought.

He wasn't in pain, but the closer he got to the door the weaker he felt. Quickly regaining his strength, the ghostly avenger defiantly made his way back to the doorway. The dizziness immediately returned, dropping him to one knee. Instead of retreating this time, the downed champion placed his hand on the solid door and concentrated. Slowly, the wooden barrier started to shimmer before him. Under his touch the dark, brown oak door became blurred and then solidified as transparent as a sheet of glass. Still on one knee, the Grey Ghost took stock of the other room through the new windowed doorway, quickly finding the cause of the sickening feeling he experienced.

In the adjacent room he saw eight men sitting at a round table playing cards under a solitary hanging light. The windowless room was full of smoke, both from the numerous ash trays and numerous lit candles adorning the room. A fireplace in the far corner was lit by three large candle wicks dancing in the updraft. Scanning the room, Joe could not see anything of importance, just a couple pieces of furniture, and a few trash cans topped off with numerous takeout boxes, nothing worth the multiple sidearms he saw adorning each card player's hip or the three shotguns and an unlit flame thrower discarded in the corner of the room.

"What is with the small army back there?" the hero thought to himself, happy that he had the foresight to only make the transparency of the door in one direction. *"There's enough muscle in there to take on half the precinct."*

Just as his strength was ebbing against the mysterious effect the candles were having on him, the Grey Ghost noticed the reflection of a small door handle on the far wall of the room. Almost invisible, the doorway was surrounded by numerous candles, some burning, some waxed over. Feeling his power growing weaker, the Grey Guardian backed away from the door. As he did the strange, overpowering effect the candles held over him immediately subsided. As his touch left the doorway so too did the magical influence he had in making the solid, oak door transparent.

"As soon as I go in there the candles will knock me for a loop and I'll be a sitting duck," the ghostly marauder, thought assessing the situation before him. *"And if Patsy and I go in there without any 'ghosty help,' I don't like our chances against eight armed goons."*

Scanning the room and its terrible tasting pastries again, the Grey Ghost found nothing of use until he came upon a small window on the left wall. Through it he noticed a sign pointing back to the Koz funeral home.

"Wait... I wonder if?" the hero said before ducking his head through the floor as a swimmer would dunk his head into a pool. Looking around for a few moments, the Grey Guardian raised his head and with a glance at the pastry trays nodded, *"Yep, that might work..."*

Reaching for his watch, Joe Bevine emerged from the back room to find Patsy watching the three prisoners handcuffed to the front bar.

"What did you find?" Patsy asked his partner.

"I'm not sure yet but I have an idea on how to find out," Joe replied. "But I have a feeling you're not going to like it."

"I was afraid you were going to say that," Patsy grimaced. "Lately you're always saying that."

CHAPTER SEVENTEEN

"Flush!" Johnny dropped his final card on the table, instantly enjoying the moans of the other players. "What do you say to that boys?"

"Oh come on! There's no way that can work!" one of the players across the small table barked. "You can't have the king of hearts when I have it right here!"

"You calling me a cheat?" Johnny swiveled back to the man. Of course he was, but the whole table knew that before they started playing. Most seemed to have the common sense to not point it out though.

"Well Johnny..." the card player stammered, suddenly understanding his mistake.

"I said, are you calling me a cheat?!?" Johnny glared, raising his voice even louder.

"You're a crazy nut! That's what you are, you know that?"

Both Johnny and the other player stared at each other wondering who had blurted it out. The new voice seemed to come out of nowhere.

"Who said that?" Johnny yelled spinning to face the rest of the boys in the room, but he was only met with confused looks. They were as stumped as much as he was.

"Will you keep it down? The sound echoes pretty loud down here."

"Why do I have to do this?"

"We went over this already. Just get on my shoulders... This will work."

"This is one of your worst ideas."

"We both know it's not even in the top ten..."

Johnny pulled his pistol from his coat pocket and started to scan the room for the two men having this invisible conversation. Following his lead the others boys in the candle lit room all dropped what they were doing and armed themselves as well.

"Okay wise guys. Who's making all the racket? Johnny yelled. "I'm going to give you to count of three to show yourself! One... two..."

"Hey big fella..."

Johnny spun, firing blindly behind him in the direction he thought the welcome had come, narrowly missing the other card player across the table.

"What? Who said that? Where are you?" Johnny yelled, a small crack of fear jumping into his voice.

"For crying out loud bud, I'm right down here," the voice responded.

Slowing looking down at his feet, Johnny screamed at the sight peering back at him. There, only reaching up to his knee was the upper torso of a larger man with a bowler on his head now coming straight through the floor!

"Hey there, you boys hungry?" Patsy asked smiling at the goons.

In a hail of creamed desert, Patsy launched a cream puff directly into Johnny's stunned face.

"Reload!" Patsy bellowed, reaching his now empty hand back down through the ceiling with an empty pastry tray.

Joe grabbed the tray away from his partner and with a quick motion handed him a fully stocked tray of cream puffs to his partner. This simple motion was no small feat since Patsy was sitting on Joe's shoulders in the small walkway tunnel directly under the bakery. Through it all, Joe never dared lose the grip he had on Patsy with his right hand. Joe was sharing the mysterious power of the Spartan Cloak with his partner, allowing him to stick half of his torso into the room and say hi.

"Ayy!" Patsy yelled from above.

"You okay up there big guy?" Joe loudly asked.

"One of these mooks keeps trying to swing a bat at my head!" Patsy yelled from above before throwing another volley of cream puffs. "Here you go pal. Here's one in your eye!"

Joe could feel the wind up and release as Patsy launched more of the cream puffs around the above room.

"Make sure you get all of the wicks!" Joe yelled to his friend as he passed another tray of cream puffs to Patsy.

"Yeah, yeah, I got it," Patsy answered through the floor. "Go a little forward!"

As Joe walked forward, Patsy waded through the wooden floorboards as if he was in a pool. Every attack from the goons above passed through him harmlessly. Neither kicks nor gun shots that tore into the floorboards around him could unnerve the intangible police officer.

"Okay, here's fine!" Patsy directed.

Once Joe settled below him, Patsy started rocketing the pastries at both the goons in the room and the lit candles surrounding the perimeter. He nailed the targets with surprising accuracy.

"Not bad shooting Tex," Patsy thought to himself, admiring his marksmanship. The second the pastries left Patsy's hand and broke the connection to the Spartan Cloak's power shared to him by Joe, they instantly became solid once again.

The one goon again tried hitting Patsy with a bat only for it to pass harmlessly through him, sending the hooligan tumbling into another man behind them.

"Yeah, serves you right you piece of trash!" Patsy spat at the two sprawled men trying to calm his nerves. The detective knew the bat swung at his head wouldn't have hurt him, but at this moment he wished he could tell his racing heart that.

Trying his best to ignore the other relentless attacks being thrown his way, Patsy continued flinging the cream puffs at every lit candle he could find. One after another the flickering lights started to extinguish under a barrage of thick and terrible tasting creamed confections. Redoubling his efforts, Patsy made sure every waxed candle in the room was completely coated in cream and not going to be able to be relit. He even stole a laugh as he saw the goons constantly slipping on the cream spread all over from his hailstorm of pastries.

"Okay bud, the place is as frosted as a cake up here," Patsy called down to Joe.

Johnny made one more attempt at Patsy throwing a folding chair at his head. The chair passed through Patsy harmlessly, but did get the officer's full attention. Patsy took note of the smears of cream puff pastry still coating his attacker's face from the bull's-eye he had nailed him with earlier. Noticing the clothing Johnny was wearing, Patsy said to the man, "Stay right there for a second..." before ducking out of sight below the wooden floorboards as if they were a lake of water he was wading through.

Johnny stared at the spot where Patsy had disappeared not believing what had just happened. He then heard the cream puff wielding maniac say to someone below.

"Brown pinstripe, blue tie..."

Looking down at his own clothing, Johnny realized the man was describing his now strained clothing. A second later, the goon fell backward in fright as an amazing figure rose through the floor as if shot from a gun! Landing in a crouched position in front of the mass of dirty henchmen, Johnny couldn't make out the figure's face past the lowered gray fedora he was wearing.

The amazing figure of the Grey Ghost slowly gazed through unseen eyes at the disheveled crowd. Those eyes and the rest of his smoke covered face was contained within the dark metal Spartan helmet, providing a deep echo to his voice.

"Brown pinstripe, blue tie..." the Grey Ghost darkly echoed Patsy's last words, motioning his head toward Johnny.

"Yeah freak, what about it?" Johnny scoffed trying to muster some moxie toward the hero. Any further attempt at that died instantly with the ghostly guardian's reply.

Walking toward the goon, the hero's ghostly, unseen face started to transform in front of Johnny, becoming unfocused for a moment until suddenly there was a dark skeleton staring back at him, its eyes furiously smoking as if they were on fire.

"My friend downstairs said you're first!" the skeletal face echoed at Johnny as the hero reached out for the goon.

CHAPTER EIGHTEEN

Patsy could hear the commotion through the ceiling. After a few minutes filled with yelling, randomly fired shots, and what sounded like numerous bodies crashing into furniture, there was a sudden silence. Illuminating the ceiling with Joe's small pocket flashlight, the large police officer waited, hoping for some confirmation that the fight had ended on the side of the white hats. Suddenly, a gloved hand stuck through the ceiling down toward him.

"Need a lift?" the Grey Ghost called down to his friend still in the dimly lit tunnel.

Grabbing his partner's hand, Patsy was quickly lifted as if he was the weight of a child through the ceiling and released in the same room where only a few minutes ago he had played target practice with a tray full of terrible tasting cream puffs. Slumped over in a corner like a sack of potatoes were the goons who earlier attempted to hurt Patsy. Smirking at the cream stained goons, Patsy turned to his friend to make a remark, but recoiled with a startled jump.

"For Pete's sake!" Patsy jumped back, seeing the hero's face for the first time since entering the room. "Will you take off the Halloween mask? You're giving me the hee-bee jee-bees!"

"You should've seen their reactions," the Grey Ghost laughed

through the burning eyes skull he still had emanating inside of his helmet. Within a second the hero's face returned to the smoke enveloped face he usually sported inside of the helmet.

"Just warn a guy before you pull that stuff," Patsy exhaled. "You can give a guy a heart attack with that mug of yours."

"It wasn't that bad you big baby," the Grey Ghost laughed in reply.

"I was talking about what you look like without the mask." Patsy smiled.

"Hardy har har," the Grey Ghost replied.

"Sorry buddy, you might be able to walk through walls but you walked right into that one," Patsy chuckled while looking over the pile of now moaning, frost-stained goons. "Anyone bring 16 pairs of handcuffs? This crew isn't going to be cat napping here that long."

"Long enough," the Grey Ghost replied. *"We are only interested in what's behind door number one here."*

"Well it definitely doesn't lead to the alley," Patsy said pointing to the back door. "Remember when we scouted around before we jumped into that tunnel? There wasn't a back door at all. Hey, how did you know about that tunnel under this place anyways?"

"Sadly I've been to one too many funerals in my day," the Grey Ghost solemnly replied. *"Funeral homes usually have a side entrance or even an underground way for the hospital to bring in the deceased. Most of the newer ones simply have a discreet entrance to the place's basement, but I figured with an old time place like Koz's it was worth a look. A quick glance through the floor and as luck would have it, it was right under this place."*

"So what's the deal with this place anyways?" Patsy asked looking around at the candles. "Why was the whole room lit up like St. Columbia on Christmas Eve?"

"Candlelight affecting me is not common knowledge in this town but," the Grey Ghost thought aloud while reaching for the small door handle. *"But I can't ignore the fact it does seem to be in the wind, especially after what happened on the bridge last year. Okay,*

you ready?"

"Ready... On three... two... one..." Patsy counted down.

At the end of the countdown, the Grey Ghost pulled at the flimsy door, his enhanced strength ripping it off at its hinges. Putting the door aside, both the Grey Ghost and Patsy looked through the open entranceway, prepared for any new threat that might be waiting for them. Instead, the heroes found two young girls, approximately seven or eight years old shivering in fear at them.

"What?" the Grey Ghost said, his words drowned out by the girls screaming at the masked, ghost-like face staring at them.

"Diabeł! Nie boli nas!" one of the girls screamed, hiding behind the other.

"What did she say?" Patsy asked, not understanding.

"I think... I think that was Polish?" the Grey Ghost answered, backing away from the door. Sending his thought to the Spartan Cloak, the Grey Ghost's helmeted face melted away becoming that of Joe Bevine again.

"This should do for now..." Joe thought to himself, still feeling the power of the Spartan Cloak surging through him. With the crowd of goons still moaning in the corner, Joe had not wanted to lower his guard in the room yet.

Motioning for Patsy to wait outside, Joe leaned back in the doorway and calmly whispered, "Relax girls. We're here to help. There is nothing to worry about."

The room couldn't have been any larger than the small broom closet in his own home, Joe thought as he took a few tentative steps toward the two young girls. With his second step, Joe felt the board directly under his foot start to give way as his weight pushed it down slightly. And that is when the world fell apart in front of them.

Directly behind the two terrified girls, a small door spun open revealing a white, unlit candle. A hidden flint struck by the spinning door suddenly set the unlit wick aflame, immediately drawing the power of the Spartan Cloak away from Joe. Crying out in pain, a sudden weakness overcame him, causing the hero to fall onto his knees in the small room. As the effect of the candle enveloped him, Joe heard a loud creaking sound of wood shifting against metal. Barely able to look up toward the sound, the downed hero saw the ceiling of the small room start to collapse on him and the two innocent girls!

Pushing through the pain, Joe grabbed at the two girls who, unaware of the deadly trap being sprung upon them, tried to push his hands away. Finding purchase around the girls' arms, Joe spun and with unforeseen strength flung the girls head over heels out of the room into Patsy who caught them in a crash. Looking back to his partner, Patsy was horrified as he witnessed the room suddenly crash down on Joe.

"Joe!" Patsy yelled as his partner disappeared inside a rain of plaster and timber.

A swift kick sent the backroom door flying off its hinges onto a large table full of empty pastry trays in the back room. The loud crashing sound of the trays didn't slow Patsy as he raced through the back and into the front room of Martensii's. His partner slung in a fireman's carry on his back, the large detective shouldered his way past Koin, still handcuffed to the front counter, as he made his way to the front door.

They're coming for you flatfoot!" Koin yelled, wildly trying to kick after the detective. "You can't outrun all of them! Boys, he's this way!"

Looking quickly behind him, Patsy made sure the two young girls made it past Koin before exiting through the front.

"Shut it Koin!" Patsy barked, motioning for the girls to head out the door. "Come on ladies!"

Patsy started off down Berwyn Street, the two girls hot on his heels. Patsy cracked a tiny smile as the girls started to race ahead of him, the large detective weighed down by his limp friend. About halfway down the block near Queens Street, Patsy's heart sank as he heard voices coming from behind them.

"Hey, there they are!"

"Keep going girls!" Patsy called ahead in between huffs. Patsy knew they had another block on Queens before they hit the intersection where they had parked the cruiser, their only chance of escape. "Why did I have to park so blasted far away?" he grumbled to himself.

Making it to the corner and turning onto Queens, Patsy could see the cruiser just as he heard the sounds of cars roaring to life behind him.

"*Almost there, almost there...*" Patsy kept thinking, not allowing himself to look behind him knowing their time was running out.

Patsy finally made it to the cruiser, almost toppling over from exertion. Patsy told the girls to get in the passenger side as he flopped Joe's still unconscious body into the back seat.

"*Man he's still completely out of it,*" Patsy thought, seeing Joe not react to being flopped down. His partner hadn't moved a muscle since Patsy had dragged him out of the rubble of the death trap from which Joe had saved the two little girls. "*I hope he's not...**"

"Oni są nadchodzący!" one of the girls interrupted Patsy's thought, pointing ahead of them.

Although he couldn't understand what she said, he could understand the intent as he followed the girl's pointing finger. About a block away on the turn from Berwyn to Queens, three sets of headlights belonging to two blue sedans and a black Rolls-Royce were turning the corner toward them. Jumping into the driver's seat Patsy, after fumbling with the keys for a moment, ignited the cruiser and kicked it into reverse, taking off down Palmer Avenue. Cutting the wheel sharply, Patsy spun the car expertly around to face away from the pursuing cars. Quickly looking over at the girls next to him as he gunned the engine trying to put some distance in between them and the pursuing thugs, Patsy called out.

"Hold on girls, this might not be a fun ride!"

CHAPTER NINETEEN

Gunning the cruiser, Patsy couldn't help himself from repeatedly checking the rear view mirror. Every glance was another bead of sweat on the detective's brow since the three chasers were closing in on him.

"Stupid mooks. Must've supercharged those buggies if they are catching up to this rig," Patsy thought, forcing his eyes to go back to the road in front of him.

Cutting the wheel sharply, Patsy skidded to the right, flooring it down a lit alley. Patsy had gotten lucky picking this alley. It was barely wide enough for the cruiser alone. As he looked back, the detective smirked when he only saw one set of headlights enter after him down the alleyway.

"That's it boys, play follow the leader," the detective smirked, unsuccessfully trying his best to avoid the various trashcans lining the side of the alley.

"I can't out race or out think these boys around here too long since I don't know this blasted area of town that well. Why couldn't they chase us around midtown or the West side? I could lose those boys there in three turns and a flash of the headlights over near Molly's," Patsy huffed, eyeing the now clear path in front of him leading to an exit from the alley. *"Half of these streets actually look like they head straight to the Scar, probably loading and unloading areas for the cranes down to the closed mills there. Sooner or later I'm going to cut down a dead-end...*"*

The detective almost didn't see the Rolls Royce before it was too late. If the car's high beams hadn't given it away causing Patsy to jam the brakes, the Rolls Royce would've broadsided the cruiser at a full tilt. Overshooting the alley exit, the Rolls Royce continued past the screeching cruiser slamming into a streetlamp on the adjacent corner.

"The mook would've nailed the side where the girls are if I hadn't seen him," Patsy grumbled to himself, looking at the two girls in the passenger seat. *"These guys are playing for keeps..."*

Getting the cruiser back into gear, Patsy followed the Rolls Royce's direction veering around the crashed car, steam now billowing out of the hood where the lamppost had crashed through it.

"BAM!"

Patsy gripped the wheel to steady himself from the jarring rear impact. Stopping to avoid the now wrecked Rolls Royce had allowed the sedan behind them to catch up. Seeing the car accelerate again to make up the small distance the first impact had put between the cars, the detective called out to the young girls to brace themselves as the sedan rear-ended the cruiser with another bone jarring...

"BAM!"

Fighting with the wheel to keep the cruiser from spinning out as it unwantedly exited the alley, Patsy never saw the second sedan until the sound of metal screeching against metal filled his ears as the other sedan veered into the cruiser's side door.

"BAM!"

Patsy could feel his teeth rattle with each hit. Fighting against the car to his right, the detective noticed his pursuers had boxed him in on the street, his car being assaulted from behind and the right. To his left ran a large concrete barrier separating the street from a row of closed shops.

"BANG! BANG!"

Gunshots started peppering the side door of the cruiser from the sedan to his right

"Bunch of cold-hearted mooks!" Patsy yelled at the sedan, trying to return fire with his sidearm while keeping control of the cruiser. "I got kids in here, you yellow-bellied punks!"

Patsy's cries of rage were met with additional shots from the sedan behind him and another jarring ram to the back end as it accelerated into them again.

"BANG! BANG!"

Patsy desperately searched for an avenue of escape from the attacking pursuers. Finding a possible glimmer of salvation, the detective noticed an upcoming alley to his right. Pushing the cruiser to its limit, Patsy rushed the car to the alley before the now trailing sedan on his right could cut him off. Screeching the tires, Patsy barely made the turn. As he straightened out, the detective prepared to gun it down the alley to make some room between them and the sedans when his heart sank. His luck had run out driving around an area he didn't know. At the bottom of the alley, about fifty feet in front of him, was a large chain-linked fence and beyond that the entrance to an industrial elevator down to the bottom of the Scar. The elevator's car was gone leaving the area opened to empty space before the death plunging drop.

"Aww crud…" Patsy barked, barely audible over the squealing of cruiser's brakes. Jamming the cruiser into reverse, the detective started to abandon his plan when suddenly.

"BAM! BAM!"

The impacts from behind sent the car veering to the right and smashed the detective into the steering wheel with a bone jarring impact. Seeing stars, Patsy looked over at the passenger seat to see the young girls crouching on the floor, probably launched there from the attack. It felt as if the Earth was spinning around him. Looking back, the detective realized it wasn't the Earth moving. Instead, both sedans, now side by side in the wide alley, were locked against the passenger side of the cruiser pushing it down the alley! Pumping the brakes, Patsy found them unresponsive as the murderous automobiles continued to inch the cruiser closer and closer to the chain-link fence. Trying the drivers-side door, Patsy pushed against it with his full weight only to find the door jammed!

"The mooks bent the frame on one of those side hits!" Patsy suddenly realized, panic now setting in.

Metal screeched in his ears as the rusted links of the fence scraped against the car's passenger door as the sedans finally wedged the cruiser near its final destination at the end of the alley. With the victims in their crosshairs, the two sedans began to back away slowly down the alley, their headlights almost pinning the cruiser in place as they started to rev their engines at the disabled police car.

"Dang it! Let the girls get out first!" Patsy yelled out the drivers-side window at his attackers, hoping to at least spare the young girls from what was about to happen.

Patsy's cries of mercy were met with the sound of squealing tires as the sedans suddenly accelerated down the alley toward the cruiser! Diving to cover the two girls, Patsy knew even this sacrificial gesture was pointless against their odds.

As the headlights of the attacking sedans overcame the cruiser, Patsy closed his eyes, hoping for the end to come quickly. The detective's eyes shot open when the expected crash never came. As Patsy looked back, he saw the right headlight of the left sedan and the left headlight of the right sedan suddenly coming through the cruiser right at him! The lights went through him as did the rest of the car! Patsy could see the sedan's occupants look over at him, mouths agape in shock. The passenger of the far right sedan even tried to grab at Patsy and the girls, his hands passing through the trio as if they were made of air.

Passing through the cruiser at breakneck speed, the sedans pulverized the chain-link fence in front of them and continued unabated through the elevator machinery and over the edge of the Scar! Hanging there for a moment as if the cars themselves were in disbelief of what had happened, gravity took hold sending the sedans falling to their doom in a fiery explosion hundreds of feet below in the Scar.

Not comprehending how they were still alive, Patsy smiled when he suddenly heard his friend in the backseat.

"That will teach them not to tailgate..." the Grey Ghost muttered, slowly sitting up from the backseat floor.

"Joe!" Patsy cheered. "About time you woke up. How long have you been joy riding back there?"

"I woke up just as they were about to hit us," the Grey Ghost explained.

"On jest żywy," the girl's cried out seeing the Grey Ghost's head over the Cruiser's back seat smiling at him

The hero was happy to see the girls no longer afraid of him. He guessed saving them from the death trap of a cell they had been in had put him in their good graces for the time being.

Concentrating his will over the magic of the Spartan Cloak, the Grey Ghost slowly dissolved the mask from around his ghostly face. Quickly, it solidified forming the handsome but bruised face of Joe Bevine. At the moment, the power of the Spartan Cloak was at work healing his battered body from the cave in, so he didn't want to release himself fully from it yet.

"Hi ladies, remember me?" Joe smiled at the girls.

"You know I still don't have a clue what these two little ladies are saying," Patsy said, straightening himself in the driver's seat as he watched the two girls jump up to hug Joe's neck.

"Neither do I, but it seems I have some fans," Joe smiled, accepting the hugs. "But I think I can solve our communication problem."

"We have an interpreter back at the station?" Patsy asked.

"No, but I've got the next best thing," Joe answered. "Do you think we can make it to Capstone General?"

"Not with the old girl as she is right now," Patsy grimaced at the sound of the gear shift grinding. "I'm surprised I can even get it to turn over after all that. Give me a little time at the station yard and I can get us going again unless you want to do your ghost car thing and get us moving."

"I'm not sure if I could ghost it along all the way back there right now," Joe replied wincing, knowing in the morning he was going to feel every single piece of rubble that had crashed on top of him today. "Let's just see how far we can get by keeping our fingers crossed."

Turning down the still deserted street, the battered officers and their new young friends slowly headed downtown toward Capstone General. Neither of them noticed the two men crawling out of the damaged Rolls Royce blocks away, its engine still steaming where the block had been cracked by the light post. Watching the cruiser putter away, both men started jogging back in the direction of Martensii's.

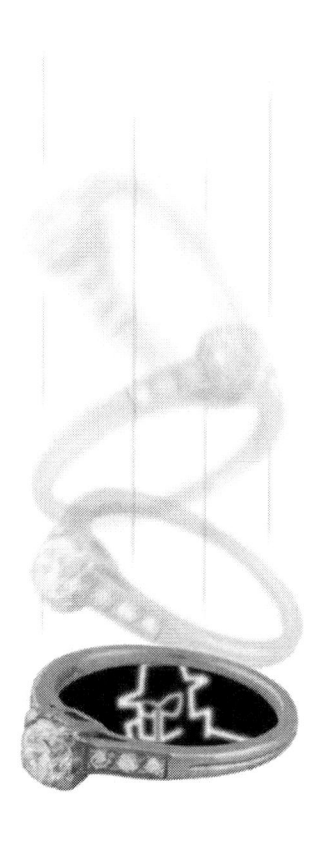

PART FOUR: THE BONDS OF FAMILY

Nicholas Cara

CHAPTER TWENTY

The sharp click of heels on the mayor's office floor was interrupted by the heavy steps of the two large, suited men following behind. The Jeweled Kiss rolled her eyes, slightly noticing the looks exchanged between the extra muscle when they insisted on escorting her inside.

"Relax boys, I don't bite," the Jeweled Kiss smirked. "That's just too messy."

The quip did nothing to de-escalate the tension building between her and the large shadows as the mysterious thief approached the center desk in the mayor's office. The large, high-back chair adorning the decorative piece was facing away from the visitors, its occupant's head barely visible over the back padding.

"Good evening my dear," the smooth voice of Lord Minos greeted her from the chair. "Thank you so much for agreeing to this meeting at such a late hour."

"Oh, I had a choice?" the Jeweled Kiss asked. "Well if that's the case, a girl does need her beauty sleep."

Smiling as she turned away from Minos, the Jeweled Kiss made a half-hearted attempt at leaving.

"How humorous," Minos drolled. "But I must insist that you stay, at least until I relay the news I brought you here for."

"And what news, darling, do you think I would care about so much that you would drag me out here at this hour?" the Jeweled Kiss asked, looking back over her shoulder at the desk. If all Minos was going to show her was his back, she was going to return the favor.

"It has to do with your sisters," Lord Minos stated, allowing the words to hang in the air of the office.

"What about them?" the Jeweled Kiss asked, turning around suddenly with fear creeping into her voice at the mention of her siblings.

"They are dead, my dear," Minos easily replied.

The words crashed into the woman as if she had just been physically attacked. Gripping the large desk for support, the Jeweled Kiss tried to steady her legs, which now seemed no longer to want to carry her weight. The world around the thief seemed to slow before her, now an after image of a darker and more dangerous world than the one she had been standing in moments ago. The wounded thief looked back at the table to find the villain still facing away from her, as if such world shattering news was something beneath his time.

"How?" the Jeweled Kiss asked, rage building behind her eyes to the point where the question had come out as more like a growl. "Why would you?"

"Oh my dear, don't blame me. It was not I that struck the heartless blow here," Minos snarked. "Why don't you take a look at the folder in front of you?"

On the dark polished table in front of her was a manila envelope. With unsteady hands, the Jeweled Kiss ripped open the paper wrapping spilling a small collection of photographs on the table. The photographs showed the remains of a small room she had seen numerous times on television screens from which Minos allowed her to view her young sisters. The small room was now decimated, debris spilling out as if the building around it had collapsed. It was impossible to see anything past the avalanche of cement and rubble enveloping the room as sand would fill the bottom of an hourglass.

"I'm sorry to say that once caught sticking their noses where they shouldn't have been, those heroes ran saving their own skins while they left your sisters behind to be... well I'm sorry to say they never left that room," Minos reported, a fake hint of sadness in his usual businesslike tone.

Looking at the other photos, the Jeweled Kiss could see two individuals escaping from the front of Martensii's, the larger man, Bevine's partner, carrying the detective over his shoulders as they fled.

"I...I want to see them," the Jeweled Kiss sputtered, barely able to speak through her grief and rage. "Take me to them!"

"Ah yes, well I would, but that is the rub my dear," Minos slowly answered, choosing each word with an absurd amount of care. "You see, up to this point we have had what most would see as a marvelous partnership filled with mutual respect and admiration in our endeavors."

A piercing glare shot from the thief on the other side of the table at the back of the chair.

"However..." Minos paused for a moment before continuing. "However, without your sisters under my... protection, I dare to say that our relationship might be well, I guess strained. So our organization has decided to, oh how do those silly Brits put it, give you the sack?"

At that the Jeweled Kiss suddenly felt the presence of the two guards behind her. The one to her right produced a small cloth from his pocket, grabbed her at the waist and quickly brought the cloth up to the thief's face. Smelling a sweet odor from the cloth, the Jeweled Kiss was shocked into action. Instead of pulling at the large arm bringing the powerful drug to her nose and mouth, the Dynamo, using every bit of her enhanced strength, actually pulled the arm toward her face! As the cloth touched her lips the rag continued through her face, head, and then directly into the face of the attacker trying to drug her! Slithering past the massive arm gripping her waist as a snake would coil around its victim, the Jeweled Kiss was suddenly behind the guard, a vice grip on the foul smelling rag now over his mouth and nose. The guard barely had time to struggle before the fast-acting narcotic took effect, sending him to dreamland. Dropping the drugged attacker to the harshly ground, the Jeweled Kiss leapt from the falling man to the other security guard. The other man was desperately trying to light a small candle he had produced from his jacket when the female thief came upon him. Before he could strike the first match, the Jeweled Kiss attacked. A quick chop at the fumbling hand ended the large man's last hope and three quick strikes to his chest and a roundhouse kick to the head later ended his day as he joined his friend, landing hard on the marble floor.

Anger burning in her eyes at the betrayal, the Jeweled Kiss turned back to Minos still facing away from her in his large backed chair. Covering the distance between them in two strides, the Jeweled Kiss struck with a solid kick to the back of the plush chair sending its occupant flailing to the ground. Pouncing on him as a cat would its prey, the Jeweled Kiss raised her fist preparing to strike the villain with every ounce of rage the news of her murdered sisters had filled her with. However, even with the blind rage in her eyes, the dynamo was able to understand the sniveling face meeting hers was not that of the villainous Minos but that of his assistant Ralph.

"Please don't kill the messenger," Ralph pleaded. Somehow his voice changed into a perfect impression of Minos's voice when he then added. "What would your sisters think?"

Picking the man up by his collar, the smaller woman brought the man nose to nose with her before smiling at him.

"Make your funny voices now, little man."

And with that remark, the Jeweled Kiss flung the assistant at the picture window to her right. Crashing through the blinds, the human projectile smashed through the plate glass window, flying into the bushes a few feet below.

Walking over to the broken window, the Jeweled Kiss looked down at the fallen man moaning in the crushed bushes below.

"Tell him little man, when I'm done with this city's hero I'm coming back here," the Jeweled Kiss ordered. "And when I do, I'm going to throw him out of a much taller window."

Seconds later the Jeweled Kiss disappeared from the office, the ripped folder and all of its photographs gone with her in the night.

The bell's chime from the elevator doors had barely receded before the nurse shoved the wheelchair onto the fifth floor.

"Easy..." a voice whispered.

"You're strangling me..." the nurse mumbled, apparently to herself in a voice three octaves too low for the petite blonde ushering the chair.

"Just make it down the hall, and don't draw attention to yourself..." the whisper replied.

The striking blonde slowed as she effortlessly pushed her patient past the information desk. Clad in a hospital gown and a large, slightly worn sweater, the vastly overweight woman napping in the wheelchair in front of her would occasionally let out a rough snore as they proceeded. Looking ahead of her, the nurse noticed the security officer peering up from the newspaper he had been skimming. Turning on the biggest smile she could muster for the uniformed man, she continued on her way past him. Transfixed by that smile, the guard never stopped to think why he had never seen the striking woman before at the hospital.

Feeling his eyes on her, the nurse was happy to see her destination at the end of the hall. Effortlessly hitting the door knob on room 515 with her hip, the nurse kept her eyes down as she started backing them in.

"What did you turn me into?" the nurse grumbled to herself, entering the room. "I thought Chris was going to ask me for my number back there."

"If it makes you feel any better he technically was staring at my behind when we walked past him," the voice answered.

"Can I help you?" Vera asked, greeting the nurse and patient at the door as they entered Kate's hospital room. "I'm sorry but this is a private room."

"Oh yeah...ah...Mom...buddy did you have a plan to explain all this?" the deep-voiced nurse said, apparently conversing with an unseen partner as she noticed Mrs. Bevine.

"It took you almost all night to get the cruiser rolling again so I was sort of hoping we would luck out and she'd still be sleeping this early," replied a voice coming out of nowhere.

"Well a lot of help you were sleeping in the back, Rip Van Winkle," the nurse grumbled. "I should be given a major award for even getting that hunk of junk to turn on without it catching on fire."

Hearing the nurse's invisible companion and recognizing the deep voice, Vera looked at the nurse and asked, "Patsy…? Joseph?"

"Mom, this is going to be a little shocking so just let me explain..." the voice answered.

"Well whatever you do, just get off me," the nurse huffed, shaking back and forth. "You're too heavy to hang there all day."

As she twisted, the nurse and her patient suddenly started to blur as if the air around them was saturating and thickening itself on command. A second later the nurse was gone and in her place Patsy stood in front of Vera twisting to get the man clinging to his back off of him. On Patsy's back was Joe riding back piggy-back style with his arms and leg wrapped around his friend.

"Will you give me a second big guy," Joe said to his bucking bronco. "It's not like I can just jump down. I need to switch places with the little ones."

Vera noticed her son wasn't wearing his prosthetic leg, the pants leg simply draped over the knee ending without a shoe.

"Ladies, can you hop out please, Granny needs her wheels," Patsy said, jerking his head at the wheelchair that he had pushed into the room. Instead of the sleeping woman in the chair, Vera was surprised to find two young girls, neither of which looked older than 10, hopping down onto the hospital room floor.

As Patsy lowered Joe into the chair, the detective looked back at his mother and raised both hands trying to get her to just give him a second. "Mom, I can explain what you just saw. I just need you to listen for a second here…"

"Is that how that watch thingy you have works?" Vera simply replied, becoming increasingly excited as she went on. "I mean, that was neat! Were you both that blonde or was it just Patsy, because I have no idea how you fit that boy into that tiny frame."

"Wait a minute!" Patsy exclaimed.

"You know about the watch?" Joe asked, dumbfounded at his mother's mention of the secret device and her calm but excited reaction to seeing a small blonde nurse turn into the two bumbling detectives.

"Oh boys, come now," Vera replied, looking cross at them. "Did you really think your Father and I wouldn't figure out your ghostly exploits? I mean Kate had to fill us in on a few things, but it was not really that hard."

"Wait, Kate spilled the beans?" Patsy asked, surprised.

"Well, I wasn't going to lie to her and she had already figured most of it out."

The voice came from behind Joe's mother. Both of the detectives instantly recognized it but neither could believe it. Joe wheeled his chair past his mom to the patient's bed near the far wall. There sitting up on the edge was Kate smiling back at him. The smile on his face soon buried itself in her shoulder as he embraced her.

"Oh thank God you're okay..." Joe said, as he clutched his love with every ounce of strength he could muster.

"I'm fine now sweetie," Kate replied, each word a gasp between breaths. "But squeeze any tighter and they aren't going to release me today like they said they would."

Noticing how hard he had been hugging the recuperated patient, Joe released his love, pulling back enough to be able to see her beautiful smile beaming at him.

"When did you wake up?" Joe asked, a million questions coming to his mind at once after the sheer joy of seeing Kate awake began to subside. "Why didn't anyone call us?"

"We've been trying all night to get a hold of you at the station but they said you left hours ago," Joe's mother answered the second question from behind him. "They said they tried to get you on the radio but you weren't answering."

Noticing his sleeve as he was holding her, Joe caught sight of the rips and tears in his suit jacket and wondered what a sight he and Patsy probably were to the two ladies.

"Must have been when we were getting dessert on the West side," Patsy shrugged, adding to the conversation as he reached down to hug Kate. "It's great to see your pretty eyes again Katie. You had us worried there for a while."

"You're just a bunch of worry warts," Kate smiled back at the two. "I'm fine, and what was so important for you two to head over to the West side?"

"These two," Patsy answered, walking back to the door to usher the two young girls forward.

"Hello you two," Joe's mother said, instantly kneeling next to the girls. Two sets of doe-like eyes turned her way, both girls nervously scanning the room, frightened out of their wits.

"They have to be exhausted by now. They have been up all night, mom, and don't seem to speak a word of English between the two of them," Joe said, looking over at his mother. "From what little I could make out, it sounded like Polish when they were answering me. That's why we brought them here to you. We're hoping you can help us out. Right now I'm not 100 percent sure of anyone, even Chris your security guard or any of the nurses. That's why we had to sneak them in here."

"Okay..." Joe's mother replied, thinking for a moment before she looked at the taller of the two girls and smiled.

Before she could say anything, the taller girl noticed something behind Joe's mother and cried out in joy. Pointing to the table in jubilation, the small girl nearly knocked Vera over as she darted for the table yelling, "Siostra, siostra."

Looking over at the table, Joe instantly saw what the young girl and her compatriot were making a beeline for. Sitting on the side table next to Kate's bed should have been the vase of carnations he had left for Kate the previous day. However, in its place was a replica of the flowery arrangement made up of pure emeralds. As the jeweled flowers glistened in the light, the obvious conclusion dawned on him.

"She's been here?" Joe asked looking back at Kate.

"It's a little more complicated than that," Kate replied.

"What do you mean?" Joe shot back.

"Joseph," his mother interrupted. "The little girl just keeps repeating 'siostra, siostra' over and over again pointing at those."

"What does siostra mean?" Patsy asked.

"It means..." Vera answered. "...Sister."

CHAPTER TWENTY-ONE

"Get your paper! Paper right here! Grey Ghost wanted by coppers!" the young boy cried out while holding a newspaper from the large stack of Capstone Vindicators next to his leg. "Mayor gives the bum the old raspberry and still wants to hold the next rally! Get your papers here!"

A coin was flipped at the boy who with practice and precision grabbed the tossed payment, never breaking his stride announcing his wares. As he did the new owner of the newspaper picked up her copy from the stack and continued on her way. Flipping open the front fold with a smack, the reader took stock of the headline.

"They definitely are eating him alive," the Jeweled Kiss said to herself, seeing the top headline through her purple-shaded glasses. "I would feel bad for the poor man, but his press clippings will be the last of his problems when I'm through with him."

The Grey Ghost: The Jeweled Kiss Mysteries

The Capstone City Vindicator
EARLY CITY EDITION
Saturday, February 28, 1942

Est. 1869

WANTED

City Wide Manhunt Called For By Mayor For Vigilante.

By: Lynda Cordova

Mayor Editar has called for a complete investigation into the attack and attempt on his life during last Thursday's G.I. Celebration. During the event, the Mayor, in front of a stunned crowd of onlookers, was seriously wounded by a brazen attack from a masked man. Witnesses to the horrible incident report the attacker to be the vigilante known as the Grey Ghost, who ruthlessly shot the official in the middle of the opening to the Celebration.

The Grey Ghost was not apprehended at the scene and still remains at large. All residents are urged to contact the Capstone City Police Department with any information on the masked attacker. While the Mayor is calling for swift action in this case, it appears that Police Captain

WITNESS'S SKETCH OF THE

Editar Rejects Cou[ncil] Plan to Postpone Sec[ond] G.I. Celebration

By: Michael Hay

Mayor Editar has made it clear that he will not entert[ain] suggestions that the second the G.I. Celebration be po[stponed] until the investigation into th[e] attack that left him woun[ded] associate professor Kathryn the hospital is complete.

"The notion that these hoo[dlums] scare the City Council i[nto] matter is frightful," Edi[tar] record saying. "The Celeb[ration] proceed as planned starti[ng] sharp. I'm making a per[sonal] the men and women

WANTED

City Wide Manhunt Called For By Mayor For Vigilante

By: Lynda Cordova

Mayor Editar has called for a complete investigation into the attack and attempt on his life during last Thursday's G.I. Celebration. During the event, the mayor, in front of a stunned crowd of onlookers, was seriously wounded by a brazen attack from a masked man. Witnesses to the horrible incident report the attacker to be the vigilante known as the Grey Ghost, who ruthlessly shot the official in the middle of the opening to the Celebration.

The Grey Ghost was not apprehended at the scene and still remains at large. All residents are urged to contact the Capstone City Police Department with any information on the masked attacker. While the mayor is calling for swift action in this case, it appears that Police Captain James Robinson is not. Calling for calm among the populace, Captain Robinson has been heard commenting that there is no evidence that the masked man was the Grey Ghost, though we could at the time of this report confirm that as a confusing statement.

Continued on A2

Editar Rejects Council Plan to Postpone Second G.I. Celebration

By: Michael Hay

Mayor Editar has made it crystal clear that he will not entertain any suggestions that the second part of the G. I. Celebration be postponed until the investigation into the daring attack that left him wounded and associate professor Kathryn Stone in the hospital is complete.

"The notion that these hooligans can scare the City Council in such a matter is frightful," Editar is on record saying. "The Celebration will proceed as planned starting at 6 PM sharp. I'm making a personal plea to the men and women of Capstone City. Do not let fear and these criminals take away the freedoms our young men are fighting for overseas. Come out and let's show them what our city is made of!"

Continued on A4

Folding the paper under her arm, the Jeweled Kiss made her way through the bustling crowds of the early morning rush. Stopping outside her destination, the thief scanned the crowd around the entrance. There wasn't a uniformed officer in sight, the police tape and markers were long gone from the storefront.

"Their dime novels do say that the criminal always returns to the scene of the crime," the Jeweled Kiss mumbled to herself as she entered Fulcher's Emporium.

Walking up to the security guard seated by the door, the thief noticed it was the same poor man who had been working the night of her first visit. As she approached him, she could see the guard start to recognize her and reach for the sidearm strapped on his belt. Before the loop of the pistol was even loosened, the gun was in the Jeweled Kiss's hand and pointing at the man who was already rethinking his career path.

"You really do get all of the fun shifts, don't you darling?" the Jeweled Kiss purred at him as she pulled the trigger twice.

BAM!!

BAM!!

*...**

CHAPTER TWENTY-TWO

"WAIT A MINUTE! One thing at a time!" Joe called out to the room holding his hands up for quiet. Far too many questions than answers, some not even in English, were flying around him that he couldn't focus on a single one of them.

"Patsy, how about you and mom take the girls over there and see if we can get the story from them about why they were in that room. I'll talk to Kate about these expensive decorations of hers," Joe suggested, throwing a thumb to the far side of the room where the neighboring bed now lay empty.

"All right, little ladies how about we sit you down over here," Patsy motioned, picking up one of the girls and sitting her on the empty bed followed by her sister.

As Joe's mother started to converse with the little girls, he turned back toward Kate. Taking her hand in his and looking over at the emerald flowers he asked, "Did she talk to you when she was here? Was she trying to hurt you?"

"Yes and no," Kate answered, following his eyes. "She wasn't trying to hurt me."

"Does this mean she knows about me, about all of us?" Joe interrupted. "Is that why she came after you at the celebration?"

"Joe stop for a second," Kate said, cupping his face with her free hand to pull his attention back to her. "I think you may have this girl all wrong. This Jeweled Kiss is complicated. I don't think she wants to hurt anyone."

"She wasn't so heavy hearted when she launched you from that stage," Joe countered as a grim look came over his face.

"That wasn't her Joe," Kate corrected. "Back at the rally I was sitting a few seats from the mayor when the first shots went off. The mayor hit the floor pretty hard. I went over to him and saw him clutching his one shoulder. I didn't see any blood but he seemed really hurt. There was chaos everywhere but you could still hear her talking over the screaming. As I knelt on the ground next to the mayor, I could see the Jeweled Kiss standing at the entrance to the stage with a tall man dressed in a dark gray trench coat and hat."

"Yeah, the shooter everyone is saying was me...I mean the Grey Ghost," Joe added.

"He looked nothing like you except the hat," Kate said, shaking her head. "Even the coat was the wrong color. And his face, he was just wearing a white stocking over his face. He looked more like a clown than you, the way his nose was smashed down under the stocking."

"Tell the papers that," Joe quipped.

"I am planning on it, especially that Cordova. Your mother showed me today's headlines and that lady definitely has it out for you," Kate added. "But like I said, she didn't have the gun; she was just giving a monologue for the crowd. She was really distracted at the podium, almost like she was trying to remember her lines, and that's when I decided to try something."

"Kate you shouldn't have..." Joe started before Kate cut him off again.

"I'm a big girl Joe. I can tie my own shoes and everything, so cut out that nonsense," Kate retorted. "These two had just shot the mayor in front of an entire crowd and heaven knows what they had planned for the rest of us. And you know, no one there had a prayer against them if they really had the same powers the cloak gives you.

Reaching over to the nightstand, Kate gathered her small clutch that had been sitting there next to the small paper bag with her belongings. "I'm just glad someone was kind enough to grab this for me when they brought me here."

Kate continued talking while fishing inside of the small purse. "You see, I've been thinking that if this lady has the same powers as you it stands to reason she has to be getting it from something like the Spartan Cloak. And if she really is getting her powers from the same source then she might also share the same weaknesses, so I've been carrying around these just in case we ever come across her again."

Pulling out her hand from the bag, Kate produced a small votive candle.

"The one I lit at the rally while she was talking got kicked out of my hand when he knocked me off the stage," Kate added.

"Did it affect them the same way it knocks me for a loop when I'm ghosted?" Joe asked, disappointed with himself that he had never thought of the idea. It didn't surprise him that Kate had been the one to figure out that the Jeweled Kiss's power might have the same vulnerability to a lit candle as the Grey Ghost's. Kate was the one who originally figured out the hero's Achilles heel from the coded field book of one of her father's students. And Joe still remembered smacking into the bedroom wall back at the house when they first tested the idea.

"It actually hurt her worse Joe," Kate replied.

"Worse? Really?" Joe asked, surprised.

"Oh yes," Kate continued. "From what I remember when we tested the candle's effects on you, your form, or at the time your leg, evaporated instantly. It was like the magic you were controlling through the Spartan Cloak was being siphoned into the burning wick."

"It left me weak... dizzy... almost as if my equilibrium was gone in an instant. After a few seconds it started to come back but it wasn't with the same power I have as the Grey Ghost. For those first few moments I was as weak as a puppy," Joe said, thinking back to the wallop he had just felt back at the bakery a few hours ago.

"The same instant reaction happened when I lit the candle around the Jeweled Kiss," Kate said. "Like you, I could almost see the power drain out of her into the candle. But her reaction to the power leaving was just so violent, she immediately clutched her chest and fell screaming to the stage floor. The poor thing looked like she was having a heart attack. She sounded like she was in so much agony. I remember almost putting out the candle before he grabbed me."

"The other gray guy?" Joe asked.

"Yes," Kate confirmed. "I was so engrossed in the horrible reaction the Jeweled Kiss was having I didn't see him coming before it was too late."

"And he wasn't affected by the candle at all?" Joe wondered.

"Not a bit that I could see," Kate nodded. "I think your doppelgänger was just a normal creep in a hat and coat. The last thing I remember seeing before I woke up here was the Jeweled Kiss looking much different reaching out to me crying for him to stop when he threw me from the stage."

"When you woke up were these here?" Joe asked pointing to the jeweled flowers.

"Not like that..." Kate answered. "But she was here."

"The Jeweled Kiss was here when you woke up?" Joe asked.

"Joe, from what the doctors tell me she was the reason I woke up," Kate added. "When I woke up she was holding my head in her hands concentrating, like this…"

Kate reached out and took Joe's hands placing his palms against each side of her temples.

"Why?"

"She was saving me, Joe," Kate said, shaking her head as if she was confused as much as he was. "Your mother and I talked to the doctors and they think my head injury from the fall was actually a blood clot from the trauma not swelling like they thought. That thing could've killed me, Joe. I might have never woken up from that."

Grabbing Kate again, Joe hugged her hoping she wouldn't see the terror on his own face. He had been worried about losing her but the realization of how close he had come to doing so never dawned on him until that second. Joe just held Kate, probably for too long but at that moment he didn't care. For those moments there was Kate and nothing else mattered.

Finally releasing his embrace, he looked in her eyes that like his own had been fighting away tears as the fear of what could have happened set in on both of them.

"She saved me," Kate whispered through tears. "Somehow she removed the clot in my brain. How could she do that? How could she know how to do that?"

"I don't know, did she say anything?" Joe asked back.

"She just said… she said she was sorry. She told me that no one there was supposed to get hurt," Kate replied. "And then she walked over to the window. I was still pretty woozy but I remember her smiling and saying these should pay for the hospital bills just before she disappeared. That was a second or two before your mom came back in the room."

"RING!!!!!"

The conversation was interrupted by the small telephone sitting next to the jeweled flowers. Reaching over, Joe answered the red phone, bringing it to his ear.

"Hello…" Joe greeted cautiously before he recognized the voice on the other end. "Ah… yes Captain, both Patsy and I are here…Yes, Kate's doing well now she's apparently... Wait she what? No we haven't been near a radio," Joe said, looking over at Kate with a confused expression. "Yes sir, we'll head over there right now."

"What's going on?" Kate asked as Joe hung up the phone.

"Patsy!" Joe called over to his partner who had tried overhearing the exchange on the phone. "Bud, the captain needs us back at Fulcher's right now."

"What's the story?" Patsy asked walking over.

"Kate, when is the hospital releasing you?" Joe asked.

"They said this morning so it could be any time," Kate replied.

"Mom, do you think you could get Dad to come pick you up and get you, Kate, and these two to the house?" Joe continued.

"I suppose so but he'll be late for work," Vera replied looking at the clock.

"Call him and ask him to take one of those hundreds of vacation days the plant owes him if he can. It's important," Joe asked. "We need to keep these two safe and out of the public eye for the time being at least until we get back."

"Joseph, what is going on?" Patsy asked again.

"Apparently the Jeweled Kiss has changed her tune from a few hours ago," Joe replied, looking over at Kate. "She's at Fulcher's again and it seems just robbing the place isn't enough anymore. She's apparently killed a guard and is now holding hostages!"

CHAPTER TWENTY-THREE

Captain Robinson didn't like what he was seeing as he scanned Meridian Drive. Police barricades blocked the street all the way to Parkman Avenue with a crowd forming at both intersections. It was definitely not the planned morning he had in mind. Before the craziness of the past few weeks, he used to say anything other than the laborious meetings he was stuck in the majority of his day would be a gift, but now he would take a lecture from the mayor on traffic patterns with a smile on his mustached face. He hated it, but he could understand the rubberneckers stopping on their way to work to see the commotion. As bad as things had gotten, a police standoff in Capstone was still something thankfully uncommon, and the few young kids ducking under the barricades to get a better view only proved the public's lack of understanding on how dangerous the situation was.

"Grootman, make sure those kids keep back!" Robinson yelled to the closest patrolman, who started after the kids.

Watching the young trespassers retreat behind the crowd, Robinson noticed a bowler peeking over the top of the crowd before Patsy finished shoving his way past the gaggle of people. Dipping under the blockade, Patsy barked something at the patrolman who apparently hadn't recognized him and made his way over to the captain with the uniformed officer in tow.

"Cap, what's the story?" Patsy asked, looking over at Fulcher's empty storefront.

"Where's Bevine?" Robinson asked, noticing Patsy's missing partner.

"He's on his way... there was a complication. I'll fill you in about it when we get a free moment," Patsy replied.

"Anything to do with the reports of a car chase and shooting from the West side last evening?" the captain asked as he eyed Thomas. "I remember you two mentioning you were headed that way."

"Like I said there were complications..." Patsy shrugged. "But he shouldn't be far behind me. How about you fill me in and I'll get him up to speed when he gets here?"

"Sure you do that..." Robinson grumbled, not liking Joe's absence. "Earlier this morning around 7:00 to 7:15, that Jeweled Kiss lady waltzed right back into Fulcher's. From reports, she apparently shot a guard and has kept an unknown number of customers and workers hostage in one of the back rooms. Weird thing about this lady is she had one of the hostages, a Mr. Sam Fowler, call the station to report what she was doing, dead guard and all before she cut the line."

"Has there been any action inside since then?" Patsy questioned.

"No, not a peep," Robinson answered. "She's in there pretty good. We can't make out a thing with all of the curtains pulled except for the one near the entrance."

Patsy looked over to the doorway and noticed the one remaining drawn back curtain. There lying next to it was the body of the shot security guard.

"It's as if she's daring us to try something with the poor devil in there," Robinson muttered, looking at the downed guard. "I wish we could at least get to the guy. We haven't seen him move since we got here."

Looking at the top part of the window the guard was lying against, Patsy could make out the splintered bullet holes from the attack.

Something isn't right here... the detective thought, observing the scene.

"How far was Bevine behind you?" Captain Robinson asked again.

"He's not that far back Cap," Patsy replied, glancing to see officer Grootman, almost forgotten in the conversation, quickly make his way from them back into the crowd. "He'll be here any minute now…"

Officer Grootman's luck seemed to be holding up. As he entered the side room, he noticed the manager's office in Fulcher's was both deserted and darkened, its lone hanging lamp switched off. Keeping low, the officer made sure to stay out of sight of the inner wall's lone window, the main floor visible through the broken blinds hanging down from its frame. As he did, his police officer disguise quickly started to fade into the costume of the Grey Ghost.

A little guile and deception had allowed him to get both an understanding of the situation and the Grey Ghost around the police barricades to the side alley of the emporium without a single creative excuse for where Officer Joe Bevine had disappeared. He took stock of the small room as he inched his way along the interior wall toward the opened door. The Ghostly Guardian noticed the room was pretty Spartan in nature; a lone desk and filing cabinet faced the opened entrance and scraps of crumpled paper were scattered along the chestnut floor. Carefully avoiding the trash, the ghostly guardian only noticed his reflection in the chrome covering of a deserted radio sitting unplugged on the desktop a step away from the doorway before...

BAM! BAM!
BAM! BAM!

The ringing shots almost deafened the hero as the ignitions invaded the silence of the captive store. Small bits of plaster and dust fell clouding the air as bullets cut through the interior wall where the Grey Ghost had been inching along, leaving pinpoints of light peeping into the darkened room. Luckily the hero had been ghosted and therefore intangible since at least three of the shots that had gone through both the wall and small window had also traveled through him before they had settled into the exterior brick wall.

Looking down at the beams of light now piercing through his ghosted form, the Grey Ghost's unseen eyes widened in surprise.

"Now I know what a piece of Swiss cheese feels like..." the hero grumbled.

Looking back at the radio, the hero could now make out the Jeweled Kiss's reflection in the shiny casing, pointing a still smoking pistol in the room's direction.

"Clever girl," the hero thought to himself, understanding that the unplugged radio had been set deliberately on the desk so the thief could observe the room from its shiny reflection.

"There is no reason for friends to hide in the dark like that," the Jeweled Kiss announced with the pistol still leveled at the doorway.

"You know you could've killed someone if it was anyone but me in here," the Grey Ghost answered, watching the thief in the reflection.

BAM!

The chrome radio exploded on the desktop, scattering metal and transistor components across the back wall.

"Why in the world do you think I would care?" the Jeweled Kiss hissed in reply. "Now come out of there. Don't make me curious to see how bullet proof this shop's other walls are."

Knowing there were reported hostages in the back room, the Grey Ghost relented, starting to rise with his hands in the air.

"That's cold, lady," the Grey Ghost replied, keeping his back to the wall but starting to step out into the doorway. *"So what's with the return to Fulcher's? You forget to get a matching set of...*"*

The hero's retort was cut off when the back of his jacket was seized and pulled through the wall. Caught off guard by the strength and speed of the attack, the hero landed in a heap on the floor in the main room. Looking up, the ghostly guardian was confused at the fury boiling in the eyes leveled at him by the Jeweled Kiss, who was still training her pistol at him.

"Whoa... Whoa...Was it something I said?" the Grey Ghost asked, seeing the hatred pointing in his direction.

Gone was the look of joy the Jeweled Kiss had beamed when they first met near the docks. Now her face looked sickly, shrunken and drawn. The only color adorning it was the bloodshot eyes whose biting gaze was as penetrating as the bullets that peppered the side room.

"I...I believed... you were actually different..." the Jeweled Kiss hissed, barely able to form the words as she stared at him.

Grabbing his collar and in a fluid motion, the Jeweled Kiss, fueled by rage, lifted the hero off the ground and flung him across the room into a display case. The glass case disintegrated under the hero's weight, shelving and jewelry exploding across the floor as he landed with a crash.

Getting to his feet, the Grey Ghost barely sidestepped a metal rack flung at him from across the room by the Jeweled Kiss as she advanced on him.

"I thought you could be the hero everyone said you were!" the Jeweled Kiss screamed, grabbing another display and throwing it at him.

"Hey lady, I'd love to discuss my attributes and why they have you in such a bend, but I make it a habit to never talk to someone who is holding people against their wills in the next room," the Grey Ghost replied, letting the second attack simply pass through his intangible form. *"I mean you're in hot water enough hurting this guard over here. How about we get him some help, huh?"*

"Oh yes, I'm the monster here you pathetic fake!" the Jeweled Kiss replied, still screaming. "You mean these lovely people? Go ahead and take them; you can have every single one of them!"

Grabbing the curtain that separated the main floor from the back room where she had placed the mysterious present on her first visit, the Jeweled Kiss tore the curtain from its rings revealing the back room where the hostages were reportedly being held. The Grey Ghost could make out six hostages being held there. All of them were standing huddled in the middle of the room, their heads down and covered by their hands. Making his way past the Jeweled Kiss, the Spirited Avenger entered the back room and placed his hand around the closest hostage to the doorway, a small brown-haired female.

"It's okay Miss, let's get you out of here..." the hero said as he started gently coaxing the small woman by the arm toward the side doorway. As he did so, the woman's arm suddenly came off in his hand! Startled by this, the Grey Ghost grabbed at the poor girl, noticing she had not made a single cry of pain...or any noise at all! The woman's ghastly arm in his gloved hand felt stiffened and dead to his touch. Looking at it, the hero could see the arm was made out of plastic as was its owner!

"They are just a bunch of dummies!" the Grey Ghost exclaimed.

"So you and they have something in common," the Jeweled Kiss stated deadpanned.

"Enough joking, where are the real hostages?" the Grey Ghost asked, now losing his temper.

"There weren't any hostages you buffoon! Fooling everyone with those was child's play!" the Jeweled Kiss exhorted, her anger rising again to match his. "Look at the guard I *shot*. I had everyone leave out of the back as soon as I shot a couple of holes in the front window. I knew you would come if you thought you would get a chance to play hero for a crowd."

Walking over to the downed guard, the Spirited Avenger saw that she was telling the truth. The guard next to the window was just another store dummy.

"So you called the report in for the hostages just to get me here?" the Grey Ghost asked, wondering what the end game was for the thief. *"You practically have the entire Capstone City Police Department outside waiting to shoot you because they think you murdered a guard in cold blood. And you haven't killed anyone..."*

"No I haven't..." the Jeweled Kiss replied, sneering at the hero. "Well not yet!"

And with that the Jeweled Kiss, throwing the pistol to the side, launched herself at the Grey Ghost.

"And that's your traffic and weather at the *tens*," Rich announced into the round screened microphone, adding a little extra emphasis to the words tens for his radio audience. "This is Rich Svenson and up next we have a special treat for you ladies and gentlemen, an encore presentation of Jody Shull and the Executive Collection's fabulous performance last night at the sold out Maple Theater. We will interrupt the presentation if there are any further developments in the police standoff reported at Fulcher's Emporium, but until then here for your listening pleasure is Jody Shull and the Executive Collection."

As soon as he placed the needle on the record sending the crooning diva along the airwaves, Rich removed his headset and tried his best to shake out the flat crease in his ruffled, thick tuft of black hair. Headphone hair was just a fact of life in this business.

"Anything from the news hounds, Jimmy?" Rich called out to his producer in the adjacent room.

Flanked by a collection of turntables and switchboards that would make a spaceman go cross-eyed, Jimmy Roche, after looking at the news tape, shook his head side to side through the small window separating the two rooms. Rich knew his longtime friend would have gotten word to him to interrupt the morning broadcast if there had been, but he figured it couldn't hurt to check before he unfolded himself from the small broom closet they called a broadcast booth.

"I'm going to grab a bite before the next round. I'll be back in 20 buddy," Rich announced looking down to grab his jacket that had fallen off his chair.

"I'll be back in 20 buddy..."

The voice echoed over the speakers into the booth. Instinctively looking around the small room and then back to Jimmy to see what the joke was, Rich was surprised to see his producer gone! Jimmy had been replaced with a shorter bald man sporting a small thin mustache and a long hooked nose now staring back at him through the studio window.

"Please say that again..." the interloper, whose face reminded Rich of a parrot, requested through the window separating them.

"What's going on? Where's Jimmy?" Rich said, standing up from the booth chair and heading to the door.

"Jim...Jim..J..J..Ji.." the man repeated back, acting like he was tasting each syllable while rolling it around in his mouth. The man kept jabbering his crooked nose up and down solidifying Rich's first fowl-like impression.

From behind the parrot of a man, Rich heard a loud crash from the production room. Looking past him, Rich could see Jimmy grappling with two other men near the far switchboard. Jimmy, swinging like a mad man, was able to get a grip on one of the large wheels of tape nearby and smashed it upside the face of one of the attackers, knocking him back. However, he wasn't fast enough to get out of the grip of the larger second man who started pummeling the producer from behind.

Rushing into the production room to help his friend, Rich's rescue attempt was stalled as the hooked nose man produced a small pistol from his jacket and pointed it at both the radio star and his friend.

"That will be enough of that!" the parrot-faced man announced. The goons violently pulled Jimmy to his feet, the one now sporting a large bruise over his eye where Jimmy had connected with the wheel of tape.

"What is the big idea?" Rich asked, still seeing red at what had happened to his friend.

"What... What... What is the big idea..." the parrot-faced man kept repeating, his voice sounding more like Rich's each time until he announced in a perfect reproduction of the radio star's voice.

"This is Rich Svenson with your news and traffic at the tens!"

"Good for you. I could hire you to cover his vacations if you weren't a nut!" Jimmy huffed, still breathing hard from the fight.

"Oh my bearded friend, I would be quiet and play nice if I were you," the impressionist wickedly smiled, walking up to Jimmy and grabbing him by the chin. "Gentlemen, my name is Mr. Tookings. I want you both to understand that the only reason either of you is still breathing is Mr.

Svenson here is going to be critical in the next stages of my employer's plans. As for you my bearded friend, you are only here to ensure his cooperation. So if that point becomes moot so will you."

The threat in Rich's voice made it all the more frightening to the radio jocks. Rich and Jimmy were lead away from the radio room by the two goons, Tookings covering them with the pistol until they were outside where a dark sedan and additional henchmen were awaiting them. The goons tossed both men in the back of the large sedan before Tookings leaned in the car door.

"Oh, and gentlemen, let me be the first to welcome you both to the distinguished organization of the Reich Hand!" Tookings said before slamming the sedan door closed.

As the dark sedan started away, Tookings walked back to the radio station repeating to himself Rich's catchphrase with the same emphasis on the word tens. "This is Rich Svenson, and here is your news and traffic at the *tens*!"

CHAPTER TWENTY-FOUR

"Now this is getting ridiculous!" the Grey Ghost barked, ducking the solid kick aimed at his face that instead smashed into a wall mirror next to him. *"Are you just trying to break things or are you trying to hit me?"*

The quip cost the hero, pausing him long enough that he couldn't dodge the follow-up punch that connected with his ribs. Grunting in pain, the spirited avenger tried to roll away from the onslaught, but his attacker pressed her advantage. Pouncing on him, the Jeweled Kiss launched a rapid set of punches into his armored face. Each connection rang off the metal plating as if the mask was being bombarded by a hammer, not a lady-sized fist. Blindly reaching out, the hero was able to grab one of the descending fists and throw his abuser off balance away from him.

Quickly backing away from her, the hero jumped behind one of the only remaining standup display cases in the store; its brothers lay broken and shattered across the floor. Hoping for a respite from the fury of the Kiss's attacks, the Grey Ghost tried to mutter a few words in between his labored breaths and the large bruise he felt puffing out underneath his disguise.

"You know we might as well break this one too," the Grey Ghost huffed. *"I mean old man Fulcher is going to have to buy all new furniture anyways."*

"Not so funny when someone else is doing the hitting, big hero?" the Jeweled Kiss spat back.

"Don't flatter yourself lady. I've been hit by prettier women than you before," the Grey Ghost countered. ***"But you are the first…what… ninja I've ever fought with…so…"***

"Joke all you want," the Jeweled Kiss taunted. "It just makes me want to hurt you more!"

Feinting to the left, the thief jumped into a spinning heel kick that slammed into the Grey Ghost's shoulder. Knocked into the wall, the spirited avenger covered his face as the follow-up blows rained down against his arms. Seeing a small opening in her attack, the Grey Ghost dove at her feet, rolling under an attempt to kick at him. Righting himself in a shooting stance behind her, the Grey Ghost focused the power of the Spartan Cloak to his hands, pointed at the thief with his finger as if it was a pistol and shot a volley of what Patsy had dubbed "the ghost gun" at his attacker.

With her speed, the attacks barely nicked the Jeweled Kiss, but they did push her back as she jumped away from his next round of shots.

"I can see you are hot at me for some reason," the Grey Ghost yelled, keeping his weapon leveled in her direction. ***"And trust me, I can 'feel' that you are not kidding when you say you want my head on a platter, but could we at least clear up why you're talking like I'm the bad guy here? I mean for Pete's sake, you're the one who has been busy leaving explosives all over the city and helping some lowlife shoot the mayor."***

"You really don't remember?" the Jeweled Kiss replied, almost growling. "Were they so little, so insignificant to you that you can't even remember?"

"They? Do you mean Hansel and Gretel?" the hero asked, catching her meaning. ***"Those two kids that you left the clues about on the bombs all over town?"***

"OF COURSE I MEAN THEM!" the Jeweled Kiss screamed, coming at him again. "They were all I had and you killed them, you monster!"

Only another volley of the ghost gun kept her at bay, murder reddening her eyes as she glared at him.

"Settle down!" the Grey Ghost cautioned. ***"I didn't kill anyone. Both of those two little girls are fine!"***

"Liar!" the Jeweled Kiss spat.

"No seriously, two young girl about this tall, no more than ten I bet," the ghostly guardian tried to explain to the incensed woman leveling his one hand to what he guessed the girl's height to be. ***"They were at Martensii's, right? Not a lick of English between the two of them?"***

"No, stop trying to trick me. I saw the photo of the room. They're dead; you left them!" the Jeweled Kiss cried out, the anger slightly dissipating in her voice. There was a slight sense of hopefulness starting to creep into her tone.

"The only worry those two have right now is getting fattened up like a Christmas goose by the people I left them with," the Grey Ghost answered, slowly lowering his hand and the ghost gun. ***"We found them at Martensii's after figuring out the birthstone and fairy tale trick you left for me on the packages. The room they were in was booby trapped for someone like us, and yeah it got hairy, but both of those two are safe and sound. You have my word on it."***

"They're... they're alive?" the Jeweled Kiss stuttered, the fury and anger in her face evaporating away.

"They are your sisters, aren't they?" the Grey Ghost asked, putting two and two together from the little girl's earlier comment and the concern the Jeweled Kiss was portraying.

"Yes..." the Jeweled Kiss answered, walking toward him, her face pleading him not to be lying. "Where are they? Take me to them."

"First you have a lot of explaining to do," the Grey Ghost replied. ***"This city is quickly boiling in hot water because of you and I'm tired of having more questions than answers here."***

"No," the Jeweled Kiss crudely said. The Grey Ghost could tell there wasn't any flexibility in her answer, though he noticed a slightly different accent in her tone. "I've been... my family has been toyed with far too long. First show me my sisters and if they are safe like you say, THEN I'll tell you everything. Not that it will help you or this city much."

"You are running out of time in there Joseph," Patsy thought to himself staring around at the officers all aiming their weapons at the emporium.

"Boys, put 'em away," Captain Robinson barked, raising his hand from his crouched position next to Patsy as he holstered his own service weapon. "We're not going to have any stray pills flying around there with those hostages still inside. And whoever is tapping their foot so loud get a grip on yourself! You're giving me a headache."

Looking down and noticing that he was the culprit of the captain's headache, Patsy smacked his leg, trying to get it to take a rest. Even though weapons were being lowered as ordered, Patsy could see the tension outside the emporium wasn't abating for anyone. About a minute ago, the entire force was starting to rush toward the front doors as the sounds of shots rang out from inside. A full display case crashing through the front window at them had been the only thing that stayed their hand momentarily.

The crashing display had been followed by an even larger racket inside the store. It sounded like the whole building itself was being thrown around by an interior twister. Shelves crashing, the sounds of yelling, more glass shattering, lights flickering on and off, whatever storm that was raging inside of the store had been violent enough to back the entire amassed group of officers to their squad cars until they knew more about what they were dealing with.

"I hope our team is winning in there," Patsy thought, brushing off a few glass shards that had peppered his coat from the crashing display.

And then almost as suddenly and as violently as it had started, everything just stopped. An eerie calm came over the scene in front of Patsy as minutes ticked by, the emporium a mask of the interior disaster they could see through the broken front window. Without notice, the lights inside the store went dark in front of the mass of united officers, daylight still illuminating the visible sections of the store but failing to hit the farther back rooms that were now bathed in shadow.

"That's it boys," Robinson softly called out, waving the squad forward. "We can't let this continue all day before that nut in there starts getting nervous especially now in the dark. Thomas, you and I are taking the front door. Grootman, take… where is he? Bishop get up here and take Jones to cover the alley's side entrance. Keep your guns low gentlemen. I don't want any crossfire in there. The first priority is those hostages, you hear me?"

The surrounding officers nodded their understanding to Robinson. As Bishop and Jones started to make their way around to the side alley, Patsy and the captain quickly made their way to the side wall of the store, inching closer to the front door. Keeping below the windows, the two hoped not to be noticed until they made it to the main entrance.

"Did we have someone cut the power?" Patsy whispered over his shoulder as he shuffled along.

"No," Robinson replied softly.

"Probably not the best idea to take this girl on in the dark, Captain," Patsy replied.

"Probably not Thomas, but we are running out of options here," the captain replied as they finally made their way to the door. "She hasn't made a single demand or really said a peep to us all morning. And now after all of the commotion in there a few minutes ago, I'm making the call. We have to try to get to those hostages."

"Fair enough. Believe it or not this isn't the worst idea I've jumped into in the last 24 hours," Patsy smirked.

Both officers pulled out their sidearms and nodded to each other before Patsy started to inch the door open. Leading the way into the store with his pistol, Patsy slowly reached over to the downed security guard by the front window. Checking for a pulse, Patsy was surprised to find the plastic neck of the downed guard. Confused, Patsy grabbed at the man's head and had to stifle a yelp when the plastic noggin came off!

"Cap, I don't think this one's going to make it…" Patsy gulped as

Robinson saw the mannequin. "Like I said outside, something was off about those bullet holes behind this fella…no mess, just straight shots."

Frowning at the downed fake, the captain slowly started to rise from his crouched position to scan the deserted room. Pointing to the back curtain separating the main floor room from the back, the two officers quickly made their way to the satin division. The captain slowly started to pull the satin curtain back when suddenly…

"RING!"

Both Patsy and Robinson nearly jumped out of their skins as the phone on the cashier's desk next to Patsy rang out, breaking the deathly silence of the besieged emporium.

"RING!"

Giving his heart a minute to fall back down from his throat into its proper place, Patsy ignored the telephone and followed Robinson as they made their way into the back room to find the "hostages." As the captain started to push aside the backroom curtain, a darkened figure quietly fell on top of him! Grabbing at the figure now tangled with the captain on the ground, Patsy tried to pull the possible attacker off of his commander when suddenly the person's upper body came off in his hands! Scrambling away from the now loose legs and lower torso of the attacker, Robinson jumped to his feet and reached for the light switch near the entranceway, which immediately illuminated the store again.

"RING!"

As Robinson cursed out loud, the two detectives could see the attacker was just another mannequin, which had been propped against the curtain on the inside of the backroom. They had been completely bamboozled by the Jeweled Kiss, who was nowhere in sight.

"RING!"

Seeing the coast was clear, Patsy walked back to the main desk and picked up the still ringing telephone. Placing it up to his ear, the detective answered harshly, "What?"

"Family meeting…time to bring them in…Kate's house, 8 o'clock" the Grey Ghost's voice echoed in the receiver before the line

went dead.

"Anything?" Robinson asked, looking at his detective from the mannequin-filled back room as Patsy placed the receiver back on the base.

Looking back at Robinson, Patsy frowned. There wasn't going to be any easy way of explaining this, and if things were really getting to a point where they had to have the "family meeting" then the detective knew things were really starting to fall off the rails.

CHAPTER TWENTY-FIVE

"It always seems to be raining when I come back here," Kate thought as Stanley pulled the family car in front of the house on Ridgefield. The dark clouds hanging in the air over their drive from the Bevine house to her childhood home had burst open into a deluge of rain only a few blocks from their destination.

Staring through the now brewing storm pelting the outside of the car, Kate could see the lights of the living room on inside. Most people would've sold the old place last year after the horrors the house had seen, but Kate could never convince herself to pull the trigger. Even living with Joe's family full time now, 22 Ridgefield Drive still pulled her back as home, a home torn away as her father had been last year.

Hiding under an umbrella, Stanley reached the passenger side and opened the front door for Vera and the younger of the two girls, holding the umbrella over the two ladies. Walking them to the front porch, he returned to the car to walk Kate and the remaining sibling through the rainfall. Looking up at the porch, Kate frowned as she and her young companion ducked under the roofed landing.

"This is what I got for hiring those kids to rebuild this after that monster threw Joe through the railing," she thought to herself, noticing the newer paint did not

match the original railing color.

"Patsy's already here," Stanley said, talking over the storm as they reached the landing.

Peering from the porch to the side driveway, Kate saw the cruiser parked there.

"I wonder if Joe is here too," she thought, opening the front door and walking into the darkened front hallway.

Making their way into the living room, Kate noticed Patsy sitting in one of her father's plush, blue chairs near the empty fireplace. Standing over him was Patsy and Joe's supervisor Captain Robinson. With his arms crossed in front of him, Robinson held a look on his face that announced to everyone that he wasn't happy being there.

"Katie," Patsy welcomed her, waving his arm as he rose from his chair.

"Ms. Stone... Mr. and Mrs. Bevine," Robinson said as he also welcomed all of the entrants. "I'm hoping one of you can shed some light on why in the blue blazes my future 'ex' detective dragged me all the way here."

"He brought you here because I asked him to," the Grey Ghost's voice echoed in the house around the visitors. Looking around the amassed collection of friends and family, the heroic form of the ghostly guardian walked into the living room from the darkened kitchen.

"Fine..." Captain Robinson answered the masked hero. "So Bevine, why did you have Thomas bring us all here?"

The masked hero quizzically tilted his helmet face to the side and slowly exhaled. "Is there anyone here that doesn't know?"

"This definitely seems a lot easier to pull off in the funny books," Patsy added, surprised himself. "Maybe you should start wearing glasses or something?"

"I figured it was one of you two a little while back," Robinson added. "You both were just a little too confident that the Grey Ghost was a fella back at Fulcher's and it all started to come together for me after that. I don't have a clue on how you're pulling it off, but from the moment the Grey Ghost first appeared, he was always tied to you two and I knew it definitely wasn't Thomas here."

"Hey why couldn't it have been me?" Patsy asked, offended.

"The Grey Ghost never talked enough, Thomas," Robinson answered. "Dark, brooding and SILENT has never been your thing, detective."

Allowing his mask and hat to fade away revealing his face underneath, the Grey Ghost looked over at his parents and asked, "What about you two? What gave away the ghost?"

"Your mother figured it out first," Stanley answered.

"I saw you...or him and Patsy outside the house last year beating the tar out of those two thugs," Vera added. "After a few minutes it was pretty obvious that it was you. Like your captain here, I don't have a clue how you do what you do, but Joseph, it is just amazing to see you standing there."

"Well the fact everyone here already knows about my night job makes having this little family meeting a lot easier," Joe said. "Patsy and I recognized long ago that one day we might come across something where we would need to bring everyone on board with us, even though I hoped it never would come to this."

"So what has happened that warranted this meeting?" Robinson asked understanding the grave meaning of Joe's statement.

"That would be me darling."

The collected group looked past Joe as another person entered the room from the darkened kitchen. The Jeweled Kiss, her customary hood and glasses discarded, walked in scanning the small crowd before continuing.

"Apparently I happened..."

"Genevieve!" The two young girls behind Vera ran out to the glamorous thief who greeted them both with an enveloping hug. The three of them broke down with tears and emotion in the embrace.

Looking back to the crowd, the Jeweled Kiss reached up to her left ear and started to loosen the diamond earring she was wearing. As soon as the golden stud was removed from her ear lobe, an amazing transformation encircled the thief, the same unfocused effect Patsy and Kate had seen overtake Joe numerous times in the past year. Within the blink of an eye the Jeweled Kiss was gone, the form of the thief seemingly falling away from the woman as if it was an oversized coat. Replacing her was a brown-haired girl who couldn't have been more than 20 years old. The young lady, who stood a foot shorter than the Jeweled Kiss, stared at the assembled crowd with large, doe-like eyes before she broke the stunned silence.

"I believe it is time we put, as your movies say, all of our cards on the table," the girl announced with a thick European accent. "My name is Genevieve Anioł..."

However, before she could finish, the mysterious Genevieve suddenly grabbed at her chest as she began to spasm, the two young girls clutching her as she pitched forward in pain. The oldest girl quickly grabbed at her clenched hand, prying the earring she had removed mere moments ago from her fist. Replacing the earring on the ill woman's left ear caused the instant transformation of Genevieve back into the larger and much healthier form of the Jeweled Kiss.

Taking a few breaths, the dynamo looked at her sister who had replaced the earring and thanked her in their native tongue, "Dziękuję, maleńka."

Watching the amazing exchange, the crowd didn't seem to know what to do after the reappearance of the enigmatic thief. Even the Grey Ghost was questioning his next step when Vera surprisingly made the first step walking toward the three girls.

Reaching down to help the Jeweled Kiss up, Vera asked her, "These are your sisters aren't they?"

The Jeweled Kiss smiled back and nodded.

"I think it would be best if you started from the beginning then," Vera replied.

CHAPTER TWENTY-SIX

"As I said, my name… my real name is Genevieve Anioł," the Jeweled Kiss started. "These are my sisters, Helen and the shorter one here is Frances."

The two young girls standing close to the thief smiled and nodded at the small audience. The Jeweled Kiss stayed on one knee with an arm wrapped around each sister as she continued.

"As you saw I have a serious condition with my heart. I remember years ago the doctors in our village telling our parents that I wouldn't make it to my 16th birthday, and honestly if not for the healing powers of a magical cloth called the Spartan Cloak, they probably would've been right."

"We've heard of it or at least a part of it," Joe commented, hearing the name of the magical piece of cloth hidden in his watch. "A second ago you had a pretty thick accent. Where are you from?"

"I…We are, as you Americans like to say, not from around this neck of the woods. Two years ago, none of us had ever left our town in Poland, let alone ever dreamed of coming all the way over here to America. My father was the chief councilman back there. It was just the five of us with our mother at home. I still remember her singing around the house as she and I would spring clean while these two cried for milk," the Jeweled Kiss replied, smiling to herself at the memory. "That was before we went to

Greece and met him. That was before the Devil himself and his foot soldiers graced our doorstep."

"Are you talking about Lord Minos?" Kate asked as the Jeweled Kiss paused in thought. "Pasty mentioned earlier they suspected he was involved in holding your sisters."

"Minos… yes…they called him Shiftlon when I first met him back then. And has that mousy face changed like his name over time? Here in America, he even goes by yet another name, Daniel Editar, your city's mayor.

"Oh come on," Captain Robinson cut in. "Are you trying to tell me that Editar, a man I've known for years, is this Minos… there is no way that can be. The mayor and I meet weekly. I would've known if something this big was up."

"Believe me or don't, Captain, that is your concern," the Jeweled Kiss snapped back. "As I told the hero here, I would tell you all that I know because he saved my sisters. I also told him there was little he could do with this information anyways. So put your fingers in your ears and stick your head in the ground for all I care. As I was saying, I first met the man back when our family found ourselves trapped in Greece as the German Army invaded. Before we knew it, Helen, Frances and I were taken from our parents once they found out the identity of our father. Even though we were promised we would see them again soon… none of us has seen our Mama or Papa since."

The Jeweled Kiss tightened her grip on the two young girls as the terrible memories rushed back to her.

"I was so weak from my condition that I could barely even cry out as our parents were pulled from the home. I actually remember our mother telling Helen to take care of me. Of me! I was so pathetic then that my young little sister was put in charge of me!" the Jeweled Kiss said, shaking her head. "Hours later, after our parents were gone they came back for us. I remember actually shaking because I was so scared of what they were going to do with us. That was when we saw him, Shiftlon, a tall, skinny German commander you could tell instilled fear into every soldier there. They wouldn't even look him in the eyes as he walked over to us. They had rounded up all of the children of the town and lined us up outside of the hotel where we had been staying. I was barely able to kneel on the dirt even with my sister's help as he approached us. The man had been walking down the line of children placing a small blanket over the shoulders of each child. The comforting gesture only lasted a moment before he would sneer and rip the blanket away. Before I knew it, it was my turn. The cad wrapped the cloth over my back and as soon as the blanket touch my exposed neck, the world seemed to spin about me. I suddenly felt…I don't know how to describe it…power…strength radiating through me as I had never felt it before."

"I know the feeling," Joe thought to himself, hearing the thief's description of the same feeling he experienced every time he transformed into the Grey Ghost.

"Without thinking, the chest pain from my heart was now gone, and I was standing eye to eye with Shiftlon. I remember him smiling and being amused at this magical newfound confidence I had, and that was when he pulled the rug out from under me…or should I say off my shoulders. With a yank, the blanket fell from my shoulders and the strength powering me vanished as quickly as it had come. And as it left, the sharp pain in my heart returned crippling me once again onto the floor before the world went black around me."

"He had a large version of the Spartan Cloak?" Kate asked. "Is that what he put on your shoulders?"

"That's what they called it, though I haven't seen the entire thing often since then. I do remember it was a very old piece of material and there was a decent gash torn off the top corner," the Jeweled Kiss replied before continuing. "I awoke hours later in a small room with Shiftlon sitting next to my bed holding Helen's headband."

"Do you love your sisters?" Shiftlon asked me. "I remember being so weak and scared that I was barely able to nod."

"Good," he replied. *"I will be honest with you little girl. How much you cooperate with us is the only thing keeping those two pretty little things in my good graces.*

I have been searching weeks for someone that could unleash the abilities of the cloak and amazingly a dying rat such as yourself turns out to be my key to it all. But such is the way of things I guess…"

"He told me of his organization and their work in the German party."

"A bunch of Nazis right?" Patsy asked.

"Not exactly," the Jeweled Kiss answered. "His group is called the *Reich Hand* or sometimes simply called the *Right Hand*. They are a branch of the military dealing with alternative weaponry and strategic planning. I remember them hating being compared to the Nazi party, as if the comparison was beneath them."

"Well, a rat is still a rat," Patsy huffed.

"A rat was all I was to those monsters, a lab rat for them to play with," the Jeweled Kiss hissed.

"Genevieve…" Joe, the first one to use the name she mentioned earlier, began to ask. "Is this symbol important to the Reich Hand organization?"

"That is their symbol," the Jeweled Kiss confirmed, looking at the piece of paper Joe had produced from his jacket with a sketch of the circled symbol they found tattooed on Otto's arm back at the Heqet. "They all have it tattooed on their arms, even Shiftlon. It is a rite of passage for them and their idea of a play on words since it literally is the right part or the right hand of the Nazi swastika on their evil flag."

"Great, we don't just have Nazis running all over. We have weird, mad scientist uppity Nazis… just perfect," Patsy continued to grumble.

"For the next six months, my every move was combat training, languages, accents, and whatever else they could think of to test the limits of mysterious cloak and make me their perfect little weapon. The threat of harm to my sisters spurred me on no matter what they demanded. They taught me to use the power of the Spartan Cloak and manipulate my form. So I came up with this appearance and act after seeing actresses in your motion pictures they let me watch. It seemed less real if I stayed like this, more like the horrors were happening to this woman than poor Genevieve Aniol." The Jeweled Kiss stopped for a moment before continuing, "They became so obsessed with using smaller and smaller pieces of the Spartan Cloak in my work that they finally supplied me with these earrings, which only contain a miniscule piece of the cloth. Sadly later on we even discovered I could manipulate the forms of others through contact and later on found out how to allow that effect to last for a predetermined amount of time. That's when they even tried walking me through medical and surgical procedures to see what possibilities there were for their injured troops. Weeks into the testing, Shiftlon disappeared, leaving me with his scientists and lieutenants until one day around a month ago, we were shipped secretly here in a U-boat. One night here in your City Hall, I met your Mayor Editar. His face had been changed and his voice modified but it was him, Shiftlon, or as you called him from the whispers on your streets... Lord Minos."

"How could they replace the mayor and none of us notice?" Robinson asked, still not believing her story.

"The Reich Hand are experts in mimicry. One of their main purposes is the infiltration and manipulation of their enemies from within," the Jeweled Kiss answered. "They have developed surgical techniques unseen by anyone that allow them to manipulate their faces so that no one would ever know the deception, even up close. Over time most of their operatives have developed the ability to mimic voices to a 'T'. You wouldn't know it even if it was your own mother calling you. That's one of the larger reasons they searched for the Spartan Cloak, besides the strength and power it provides. As you know it allows the user to manipulate the matter around them at their will. It is the ultimate disguise if you want it to be."

"They could impersonate the President himself and no one would even know," Joe added.

"However, they have never been able to get the Spartan Cloak to work on anyone but me so far as I know," the Jeweled Kiss added.

"We've run into the same issues here. Joe is the only person it seems to affect," Kate added.

"Is it because we are broken goods... my leg... her heart?" Joe thought to himself. *"She's shown a different and higher level of abilities than me at times...could it*

be because her injury is more severe? Is that how this thing works?"

Lost in his thoughts, Joe missed part of the conversation until he heard the Jeweled Kiss say something to his mother.

"Don't waste your tears on me dear lady… This…all of this is my fault. My worthless heart was the reason my family was in Greece to begin with. My father had heard of a specialist there who might've been able to help. We were there because of me and now my parents are gone. My sisters have been in the grasp of those monsters for almost a year because of me, their lives dangling by a thread on my performance. And that doesn't even count the packages I've hand delivered all over this city just awaiting the order to erase it from the map."

No one spoke for a moment after she mentioned the packages, which they all knew were around the city. Her confirming they were as destructive as they had thought had finally let the horror sink in that their entire city was in desperate peril.

"It wasn't until they briefed me on both your work and abilities as the Grey Ghost here in Capstone that I saw the opportunity to get my sisters away from them," the Jeweled Kiss continued. "Shiftlon continued to show me images of my helpless sisters in that small room of theirs. So confident in his planning, he let the location and name of the store eventually slip and that's where I came up with the trail of breadcrumbs as it were."

"Why not go after them yourself once he told you?" Patsy asked.

"Because I was always being watched," the Jeweled Kiss replied. "Shiftlon's men have eyes everywhere. I was warned on multiple occasions that even an attempt to rescue my sisters would lead to their deaths."

"With your condition and the trap they had laid out, it might've ended that way for you and without Patsy here I might not have made it either," Joe nodded. "It took us a while but we finally figured out the line connecting all of the mysteries in front of us. My mom was the one who finally noticed the quotes you were leaving for us were from the Hansel and Gretel fairytale."

"I owe you more than I can say dear lady," the Jeweled Kiss said nodding to Vera. "It was one of the stories our mother always told us. I wasn't sure if anyone here would be able to find the connections to them, but I had to make sure no one in Shiftlon's organization would know what I was doing."

"They are safe now," Joe commented. "And now with your help we can…"

"I'm not helping you," the Jeweled Kiss defiantly stated.

"What?' Joe replied.

"I've told you numerous times there is nothing you can do to stop what is coming," the Jeweled Kiss said, shaking her head. "They have planned out every step of this to the letter. You probably think stopping them from destroying your city's bridge last year was a great success. But it was one of many calculated scenarios Shiftlon already had planned."

"Wait, the bridge was the target and not the military equipment below in the warehouses?" Joe asked surprised.

"Two birds…one stone," the Jeweled Kiss answered. "You all have been kind to us which is something neither my sisters nor I honestly have experienced in years, so I will be truthful with you. The only way to survive what is coming is… to… run!"

"The red tie should do nicely Ms. Penmen," Mayor Editar nodded, admiring himself in the full length mirror. Peering at the suit ensemble the seamstress laid out for him, the evil politician smoothed down the small goatee on his chin as he smiled to himself. Seeing Ralph's reflection behind him limping to the doorway, his face still quite bruised from the beating he took from the Jeweled Kiss the previous night, Editar looked down at Penman who was in the middle of marking a hem on his trousers and politely said, "That will be all for right now, Ms. Penman. Please give my associate and I a few moments of privacy."

Knowing better than to question the mayor, Penman immediately finished the hem mark and left the room. Waiting until the seamstress was out of sight, Editar waved for his minion to enter.

"So do you have anything to say that would put a smile on my face, Ralph? I'm still quite upset with you bungling the operation last night that led to that limp of yours."

"All reports from our men in the police department leave the matter of our Jeweled Kiss still in the air. She was not apprehended at the scene and they do not have any leads on her at this time," Ralph began.

"I'm honestly not surprised, the police taking care of that matter for us was a bit of a long shot, however I am a little surprised that Captain Robinson himself hasn't relayed that information to me personally... I wonder where he is." Editar frowned. "Oh, and by the way Ralph, I'm not smiling...

"Mr....Mr. Tookings did report in while you were out earlier this morning and the radio station has been secured as planned," Ralph quickly answered.

"Good," Editar nodded, still peering at the minion.

"We... we were also successful in securing the 'release' of the asset from his detention cell," Ralph stammered. "He is changing his clothes downstairs as we speak and will be here in a few moments."

"Excellent," Editar said, clapping his hands. "I like how you did that, get the bad news out of the way and end on a positive note, a good way to keep your head little man. I do assume you arranged that his disappearance will go unnoticed until well after tonight's events?"

"The only guard who would have gone near that cell tonight has been replaced by one of our men," the assistant nodded. "So anything out of the norm there won't be noticed until the planned guard change tomorrow morning."

"And by then, I would wager the authorities will be too busy to care," Editar smiled.

"I would agree," Ralph again nodded, slightly relaxing. "And here he comes now."

Looking back at the door frame, Editar smiled noticing the complete threshold darkened. The shape of an incredibly large person blocked most of the light from the adjoining room as he twisted his broad shoulders to fit through the enormous door frame.

"Mr. Vega! Welcome back to the fold, my good man!" Editar smiled as the giant walked toward the two. "I'm sorry to have thrown a wrench in your workings at the prison, however we have found numerous members of our organization falling under the vision of this city's ghostly hero recently so it became important to solidify the ranks for the celebration conclusion this evening."

"I was still able to organize the needed assets inside of their prison as you requested and they await your orders. I am, as always, at your heed Lord... I mean Mr. Mayor" Vega corrected himself, looking attuned to the room.

"Oh my good man," Editar laughed. "I believe we are close to the end for the need of this subterfuge. In a mere few hours, everyone in this pitiful city will know the name Lord Minos, well... at least those who are still alive when the sun rises tomorrow.

CHAPTER TWENTY-SEVEN

"Running is not a plan," Joe rebuked the Jeweled Kiss. "I know you've been through a lot."

"But you also have a lot to answer for young lady," Captain Robinson cut in. "From what you're telling us you have been working with enemy agents on U.S. soil to destroy this city. Sisters or not, there is no get out of jail free card from something like that."

"Dear Captain, I understand," the Jeweled Kiss replied, her voice dropping back to its usual purr as she knelt next to her two sisters who had moved next to one of the end tables.

"Oh that's not good," Joe thought, catching the change in demeanor.

"I've caused you a lot of problems and frankly I'm quite sorry about that, BUT you have to see, this isn't my war," the thief continued, patting the table. "My family has been dangled on strings by one side of this conflict of yours for too long now and I'm not about to let you continue that just for what you deem the *good guys*."

"But you might be our only chance of stopping whatever Minos' plan is," Kate started. "You said it was too late for us to do anything, which must mean we are running out of time. You can't just run away from this."

"I knew coming here that none of you would be smart enough to get away while you still can just on my word alone," the Jeweled Kiss shook her head in disgust. "That's why I brought those files over there. Let's just say they were my severance package along with a few others I've secretly collected during my time with the Reich Hand. I can only hope that you will reconsider once you see what you are really up against."

The assembled group looked over in the direction the Jeweled Kiss had motioned and there on the left side of the living room couch were two folders. Each brown envelope wrapped in twine was overstuffed with papers of every size, small posts spilling out from the top envelope. Kate walked over to the gifts, carefully unwrapping the top layer first.

"Ms. Stone, you might want to check the second packet first. I think you'll find page eight very interesting," the Jeweled Kiss said out loud before abruptly adding. "And best of luck…"

Joe, looking in the direction of the envelopes, quickly turned back to where the Jeweled Kiss had been kneeling next to her sisters, surprised at her last statement. He relaxed for a split second when he saw they were still there, the Jeweled Kiss looking back at him smiling, her two sisters holding each of her arms. But then he saw it.

"Wait a minute," Joe said, walking over to the sisters. As he approached the three, all of them just smiled silently at him, worrying Joe even more. Reaching out, Joe grasped the Jeweled Kiss's shoulder and instantly the girls all disappeared in a cloudy haze leaving the side table they had been kneeling next to in his grip. "They're gone!"

The shocked silence of the room was jolted alive as they heard, through the pouring rain outside, the sound of a car's engine turning over.

"Oh for Pete's sake!" Patsy shouted, patting his jacket. "She lifted the keys to the cruiser!"

Racing toward the front door, Joe and Patsy barely made it to the front porch before the cruiser sped away from Ridgefield, spraying rain from the soaked streets in its wake. The car's taillights quickly disappeared in the storm as the car accelerated down and over the hillside toward the Trumbull Bridge.

"Let me get your Dad's keys; that car was barely hanging on by a thread after the beating it took the other night," Patsy called, running back into the house. "We should be able to catch up to them."

"Never mind Patsy, it's no use. She got what she wanted," Joe called out after him, seeing that their chances were slim at best. With her powers, Joe knew she could change the look of the car so much that they would drive right past it and never know, especially in this storm, which was probably part of her plan from the beginning.

Sighing into the storm after her, Joe realized he had secretly enjoyed having someone around who really understood the craziness the Spartan Cloak could bring into their lives. However, he had always thought her helping them was wishful thinking. She wasn't someone who wanted to play a hero or even a villain at that; she was just a scared young girl thrown by no fault of her own into a nightmare. It shouldn't have surprised anyone that her first reaction was to run with her sisters. They were all she had left.

"You know these papers are just copies of the plans Editar had the University look at a few weeks ago for his G.I. Celebration," Kate mentioned out loud to the group as Joe and Patsy walked back into the living room.

"That's disconcerting since she mentioned these packets were supposed to show us Minos' plans," Robinson commented. "I still can't buy that Editar and this Minos character are the same guy. I take from your faces she's long gone."

"I hope that car has four flats on her in the middle of a snowstorm," Patsy grumbled, thinking about his beloved vehicle. "Hey, that looks familiar."

Looking at the map she just unfolded, Kate motioned to the markings on the image of the city asking, "These? What are these Patsy?"

"Those look exactly like the locations we mapped out earlier where the Jeweled Kiss dropped off her packages when we were figuring out where her sisters were being kept," Patsy answered. "Except for those yellow ones in the middle."

Kate pointed to the two additional markings on the map Patsy had mentioned. Both markings were located downtown at the exact opposite ends of Main Street. "So what are these two?"

"We never found any packages near downtown," Robinson commented. "And after all of the officers I've had stationed there since the attack during the first G.I. Celebration, there is no way I can see us missing one of those."

"Aren't those the balloons the mayor wants to launch at each celebration?" Vera added from behind the group. "I remember reading in that Lynda Cordova's article a few days ago there would be one balloon released at each end of Main Street during the celebration."

"You're right, Mom," Kate answered, pointing to the one marking right next to Town Hall. "The first one was raised just before the attack during the first Celebration. It's still up there like a huge Christmas star hanging right here."

"You don't think there are explosives in those balloons?" Robinson asked.

"With that girl there's no telling," Kate answered. "But if there are, why hide the explosives when you went out of your way to make sure everyone knew where the others were placed like she did?"

"Since we know where all of the other explosives are located, is there any way we can defuse them before the mayor does what he wants?" Stanley asked, looking over the map. "Can we call in the Army or someone who really knows what they are doing?"

"I've had military specialists looking at those packages for weeks now ever since they started showing up and they can't even touch them," Robinson reminded the group.

"Yeah that was a nice little feature the Jeweled Kiss left on all of those," Joe commented. "Even the best I can do is lift the top lid off of the boxes. She's made it impossible for anyone to get to the cylinders inside them and from what I've seen of her abilities, those packages will more than likely stay untouchable right up to the moment before they go off."

"I don't remember your friend Marcus mentioning a timer in any of the explosives we found on his ship?" Patsy asked looking over at Joe.

"Not from what he saw," Joe answered. "And I don't remember any ticking from the packages we've looked over."

"That would be a really long timer. Could they be remotely activated?" Robinson asked coming over to his two detectives.

"That is exactly how they are going to be activated," Kate answered interrupting.

The officers looked over at the engineer who was still rifling through papers.

"Take a peek at these," Kate motioned to the officers. "Do any of you know what this is?"

"That looks like an AM radio," Joe answered.

"Good eye, sweetie," Kate commended.

"You sure?" Patsy asked.

"Let my Mom tell you about the time I took our radio apart when I was younger to see how it worked. She loves to tell that one and how badly I busted it," Joe mentioned, looking at Patsy.

"It was still better than what you did to our cuckoo clock that one time," Joe's father couldn't help himself from adding.

"Well when I took my father's radio apart I made sure I knew how it went back together, so believe me when I tell you Joe is right," Kate added continuing, "except take out the AM signal from that definition. This is more a HAM radio schematic but see here, it's only configured for a single output and input signal."

"You mean it will only receive and transmit on one channel?" Joe asked.

"Yep," Kate nodded. "And I'm not an expert in explosives but if you were trying to signal something, this is definitely how to do it at a long range."

"So that's it," Robinson grimly added, lowering his eyes. "These packages are all primed to go and we are just a radio beep away from the city going up in a bang."

"Yes, but I still don't see how and when they are planning on activating the signal," Kate kept going. "I mean these packages have been around town for weeks now and not a single one of them has made a peep. So what are they waiting for?"

"They are waiting for these..." Joe said, pulling out another map from the folder. He had been flipping through the papers when he saw the map, this one not of the city but of Capstone Pier.

Walking over to the dining room table, Joe unfolded the map, which was double the size of the city-package marked one they had been looking at a moment ago, and pointed to three stamped marks on it.

"Are those what I think they are?" Robinson asked, seeing the straight line markings triangulated to Capstone Pier, each line with a red triangle with multiple markings near it."

"Yes those are ship patrol estimates. We had these marked all over the coast back overseas based on reported U-boat sightings. According to these time markings, these two apparently have been circling the harbor for days and we haven't heard a peep about them."

"And these three are estimated to arrive at 1800 hours tomorrow," Patsy said, pointing to the markings next to the remaining triangles only marked with a straight line courses.

"That's 6:00 p.m., right around the time the mayor's second G.I. Celebration is planned to start," Stanley added from behind the officers. "Are we talking about an invasion here?"

"Joe, when you were at the docks earlier could you see downtown?" Kate asked. "It's been a long time since I've gone down there."

"You can see downtown's outline but nothing specific," Joe answered.

"Can you see the Seaman Towers?" Kate asked.

"Yeah probably," Joe answered.

"That's his signal then," Kate nodded. "Think about it, if we can believe these charts and that conniving thief, there are U-boats incoming to Capstone here at the docks, the last ones arriving right at the planned beginning of Editar's second part to the G.I. Celebration. That's the moment the city will be raising the second of two large lit balloons next to the Pathfinder Building."

"And that second balloon could be seen from the water and more than likely by these ships," Joe nodded. "Editar has his own little Trojan Horse. He's telling the city these raised lights are there to symbolically show the way home for our troops and they're really signaling to these boats."

"I bet you that second balloon will signal the explosives Joe," Kate added. "A hidden transmitter raised that high will be able to broadcast all around the city to every one of these packages. It is almost like he's raising his own radio antenna."

"If those bombs go off there won't be much standing in anyone's way to walk directly from the docks to downtown and take over this entire city," Patsy said dragging his finger from the dock area in a straight path downtown.

"People, this is a lot of IF's" Robinson added rubbing his hair. "I mean we are making a lot of leaps here based on maps and drawings that a completely untrustworthy individual dropped on us just before she ran away. One minute we are assuming the mayor of our city wants to destroy it with explosives he's placed all over town and now we have Germans invading with hidden submarines. I mean, doesn't this just sound crazy?"

"It does, but so did using the wind to destroy the Trumbull Bridge last year, sir. You might want to take a peek in this second folder she left," Joe answered, handing his captain the brown folder. "The one thing the Jeweled Kiss did get wrong was when she said we were out of time. If we are right, none of this will happen until tomorrow night at 6:00 as long as Editar or Minos doesn't move his timetable up."

"And he might, knowing the Jeweled Kiss isn't on his payroll anymore," Kate added.

"Well he is still waiting on this one boat," Patsy mentioned pointing back to the map.

"True, but if he blows these packages all around town two boats would be more than enough to march in here if he really wanted to," Joe countered. "We have time to at least check out a few of these ideas to see if we are on the right track, but we have to be careful not to show our hand.

We still might be able to throw a monkey wrench in Minos' plans."

"Just the five or six of us?" Patsy asked. "Remember the fiasco with your friends on the boat and the fake officer Parks? We really don't know who on the force right now isn't on Editar's payroll. If we try to bring in any help we could be tipping our hand early."

"I can help with that," Robinson nodded, still studying the contents of the second folder. "I have a guy."

"A guy?" Patsy asked surprised. "Who?"

"A guy," was Robinson's only reply; the captain never looked up from the contents he was studying.

"Oooookay," Joe stretched, eyeing Robinson. "Get in contact with your guy then. I have a call to make to a couple of friends of mine that I think could help us with our unwelcome guests in the harbor."

PART FIVE: ONLY A GHOST OF A CHANCE

Nicholas Cara

CHAPTER TWENTY-EIGHT

Kate tried her best to look as nonchalant as she could as she turned the corner heading to Main Street. Focusing on each breath, the engineer tried to will each inhale and exhale as slowly as possible over the pounding in her chest. As it raced in her chest, the crazed rhythm of her heart echoing in her head was not helping matters as she continued walking alone. Joe and Patsy hated the idea, but out of their rag tag group of heroes and based on her experience with the Celebration's plans, she was the logical choice to scout the area early that morning. But as she closed in on the square and began mingling with the crowd in front of the Seaman Towers, Kate was beginning to have second thoughts.

It was the first time she had come back here since the attack during the first G.I. Celebration and as much as she tried to put it out of her mind, Kate couldn't stop herself from gazing at the erected stage still standing next to Town Hall. The memory of the feeling of weightlessness when she was thrown by the imposter Grey Ghost replayed through her mind like a terrible film.

"Get a grip, they're depending on you..." the engineer steeled herself as she continued on.

Making her way down the sidewalk toward the Pathfinder Building, Kate continually gazed at the glowing orb still visible in the early afternoon haze suspended between the two Seaman Towers. Too far away for any real inspection, the orb hung like a glowing miniature sun over the streets of Capstone. The engineer had hoped even at this distance to see some sort of evidence of the radio transmitter in the globe. However, the orb revealed nothing in its design to suggest it was there. A radio dish, wires, even a shadow in the plastic beacon would've given her an inkling of the nature of the large decoration. But there it hung, 42 floors up, a blank slate to the world not portraying a single one of its possible destructive secrets.

Not wanting to attract too much attention, Kate continued moving as she scanned the orb. Noticing though that she couldn't walk a few feet without seeing a different Capstone Police Officer scanning the crowd, Kate stopped her attempts to study the glowing orb and moved farther down the street. This wouldn't usually bother her except for the fact she had no idea which of these officers were with or against her. The engineer sadly understood even if they stopped the maniac's plans tonight, the crooked official had still succeeded in dulling the luster and shine that once glistened on Capstone City, and it was going to be a long road back for the people and the city.

Following the crowd, Kate entered a small drug store, surprisingly open on a Sunday morning, off the square and tried her best to act interested in the shop's wares for a few minutes until she started out again down the street toward the Pathfinder Building. Looking ahead, Kate found a small crowd starting to gather around the front steps. The trip was only a few small blocks yet Kate couldn't help but feel her skin crawl as if there were eyes watching her every move, feeling especially conspicuous the closer she got to the small, gathered crowd. Reaching the crowd, Kate started to squeeze her way toward the front to see the cause of the gathering. Halfway through, she stopped and looked up as the reason for the gathering became evident. Above their heads a large circular shape started to rise in the air.

"*A hot air balloon? That wasn't in the plans he showed us for the Celebration. It was supposed to be another lit orb,*" Kate thought to herself as the partially inflated envelope colored in red, white and blue lofted over a large tied down basket.

The balloon operator stationed in the large basket waved at the crowd to get back as he wrestled with multiple burners that sent jets of flame into the inflatable. After a few moments of activity, the operator proudly beamed at the crowd after he successfully obtained the correct pressure inside the balloon allowing it to fully inflate.

There it sat as a beautiful decoration of the American spirit just waiting for its bounds tying it to the Earth to be cut allowing the heated envelope to rise into the afternoon sky. The operator pointed to the balloon for the crowd to look up as he manipulated a few levers on an interior panel in the basket. For a few moments, the large balloon lit up like a star in front of them amazing the crowd. Kate took notice of the small wires that had been sewn into the seams of the balloon allowing multiple rows of white decorative lights to travel the shape of the large inflatable.

"So this is what Editar has planned for the second part of the G.I. Celebration tonight," Kate thought to herself as the operator switched off the exterior lights. *"You definitely would be able to see this lit monstrosity from the docks…"*

And on that thought is when Kate saw it. Just as the balloon operator shut the decorative lights off, there in the large basket was the shape of a curved antenna. It was smaller than she had expected, so much so that the engineer could've missed it altogether had luck not been on her side when she caught the tiniest reflection of it from the display lights. Kate tried to make her way closer to the balloon but started to feel the crowd around her moving back. Surrounding the balloon was a small group of police officers barking at the crowd.

"Okay folks, show's over until tonight!" one of the officers barked roughly as the armed guard motioned for the crowd to disperse.

Thinking she could get one more look at the components in the basket, Kate tried to sneak past the scattering crowd until she saw one of the officers notice where she was looking and lock in on her. Kate had been around the Capstone City Police department for years, recently even helping out on cases, and never before had she seen the officer staring daggers at her. Knowing she was pressing her luck, Kate immediately turned around and started walking with the leaving crowd. Waiting a moment before glancing over her shoulder, she was startled to see the unknown officer following her! Picking up her pace, Kate tried her best to not pull attention to herself by running. One more glance behind her revealed she was in trouble as the officer quickly made his way closer and closer to her. Looking around the crowd for a possible avenue of escape, Kate regrettably found the crowd thinning around her the farther up the street she traveled away from the Pathfinder Building. Ducking down a side street toward Banks Avenue, Kate hoped to make her way to the bus stop from where she had arrived. Looking down the street, Kate's racing heart almost skipped a beat when she found the side street deserted except for an elderly woman, her face covered with a purple shawl, slowly walking past her.

"Flee into an isolated area, brilliant," Kate grumbled to herself as she noticed the empty bus stop. "Why don't you twist your ankle now and really complete the stereotype."

Looking back up the street, Kate's annoyance with her bad decision was forgotten when she saw the unknown police officer turning the corner. There was no mistaking his intent as the cop walked deliberately and silently toward her. As the man began to pass the elderly woman who had made it nearly to the corner, she looked at him and spoke.

"Sir, can you help me find where...?" the small woman started in a weak and tired voice before she was cut off as the officer roughly pushed her to the side.

"Out of the way Grandma..." the stalking man growled as he deliberately elbowed the elderly woman.

Kate felt her teeth clench as she saw the elderly woman's shawl fall to the paved street along with the form of its owner. She was so outraged at the man's disregard that she unknowingly started back toward the officer with her fists balled, any fear now replaced with fury and conviction from the attack on the poor woman.

"Oh such a big guy! Knocking over little old ladies, aren't you a tough guy..?" but Kate quickly stopped when she noticed she had been mistaken.

It had not been the form of the older woman who had ended up sprawled on the ground but that of the officer himself!

"Oh dear, you really should be more careful sonny," the unfazed senior said, reaching down to the surprised officer. "You wouldn't want to hurt yourself."

With that the senior citizen shot a right hook directly into the jaw of the surprised bully. The next sound Kate heard was the back of the officer's head smacking the pavement, where he stayed unmoving.

"What?" Kate asked, confused by what she had witnessed.

"For as nice as a place this city used to be, my mother still walks around with two rolls of quarters in her purse," the elderly woman said, looking back at Kate. "Just think if I had hit him with that thing?"

And as if this situation couldn't get any stranger for Kate, the senior woman grabbed the fallen officer by the back of his shirt and with one arm flung him into a large trash bin on the side of the street. She slammed the metal lid down on the crooked officer and in one motion broke the handle on the lid, effectively locking the unconscious man in with yesterday's trash.

"That should hold him for the time being…" the woman said, her voice slightly deepening as she rolled the large trash bin into a side alley.

"Joe?" Kate asked coming nearer to her rescuer, now recognizing his voice.

"Nope, no Joes here, just us bingo players," the sweet woman smiled.

"Oh for Pete's sake, I thought that lady looked a little like your mother," Kate replied, peering at the woman. "I thought you were going to head to the dock with Patsy?"

"Patsy figured he could handle updating Marcus and his brother so I decided to keep an eye on you," Joe answered, still in the form of the elderly woman. "I thought you said you were going to keep out of trouble?"

"Well our trash man here noticed me checking out their new hot air balloon a little too much," Kate shrugged. "I guess I'm lucky I had my friendly neighborhood bingo player here to save the day."

"Oh shucks, dearie," Joe replied coyly. "So what did you find?"

Pulling the cruiser over, the Jeweled Kiss scanned the deserted road for any oncoming traffic. Seeing none, the exhausted thief took a moment to close her eyes and rest. They had not stopped since running from the Grey Ghost's meeting the previous night and coupled with the events of the two days before, she could barely keep herself awake. Never relinquishing the hold on the power of the Spartan Cloak hidden in her earring, the Jeweled Kiss camouflaged the cruiser as a green Buick she had remembered passing earlier and discarded the Jeweled Kiss persona to her true form as Genevieve Aniol before resting her head back on the headrest.

"I can't believe they actually let us leave..." Genevieve thought to herself. All night she had been driving expecting to see someone following them. It was beyond her belief that Bevine and his cohorts would allow them to walk away after everything she had done.

Opening her eyes to peer in the rear seat, Genevieve saw that both Helen and Frances were silently sleeping next to each other under a small blanket. The two young girls had been through so much misery because of her and as much as she just wanted to hold them right now, she didn't have the heart to wake them. Watching them peacefully sleep, Genevieve knew although they were united once again, it didn't mean the young girls' torment was completely over. Shiftlon's plan was going to happen tonight, and everything that came to pass with it was set into motion by her unwilling hands.

"They are all fools," she thought every time she wondered if Bevine and his family were going to follow her lead and get out of town. She knew they wouldn't...but hey, she had tried to warn them. That was on them.

"I tried...not my problem," she barked at herself, smacking the steering wheel, her conscience starting to itch at her for leaving. "I didn't ask to be involved in this war. They made their decision. They can all jump off a cliff for all I care..."

Hearing Helen stir in the back at her rantings, Genevieve silenced herself. She knew she had to keep going. The farther away from Capstone City, the better her and her sisters would be.

"*But what then?*" the thief thought to herself, looking at her slumbering sisters. "*How far will ever be far enough from a man like Shiftlon? If his plan works tonight, what is going to stop him from coming after us? This country like Greece, like Poland, and all those others will be under his command. How long until I see his troopers' headlights in this rear view mirror?*"

CHAPTER TWENTY-NINE

"Well doesn't this look lovely?" Editar thought to himself as he scanned the crowd from the front steps of town hall.

The crowd, larger than the one that attended the first rally, was settling in and enjoying the local bands that had been hired to entertain them while they waited for the festivities to start.

"One can never say these Americans scare easily," the politician chuckled to himself. "I actually thought this crowd would be smaller after the attack at the first rally."

"Mr. Mayor," Ralph interrupted the mayor's musings.

"Yes Ralph, what is it?" Editar droned in reply.

"We just received a report from outside saying that everything is now in place," the nervous assistant started. "All of the instrumentation in the balloon has been double checked and is in working order according to our operator."

"And what of the additional precautions I asked for?" the mayor questioned.

"I have personally seen that all of those have been implemented," Ralph confirmed. "And as you requested, no one but the two of us are aware of these changes."

"Excellent, but sadly my boy you do know that means I have to kill you now," Editar smiled at his assistant.

"Wait…what?" the underling replied, shocked at his supervisor's response.

"Just kidding my good man…" Editar laughed, enjoying the look of fear crossing the face of his assistant. "I read once that was the way the ancient Egyptians kept their secrets so well. Bury the secret and then bury the slaves that did the digging right next to it."

"Sounds like an awful waste of personnel," Ralph answered.

"Numbers were never something the Egyptians worried about back then," Editar replied, looking back through the glass windows at the assembled crowd. "One would think after this war is concluded that might not be an issue for us either."

Looking at his watch, Editar smoothly left the front entrance and proceeded back to his office, Ralph's steps echoing on the marble floor of the hallway behind him. The building per his instructions had been cleared earlier, leaving him alone with his assistant. Even Mrs. Renae had been sent away for the evening, leaving the politician slightly amused he would no longer have to bow to the secretary's scheduling whims.

"You know," Editar started as he looked around the office. "I will miss this place. It was my only respite at times from the mind-numbing chores of pretending to be this city's mayor. I think I'll have them rebuild this office exactly as it is when we are through here."

"I'm still a little confused, sir, at the need to destroy this building. This could easily stay our base of operations after tonight," Ralph replied, joining with his superior in looking around the office.

"And that is simply your short sightedness talking," Editar scoffed. "Forgetting the fact it will allow me to wash my hands of our unneeded guests downstairs, it also preempts a future problem my time as mayor of these people has allowed me to foresee. There will be a rebellion against what we do tonight. As futile as it will be, the people of this shameless little metropolis will never bow to our will simply because they took a good clip to the chin."

Walking to his desk, Editar reached over to a small replica of the city's seal and exaggeratedly tipped it off the desk before continuing. "You see these people enjoy getting back up from the floor, they cheer for it, and that is why we must break both their back AND spirit before they will truly understand their position in the new world. And Ralph, that is why we must destroy this building. It along with the other key buildings and structures in this city are institutions to these silly people. They feel a connection to them, one would even say they love them. So while these institutions remain, so too does *hope*, which will be a dangerous word for us. *Hope* will allow the common man to think they can still win even after most of their city lies in ruin around them. *Hope* will tell them they can reclaim this building from us and maybe flush us out of their destroyed town... No Ralph, *hope* is not a word I want to deal with after tonight. This building, like the rest of them where our jeweled turncoat left her dangerous packages, will have to be torn down and with it the spirit of this city and its people."

Walking from the desk to a filing cabinet near the far wall, the villainous politician expertly entered a combination into the small lock on the top drawer. At the sound of the small tumblers in the cabinet's lock falling, the villain pulled at the two top drawers which gave way revealing the exterior of the cabinet to be nothing more than a metal covered wooden facade. Inside the remaining shelving of the fake cabinet sat two wrapped packages, each an exact copy of the wrapped packages the Jeweled Kiss had delivered across the city during her crime spree.

"I even wonder if that creature remembered these two explosives I had her place here?" Editar mused, waving his hand through both packages that, like all of the others offered no resistance. "They were the first and to be honest, I wasn't completely sure it would be possible for her to project her influence on these for such a long time. However, here they sit all the while awaiting the clock's sixth strike tonight to solidify for their deadly purpose."

"Sir, your police escort has arrived for the celebration," Ralph announced, seeing the men start to file into the main entranceway. "It is twenty til sir."

"Yes... we of course will not have any troubles with these young men, correct?" Editar asked, hearing the sounds of the officers.

"No sir, they are all *replacements*," Ralph replied indicating the officers as they entered the office. Each man was a complete duplicate of the Capstone Police officer they had replaced over the past few months. "The rest of our operatives have been assigned as security outside for the Celebration."

"Excellent, make sure Mr. Vega doesn't delay too long. I wouldn't want him with his playmates at 6:00 pm," Editar smiled before looking at his assembled guard. "Gentlemen, tonight we change the world. Let us not leave our adoring public waiting."

Leaving Editar with his assembled guard, as they started to proceed toward the exit, Ralph turned down an adjacent hallway never noticing the wooden boards covering the shattered window the Jeweled Kiss had thrown him through days before, start to move.

Even if the guards and mayor had been paying attention, the cheering crowd surrounding them as they exited City Hall easily drowned out the sound of the two boards nailed over the broken window being pulled away with a jerk. Peering up through the opening, Patsy's face started to scan the empty office for any stragglers.

"The coast is clear; give me a boost," Patsy whispered from the opening.

Somehow able to fit his large frame through the opening, Patsy reached back through the smashed window to help his fellow burglar. Crawling inside the office next to him was officer Joel Bishop, who landed in a heap next to his fellow policeman.

"Thanks," Bishop grimaced, rubbing his backside where he landed. "Why did we think me having YOU on my shoulders was a good idea again big guy?"

"Search me…" Patsy shrugged. "I'm still trying to get my head around the fact you've been a mole for Robinson all of these months with this group."

"Like I told you guys, it was the captain's idea," Bishop answered. "I guess they thought they could buy me off just like they did my stupid brother last year. When I told Robinson he had me play along, at least until he called me this morning."

"And you're sure that everyone on Editar's payroll will be outside in the square tonight?" Patsy asked. "That just seems like a stupid move for this guy."

"Definitely," Bishop replied. "The word we got back at the station this morning was either you make it to the square tonight or get out of town. The Jeweled Kiss never delivered a package anywhere near the square so from what you were telling me about the mayor's plans, outside in the square might be the safest place in the city tonight. He wouldn't want to blow up any of his own men."

"How many are we talking about here?" Patsy asked, starting to scan the office.

"That depends on what you mean," Joel replied. "The way this group works is twofold. When they come for you, you either buy in or they replace you. So outside there are guys who took the bribes and smiled but then there are officers who have been replaced. When I first came to him after they approached me, Robinson told me to take the money like Jimmy did and play along. We really needed to know how deep this operation went."

"These guys can really replace boys that easily?" Patsy asked in return.

"It is scary how good they can be," Bishop nodded. "Appearance, voice, small little tics… you almost can't tell a difference. They never went after guys with families. This group isn't that good, but single boys on the force who maybe no one but their mother would notice the differences, those were the prime targets for the Reich Hand."

"And you're sure our guys that have been switched are here in City

Hall of all places?" Patsy continued to question Bishop as he checked every closet in the office. "This place really isn't that big. It would be pretty hard to hide a lot of people in here."

"That's what I heard. Apparently these guys can only mimic one person at a time so if they move on to another guy for some reason they need to hear and study the first one again to switch back. That's why they've been keeping our boys alive," Bishop nodded, pointing to the two packages Editar had not even bothered to cover. "But remember what Editar said about the guests downstairs and washing his hands."

"Yeah, I've been thinking about that. They won't have to pretend anymore after tonight," Patsy replied, moving out of the small office. "He did say downstairs right?... but from what I know City Hall doesn't have a basement so... hey wait a minute, check this out."

Walking over to Patsy who was now kneeling at the far wall in the carpeted section of hallway, Bishop could see the larger detective pull out a flashlight and illuminate the edge of the light brown carpet. "What do you have there?"

"See here, this brown spot," Patsy answered, pointing to the carpet. "It looks like someone tried to clean up something from here, something brown, maybe ink or coffee, but it still left a stain in the carpet."

"So the mayor is clumsy, I don't see what the deal..." Bishop started before Patsy cut him off.

"The stain doesn't start here on this side of the wall; it is bleeding out from behind the wall," Patsy explained, pointing at the small half circle mark.

Pushing at the wall Patsy found it to be as solid as it appeared. The detective started knocking softly on the structure nodding when his ear was rewarded with a hollow reply. "You hear that?"

"Yes, there is nothing behind that section," Bishop confirmed, knocking on the wall farther down. "You can definitely hear a difference."

Pasty and Joel began fruitlessly searching the seamlessly curved wall of the hallway until Patsy decided to return to the ground where he found the stain on the carpet and retrace his steps. After a few moments of searching he found the smallest notch in the carpeting, barely visible, but a notch as if the carpeting had been rubbed slightly over and over again. Following the white wall up from that point, Patsy finally hit pay dirt. Keeping his eyes level to the curvature of the wall, Patsy noticed at about waist height on the white-washed wall a slight dip in the panel. The mark was more of an indentation in the smooth white paneling than anything, but with his eyes following the wall the dent jumped out at him. Pushing gently at the dent, Patsy smiled as he heard a small audible click behind his finger. The entire section of the wall silently started to rotate toward him, pivoting on unseen hinges.

"Well lookie what I found?" Patsy said, looking through the doorway. "I think I found downstairs."

Joining Patsy, Bishop peered into the dimly lit hallway. "That's a lot of doors for a spooky, dark hallway."

"Well let's get knocking," Patsy replied stepping into the darkened hall. "We don't have that much time before Joe and the captain need us outside. Hopefully we can bring some friends to the party."

CHAPTER THIRTY

"The sight just brings a tear to your eye doesn't it?" Mayor Editar exclaimed, tapping his top hat in place as they exited the main doors of City Hall.

"It was a brilliant stroke to pass out candles to the crowd," the officer to his immediate right replied, looking at the crowd down the square all holding lit candles. The security teams flanked each side of them. "To pray for their boys in uniform of course."

"Of course it was, and may I ask who in this world told you that you could speak to me?" Editar gruffly replied, never looking at the officer but mentally filing his offense away for a later date.

Losing a step away from the mayor, the cowed officer filed into the procession as it continued down the main steps of City Hall before starting up the square to the Pathfinder Building where the crowd and hot air balloon were awaiting them a few blocks ahead. As they started toward the crowd, Editar was surprised to see a small group of men, all uniformed Capstone Police officers, blocking their way barely a few steps from the bottom of the steps.

"Captain Robinson? Here to help escort us to the celebration?" Editar asked, seeing the central interloper. "How thoughtful..."

"Mr. Mayor, information has come across my desk that I would like to discuss with you," Captain Robinson announced, backed up by Officer Jones and the two Lape brothers. "I would like you to please come with us peacefully to the station so we can sort these issues out."

"What? You must be joking Robinson!" Editar scoffed. "I have half the city waiting for me at the end of the square. What information would be so important that you would bother me on such a momentous day?"

"Murder, arson, espionage, possibly treason to name a few..." Robinson started, raising a brown envelope, the second left to them by the Jeweled Kiss. Removing a handful of the folder's contents, Robinson started flipping through numerous photographs and reports of the mayor and other individuals marked with the Reich Hand's symbol for the assembled officers. "We probably will have to start with the murder of Officer Jim Bishop last year and go from there Mr. Mayor, or should I call you Mr. Shiftlon?"

"Shiftlon? Really? Well my good Captain, you really have done your homework!" Editar complemented nodding. "I would wager that a certain jeweled canary may have sung a little song in your ear if you know that name. Sadly dear Captain, I am quite busy today so we'll have to see if we can fit you in sometime tomorrow to deal with these matters."

"And I'm sorry to say I must insist Mr. Mayor," Robinson replied the three of them holding their ground.

"My dear Captain, as amusing as this is I am on a bit of a tight schedule right now and as you can see, your little rabble here is slightly outnumbered," Editar replied, now annoyed at the intrusion. "So if you could please move before we move you."

"We?" Robinson asked, eyeing the security escort. "Last time I checked those officers were Capstone City Police officers sworn to uphold the law of our city, so I'm a little confused by what you mean, your honor."

"Really... are we going to have this scene now?" Editar sighed, annoyed as he checked his watch. "Fine... this charade was really only going to last another few minutes anyways."

"Gentlemen, which hand holds up the new world?" the mayor yelled out.

"THE REICH HAND!" the crowd of officers behind him yelled in unison.

"Which hand will crush the old world?" Editar asked even louder.

"THE REICH HAND!" the officers again yelled.

"What hand do we raise in triumph?" Minos' dark voice now echoed from Editar.

"THE REICH HAND!" the officers finished, reaching their right shoulders and ripping the sleeves of their shirts all revealing the crooked L tattoo that was found earlier on Otto and Horst back on the Heqet.

"Well it looks like this year's Christmas party just got a little smaller," Robinson remarked, looking at the turncoats standing in front of him. "I'm going to ask everyone to stand down. We don't want anyone to do something they might regret."

"Ha! My dear Captain," Minos laughed, almost doubling over at the notion. "You really do not flinch in the face of death. May I ask you, do you still wish to take me in for whatever you might have found in that little folder of yours? It probably doesn't even contain my personal top 20 greatest atrocities... Ha... Take me in? Tonight of all days? What is the saying you Americans like to use? You and what army?"

"We'd like to have a say in that your honor!" Stanley yelled from one of the side alleys as he and a large group of men started walking toward the gathering.

Robinson recognized the men from a meeting he would occasionally have at the Barnes plant down in the Scar. Knowing the number of uncorrupted officers left could be counted on two hands, Mr. Bevine said he would get as many men from the plants as he could and to the captain it seemed as the entire shift had followed him to the square. Luckily, Mr. Bevine was able to talk his wife out of showing up there with a rolling pin and her sisters.

"Well isn't this a fun gathering?" Minos addressed the crowd, seeing his way to the square now blocked. Looking past the gathering of troublemakers, Minos noticed a group of men and Ms. Stone reaching the hot air balloon at the end of the square. "No, this will not do. Men! I have somewhere to be, please clear the road of this rabble!"

On the command, the group of Reich Hand police officers unholstered their side arms and leveled them at Robinson, Stanley and his friends. The group of men started to back away at the armed threat. However, simply moving the crowd wasn't the Reich Hand's agenda as the officers cocked their weapons and prepared to fire!

Just before the murderous officers fired their weapons into the crowd, the scene was interrupted by the loud sound of a peculiar rainfall echoing around them. Hearing the sound of metal hitting concrete, all of the officers looked on in shock as the bullets from each of their weapons fell through their cylinders and disappeared into the now intangible concrete ground below them! Not only the bullets in the ready to fire weapons, but the ammunition in the pockets and belts of the officers proceeded the other bullets as they too disappeared into the ground below the shocked officers.

Puzzled looks were thrown back and forth between the murderous gang as they lowered their useless weapons and looked to Minos for new orders. The corrupt officers were beside themselves at the bizarre events unfolding before them.

"I would be willing to wager that you just lost a few votes Mr. Mayor," a dark voice growled behind the gathered Reich Hand officers, scaring the wits out of those closest to the terrifying voice.

Hearing the voice, Minos rolled his eyes at the intervention as he turned around to face the newest member of the party.

"Of course you had to be here," Minos sighed, seeing the reason perfectly good bullets could suddenly fall away from his officers and pass harmlessly into the concrete.

"I wouldn't have missed this for the world, Lord Minos," the Grey Ghost replied, looking up through unseen eyes from his crouched position. He had been transferring the power of the Spartan Cloak through the ground and into the officers allowing the dangerous ammunition to fall away harmlessly.

"Dear hero, I really don't know what you hope to accomplish here, but in… fifteen minutes… all of your heroics will just be a huge waste of time," Minos tsked, looking at his watch.

"Fifteen minutes? Well then we better finish this up in ten…" the Grey Ghost replied launching himself toward Minos and the crowd of Reich Hand officers.

As the cage finally disappeared from sight, James made sure to slacken the waterproof cord behind it as the Heqet continued on its slow path across the water a few miles out from the docks. Seeing that the cord wasn't caught and was unraveling smoothly from the large spool they had connected, James threw the green floatable buoy overboard attached to the line. The tall man smiled slightly as he noticed the green inflatable bobbing in the water in the dimming light.

This little trip had started earlier in the afternoon, however with his brother Marcus at the controls slowly gliding the vessel across the water and him being the only hand on deck, it had taken the two man operation over three hours to deploy the cages in the Heqet's wake while the temperature continued dropping with the waning sunlight. But the chill in the air wasn't going to bother James right now if he had anything to say about it. Since meeting with Patsy earlier and hearing him explain what was going to happen tonight at the city's G.I. Celebration, James noticed his usual aches and pains had taken a backseat for the day. Whether it was the adrenaline or just the thought of erasing the secret shame he carried all these years when he'd seen that 4-F stamp on his paperwork and had to watch his brother go off without him overseas, James would not allow his body to skip a step tonight. The Heqet, this little want-to-be fishing boat, was primed to be this city's last line of defense if things went south downtown and if it was the last thing he ever did, the tall sailor was going to make sure they were ready.

Making his way up to the front of the boat, James discarded his ripped gloves, the leather long ago worn off from the sharp cages now sitting on the bottom of the ocean lining a perimeter around the docks. Signaling his brother in the wheelhouse that he was finished, he saw the large man stick his head out of the window to look down at him.

"Great job Washington, just in time!" Marcus called out over the surf. "Make sure that spool doesn't get caught and I'm going to hightail it closer to the docks. I don't want to be anywhere near here in a few minutes."

"Roger that. Hey, you think old man Ridley will notice his crab cages missing tonight?" James asked.

"If that old vet had any idea what we stuffed in them and why, he probably wouldn't care. Bengy's friend did say the city would replace them for him after this was over," the large captain replied, looking at the jury-rigged ignition control taped to his vessel's controls as he increased the speed of the boat heading back to the docks. "As long as after tonight there is a city left to foot the bill."

CHAPTER THIRTY-ONE

"Head up the hall and get out of here. The captain and our boys need your help outside," Patsy whispered, waving the officer he had just freed from one of the rooms up the hidden hallway.

Patsy remembered the man's name as Broome, a young kid on the force but a good egg. What concerned Patsy, though was the fact that he just saw Broome in uniform escorting the mayor out of his office only a few minutes ago.

"The same thing with Knox, Taylor and Broshears in the last few rooms," Patsy thought as he made his way down to the next door. Although the rooms were not locked, Patsy noticed when he entered the first room that the inside of each heavy door was void of a door handle, effectively locking the occupant inside. While he saw Bishop make it to the room across the hall, Patsy opened the fourth door on his side and was pleasantly surprised to see its occupant.

"Professor Stone?" Patsy asked, seeing the elderly man lying on the room's lone cot. After seeing a file on the professor in the folders the Jeweled Kiss had left them, Patsy and Joe had theorized they might find Kate's father here but neither wanted to get Kate's hopes up. Making sure to avoid the smashed pieces of wood he found littering the doorway, the detective entered the room and was overjoyed his eyes were not playing tricks on him. "Professor, get up. We've got to get out of here…"

Hearing the officer, Stone looked up from his bed, his eyes widening at the sight of Patsy standing in the doorway. "Patsy? Patsy is that you?"

"The one and only," Patsy smiled back softly, looking at the disheveled man. *"He's a lot worse off than the other boys for sure."*

"Come on, no sitting around during a jail break," Patsy commanded, helping the Professor to his feet

"I can't go Patsy, not without my student Roger. Have you found a young boy around college age?" Professor Stone asked, shoving the detective away. "If I leave and we don't take him they'll kill him for sure. He's my responsibility Patsy and they've already done such horrible things to him. I can't leave here without him."

"I haven't seen anyone like that yet, but we've only searched a couple of rooms in this crazy place," Patsy replied shaking his head. "Let's see if Bishop knows anything about a kid. If he is here we'll find him Professor, I promise, but we can't stay around here forever. We need to get as many of these guys outside to help Joe and Katie."

"Kate? She's here?" the Professor asked, jostled by his daughter's name.

"Right in the thick of it as usual," Patsy replied. "Come on, let's check the rest of this hallway and see if we can find this kid of yours."

"Professor?" the voice echoed from down the darkened hallway.

"That's him!" Stone exclaimed. "Roger? Where are you my boy?"

"Shhh! Professor keep it down!" Patsy tried to hush the man.

"Roger!" I'm coming, where are you?" Stone continued, ignoring Patsy. Running past the detective, the Professor started blindly down the hall calling out for his student. "Roger? ROGER?"

"Professor, help me!" the voice of his student continued somewhere in the hall.

"Professor!" Patsy called after Stone as the man disappeared down the hall. "Bishop, keep getting these guys out of here. I've got to get that nutty professor or Katie will kill me," Patsy called out to Bishop, still making his way down the other side of the hallway.

Taking out his small flashlight to check his watch, Patsy exhaled in frustration. *"Blast, I need to wrap this up. We're running out of time down here."*

"Professor, where are you, you blasted mook!" Patsy yelled ahead.

Illuminating the hall with his light, Patsy could see the carpeted hallway become more barren and unfurnished the farther he traveled along it. The floors became concrete pavers while the walls bared the brick structure underneath the plastered walls farther toward City Hall.

"How far down does this go?" Patsy thought to himself noticing the temperature in the hall start to fall the farther he went. Illuminating the way ahead of him, Patsy saw it was blocked.

"Where did the Professor go then?" Patsy thought to himself, just before he noticed what seemed to be a wall at the end of the hall start moving toward him. Barely ducking the monstrous hand that reached for him, Patsy rolled under the attack to find himself behind the mountain of a man who slowly turned to face him. Quickly retrieving his flashlight that had bounced away, Patsy noticed a body next to him on the floor. It was Professor Stone.

Placing his hand on the unmoving man's chest, Patsy was relieved to find him still breathing. Before Patsy could say anything, their giant attacker hurled a small, metallic object at the two that landed on the concrete floor next to him. Patsy illuminated the object to find a small tape player.

"Professor! Professor! Help me!" the cries of Stone's student echoed in the hallway from the recording device. **"Professor! Professor!"**

Reaching over to the player, Patsy clicked off the device. *"This is a lot smaller than the reel to reels we have back at the station,"* Patsy thought looking at the miniature device, the student's pleas dying in the echoes of the hallway. "Well aren't we the tricky gorilla man?"

"Ha, ha, ha," Mr. Vega chuckled at the comment, the laugh sounding more like gravel scraping across stone. "What would you say if I told you we've been playing this old fool for months with something like that?"

"You mean the kid's not here?" Patsy asked. "You've been playing recordings to torture the old man all this time?"

"In so many words…" Vega replied, starting to stalk forward in the hallway. The Reich Hand's skill in mimicking their targets is without compare. We didn't even need to keep that one alive this time."

"You killed a kid?" Patsy growled.

"Many, but not that one. From what they tell me that boy on the recording never made it back from overseas," Vega snickered. "But that has never stopped us from using sentimental fools like this old man to do our bidding before. From what I hear Lord Minos enjoyed toying with him the most. The strongest wills are always the most fun to break."

Pulling his service piece, Patsy, still in a crouched position on the floor, got a bead on the monstrous man coming toward them. "That will be far enough big guy. I think you're a piece of trash but that doesn't make me want to put a plug in you unless I really have to."

"Funny thing about that flatfoot, is I don't have the same misgivings," Roger's voice suddenly hissed from behind Patsy, the cold steel of a revolver pressing against the officer's back.

"Patsy, you stupid lug," the detective berated himself. He had been so focused on the monster in front of him he had never heard the man creeping up behind him until it was too late.

"Mr. Vega, you're lucky Lord Minos had me come down here to make sure you left the building before 6:00," Ralph added now using his own voice. "Now keep those hands in the air, officer."

"I was fine little man," Vega grunted.

"Ha! Really, the last time you met this man he tore you limb from limb," Ralph commented. "You're just lucky I was able to get the drop on him before he transformed."

"Transformed into what?" Patsy asked, confused about what the man behind him was talking about.

"There is no need to play coy anymore with us, Detective Patsy Thomas," Ralph replied. "The Reich Hand has known you are the Grey Ghost for months now."

"Me? Ha, you boys should start calling yourself the wrong hand if that's what you came up with!" Patsy scoffed. "I'm not the Grey Ghost, though I appreciate that at least you numbskulls thought I could be."

"No, he's not," Vega stated. "I've fought the Grey Ghost and I saw what he looks like without his mask. This one is much too flabby to be the Grey Ghost."

"Hey!" Patsy protested.

"Are you sure?" Ralph asked confused. "We've been putting this together for months."

"You should've simply asked me," Vega grunted.

"You being in jail until this morning made that slightly difficult," Ralph barked, annoyed at being so wrong. "Fine, so you're not the Grey Ghost detective, but that makes my job slightly easier here. If there isn't anything special about you then we don't have any use for you at all."

At that, Ralph cocked the hammer on his pistol and jammed it into Patsy's back.

Two quick jabs to the jaws of the men next to Minos sent the Reich Hand officers falling away from their leader. The surrounding security detail sprang into action, almost tripping over their fallen comrades in an effort to get between the Grey Ghost and Minos. However, even with their superior numbers, the ghostly guardian refused to allow the fake policemen to block him from the villainous man. Grabbing the nearest attacker, the Grey Ghost, using his enhanced strength, flung the man into a grouping of the advancing men sending them scattering to the ground. Ducking under a punch thrown from behind, the Grey Ghost returned the favor with a vicious uppercut to the heel sending him skyward like a rocket launching into space.

"We can do this dance all day Minos," the Grey Ghost said, never losing eye contact with the retreating villain. Using his guards as a barrier, Minos tried retreating from the advancing hero, however, the corrupt politician found his path to the square blocked by Robinson and the assembled men.

Sending a sharp kick to another attacking guard, the Grey Ghost knelt, aimed and sent two volleys of the his powerful Ghost Gun into the wall of guards that lined his way between himself and Minos stunning a handful of them. Hearing a commotion behind him, the hero noticed a cascade of men, the original police officers that the Reich Hand doubles were impersonating, start to flood out of City Hall.

"*Thank you Patsy and Joel,*" the Grey Ghost thought, sparing a quick glance at the cavalry of men the two detectives had rescued from somewhere in City Hall.

With only two guards lined in front of the hero, the spirited avenger phased his hand past the shoulder of the guard in front of him and grabbed onto the corrupt politician. Effortlessly pulling Minos toward him, the Grey Ghost knocked aside the two remaining guards with the solid form of the commander they were so helplessly trying to protect.

"It's over Minos! Tell your men to surrender" the Grey Ghost growled at the villain, pulling him by the collar to bring his goateed face inches from his eyes hidden under the Spartan mask. **"There is nowhere left to run and if you think you or any of them are getting even close to that balloon…"**

"You stupid fool," Minos cut off the Grey Ghost. "It bothers me that I can tell you over and over again there isn't anything you can do to stop us and you don't believe me. Did you and your band of merry men really think it would be so obvious, that I would base all of these years of work to rely on some conflated plan based on that stupid balloon?"

"Give it up. We found the radio transmitter in the basket this morning. Without it you can't signal the explosives," the Grey Ghost replied, not believing the boasts of the captured villain.

As the hero stood there holding Minos by the collar, his guards not occupied by Captain Robinson's forces were hopelessly trying to free their leader from the hero's grasp. In a desperate attempt to pry Minos away from the hero, one attacker swung a large pipe at his back.

"Ooof!" Minos winced in pain as the pipe passed effortlessly through the intangible hero and struck the villainous leader's face. The blow was so direct that if not for the Grey Ghost's grip on the man, Minos would have fallen over in pain. "Stop it... you... idiot!" Minos snarled at the guard who inadvertently struck him, rage bleeding into the man's eyes.

Peering up at the large clock adoring City Hall, Minos smiled through his bloody lip. "Your city has five minutes left until the packages solidify," Minos said as the large hand on the clock moved closer to the hour. "You see my friendly specter, that mechanism in the basket you found is simply to activate the real transmitter that has been hanging over your head for over a week now you fool."

"And what if that signal is never given..." the Grey Ghost asked roughly dropping the villain to the ground to look up at the first celebration's orb hanging above their heads.

"It won't matter, even though it would've been delicious to see that crowd watch the balloon rise in the air as the altimeter in the basket signaled the explosion. I will sleep just as soundly if the backup timer on the transmitter does its job. One minute after 6:00...boom!" Minos laughed, looking up at the hero. "What? Did you think this was one of your American funny books where I would spill my entire plan to you so you had just enough time to stop it? Ha-ha, I just want you to understand how useless you are. Even with all of your skill and powers, even with all of your strength and cunning there is nothing you can do to stop the explosives from going off!"

"You're... right..." the Grey Ghost replied the weight of the situation falling on him.

Minos had outmaneuvered them. Once they found the transmitter in the basket of the hot air balloon, they assumed that preventing its flight would stop the signal from reaching the hidden explosives the Jeweled Kiss had placed around the city. However, it had only been for show. The Jeweled Kiss and now Minos had repeatedly told him there was nothing he or anyone could do to stop the explosives and they had both been right. Looking at the City Hall clock, the Grey Ghost knew there was little time left before the untouchable explosives would solidify and be signaled to decimate his beloved town. Thousands would perish just in the explosions alone even before the U-boats off shore landed and there wasn't anything he could do to stop them from exploding…. And then the one possible flaw in Minos's plan dawned on him.

"You are absolutely right… I can't stop the bombs…" the Grey Ghost said out loud looking at the gloating villain. *"How about I help them along then?"*

Before Minos could reply, the Grey Ghost spun and took off at breakneck speed toward the other side of the square. Looking ahead, the ghostly guardian saw the assembled crowd near the base of the Pathfinder Building, all unknowing pawns in Minos' plan, holding the distributed lit candles in vigil. The hero continued sprinting directly toward the obvious trap, his internal clock screaming at him that he had less than five minutes remaining and only a ghost of a chance of pulling this off.

CHAPTER THIRTY-TWO

Kate knew something was wrong. According to the Jeweled Kiss's notes, Minos and the Reich Hand had been planning this attack for months, maybe even years and all they had to do was stop this balloon from rising into the air to short circuit everything?

"It can't be this easy," Kate thought to herself looking at the three men sitting on the stage.

The engineer, following four of Capstone's finest that Robinson had vouched for, had gotten the drop on the security but it was just the way they gave up that bothered Kate. She had watched the men's eyes when they arrived and fighting back had never even crossed a single one of their minds. Their timid reactions had worried Kate into thinking they were completely wrong about Minos's plans, but there inside the balloon was exactly what she had thought would be there, a miniature transmitter attached to a steel frame in the basket. It was smaller than what Kate had originally estimated, but probably good enough to do the trick. She was, however, surprised to see an altimeter attached to the transmitter's wiring next to something she thought looked like a battery house.

"What do they need that extra battery casing for?" Kate questioned, just before she heard him coming.

"Get out of the way!"

Looking away from the destructive hot air balloon, Kate followed the stares of the crowd gathered around the balloon, some still holding the lit candles, to the sight of the Grey Ghost sprinting toward her and the balloon.

"Move! Move!" the ghostly guardian yelled at the crowd never slowing down, even ghosting through a few of the pedestrians farther up the square.

"Joe what are you doing? Don't come down here. We haven't gotten everyone to put out their candles yet," Kate thought, waving the Grey Ghost away, the hero heedless to her warning.

"Everyone please put out your candles!" the engineer desperately screamed at the crowd, which was starting to panic at the appearance of the alleged would-be assassin.

However, Kate had been too late. Still sprinting toward the crowd, the Grey Ghost finally was enveloped by the strange reaction the Spartan Cloak had to a lit candle. Before everyone's eyes the spirited avenger dropped, the form of Joe Bevine left too weak from the instant reaction of the burning candles to even hold himself up. The momentum of his run caused him to crash into a group of onlookers, with chaos erupting as bodies flew everywhere, the injured left to untangle themselves from the pile.

"I'm not going to make it!" Joe feared, struggling to pull himself from the mess, adrenaline the only thing allowing him to make it to his feet with his repaired prosthetic. Looking at the balloon area ahead, his eyes locked with Kate's, her eyes now reflecting the terror that was drawn across his face.

Seeing too many panicking bodies between him and his target, Joe knew his options and time had all but run out. *"I'm not going to be able to push past all of those people to get there in time!"*

Desperately looking for another option, Joe repeatedly came up empty as he quickly racked his brain over and over on a way to get to the balloon before they passed the point of no turn. The hero was on the brink of giving up hope when the most miraculous event unfolded before him; a drop of water hit his cheek! Another drop and then another until a steady spray of water was enveloping the crowd around him!

"It's raining?" Joe thought, flabbergasted seeing the lit candles all around him petering out as they and their owners became drenched in the now pouring precipitation.

As the power of the Grey Ghost started to return, Joe noticed the spray of water wasn't falling directly from above. Following the spray to its origin, the hero smiled just before the clouded Spartan mask returned, covering his face. There, stationed at the edge of the square just far enough from the effects of the crowd's candles, was the Jeweled Kiss who gave a quick nod to him. The dynamic thief had opened a city fire hydrant, angling its water directly into the crowd in front of Joe!

Seeing this as his last opportunity, the Grey Ghost pushed into the crazed crowd, becoming intangible so as to pass directly through everyone in front of him. Screams of both men and women followed the hero as he sprinted directly through the solid wall of soaked people blocking his way.

Unfortunately, the small triumph was short lived. Just as the Grey Ghost reached Kate and the stationed hot air balloon, the large clock back at City Hall struck it first chime.

"DING!"

"It's 6:00, no time for explanations…" the Grey Ghost thought to himself before he moved past Kate and jumped into the balloon's basket, firing the burners and sending a jet of hot air into the inflated balloon. Loosening the tie downs and releasing all of the weights attached to the basket with a thought of intangibility from the Spartan Cloak, the balloon launched itself into the air.

"DING!"

"What are you doing?" Kate screamed at the Grey Ghost as the balloon began to rise higher and higher into the air around the square.

"Trust me! And hold this for me until I get back down!" the Grey Ghost yelled to his love as he fired the burners causing the balloon to rise at near breakneck speed. As he did the ghostly guardian flipped a small package from his coat down to the engineer who caught it midair.

"DING!"

Looking down at the small black box, Kate immediately understood what it was.

"DING!"

Glancing back at the rising hero, Kate's senses were overcome with a as the world around her was bathed in a series of blinding flashes!

CHAPTER THIRTY-THREE

After what seemed like an eternity, the world slowly returned around Kate. Surprised to even be alive, the engineer, who had thrown herself to the ground desperately trying to shelter her eyes from the glaring explosions, stubbornly laid there too horrified to open her eyes at the sight awaiting her.

"*How were we so wrong? How could we have thought we had figured it all out?*" the engineer berated herself. "*We missed something, somewhere. Just like she told us, in the end it hadn't mattered, even with all of our plans. One way or another Minos had outwitted us and won.*"

As her fear began to dissipate, Kate finally relented to her curiosity and dared to open her eyes to take in the catastrophe around her. Trying her best to rub away the flashing dots flaring in her vision, Kate became more confused and disorientated as her mind screamed at her that what she was seeing simply didn't make sense.

There was no fire, no smoke rising beyond the buildings surrounding them, no sirens, nothing but a silent stillness as the crowd some rising themselves searched the area with shocked faces.

"*This just can't be right,*" Kate thought to herself refusing to believe her own eyes. "*There's no way that after all that there is just…nothing…*"

Seeing a two-story shop across the street from the Pathfinder Building, Kate ran to the downed ladder of the side fire escape. Scraping her hand on the rusted metal, Kate climbed the escape to the second story roof and scanned the visible square in bewildered shock.

"Everything is... fine..." Kate thought, baffled as she looked around the square.

But that wasn't where the miraculous mystery ended. No matter where she looked in the city from her elevated vantage point, there wasn't any evidence of destruction from the explosions. From her view, the entire city had somehow been spared from any devastation. None of the surrounding buildings showed any damage. There was no rubble, no smoke, or even distant cries of alarm. THERE WAS JUST NOTHING! She could even see Fulcher's Emporium a few blocks away, the place where the Jeweled Kiss had planted an explosive, the first one to be precise, and there it sat, even its large glass display window perfectly intact.

"Am I dead?" Kate thought in a confused daze as she climbed back down to street level, almost relieved to feel the pain from the scrape on her hand. *"Is this Heaven because none of this makes a lick of sense beyond that..."*

"Ms. Stone!" a voice called out to her from farther up the square. Looking in the direction of the voice, Kate saw Captain Robinson walking toward her, the City's mayor cuffed and in his custody stomping along in front of the triumphant officer.

"Captain!" Kate shouted. "What is going on? Have you heard anything from around the city?"

"Not yet. My officers are rounding up this man's henchmen back at City Hall," Captain Robinson answered. "I saw you climbing down from there. What did you see? I... honestly was sort of hoping you might be able to make sense of this. I mean well we lost... the explosions went off and not that I'm complaining but I expected to see the world falling apart around me when I opened my eyes and there is just... nothing..."

"I know what you mean," Kate replied "There isn't a sign of anything from what I saw up there. I mean it looks exactly the same as before. I saw people walking around dazed but seemly fine. None of it makes sense to me. I just don't know what happened!"

"Your hero happened," Minos grumbled blankly.

"What?" Captain Robinson asked pulling the politician to face him.

"Captain, please my shoulder," Minos winced nodding to the still healing wound he had received from the fake Grey Ghost earlier this week. "He found the one weak link in my plan that I hadn't foreseen. It does give me much delight, however, to see you two still don't understand what he did when he launched the balloon."

"But launching the balloon caused the explosions..." Kate started.

"Yes and at 6:00 pm on the nose those explosives were set to solidify..." Minos added.

"So he... Wait are you saying he triggered them early?" Kate added understanding. "I remember the clock on City Hall had only hit its fourth chime. The balloon was released early sending the ignition signal to the explosives before they solidified! They all exploded still out of phase without any solid force!

"Well at least one of you simpletons has the ability to figure things out for yourself," Minos grumbled.

"You made the Jeweled Kiss create the packaged bombs all intangible so we couldn't tamper with them, but in reality while they were like that they were already defused to the physical world," Kate smiled. "And since they exploded like that all of the bombs and all of your plans ended up being nothing more than just a lot of flashing lights, nothing more! That's why we didn't hear anything, not a single explosive sound! There wasn't anything in those bombs tangible enough to make contact with the air. No contact meaning no sound and therefore no pressure wave. That's why there isn't any damage!"

"Don't be too excited Ms. Stone," Minos snarled.

"BOOM!"

The distant explosion echoed from the direction of the docks pulling the crowd's attention, screams of fright ringing out with the gathered people's nerves already on edge.

"That, Mr. Mayor, IS the beautiful sound of freedom ringing as your tiny Navy was just introduced to a very solid surprise we left for them out at the bay," Captain Robinson smiled at the captured leader. "You really should keep track of all of the explosives you tried smuggling into my city. You just never know where they might end up."

"The lost shipment... well played Robinson, well played," Minos slightly nodded to the captain before straightening as much as he could in the man's grasp. "My dear Captain, Ms. Stone, I want you to take in this moment. I want you to enjoy this fleeting moment where you think you've stopped the Reich Hand, where you and your rag tag group can breathe easy thinking this city is safe and you're all going to head home tonight to your comfy beds."

"Oh get off it," Robinson barked. "You had your roll and came up snake eyes, Mr. Mayor or whatever your name is. The plans you've been terrorizing this city with for weeks ended up being all flash and no bang."

"Not all of them," Minos smiled back.

"What do you mean?" Kate asked, Minos' confidence starting to worry her.

"Allow me to key you two in on a little secret. The plan was never to reveal myself until this city was firmly in the Reich Hand's control. We never thought we could just march across the city and raise a flag, you simpletons. So with that in mind I ask you, do you think I would simply leave all of the evidence of what I did to your city floating above your heads?" Minos smiled looking at the two. "And this is the part where one of you turns out to be the smart one. Go ahead and take a second. I'm curious to see who gets it first."

Annoyed by the villain's arrogance, Kate felt her hand grip tightly around something in her right palm. Looking down, she realized she was still clutching the black box Joe had dropped to her before launching the balloon. Seeing that box was when it dawned on her. Kate suddenly remembered another box, the small battery house next to the altimeter in the balloon. There had been no reason for it to be there unless it was...

Seeing the realization dawning in her eyes, Minos cackled before adding, "That's my girl.... Go ahead, say goodbye to him for me..."

Turning away from the laughing villain Kate started to run as fast as she could toward the Pathfinder Building all the while screaming as loud as she could at the still rising inflatable.

"Joe! Joe! Get out of there! No Joe, NOOOOOOOO!!!!!!!"

But her frantic screams were stopped as she was violently knocked off her feet by a concussive wave from above her when the brightly lit hot air balloon holding the Grey Ghost erupted in a ***fiery explosion!!!!***

Nicholas Cara

HORROR OF HORRORS!!!

Can it be???

Our ghostly guardian,

THE GREY GHOST

BLOWN TO SMITHEREENS??

And what of Patsy, trapped in the catacombs under City Hall with the murderous Mr. Vega?

Is **THIS** the **GHASTLY END** for our Heroes? Has the Reich Hand finally prevailed???

FIND OUT the answers to **THIS** and **MORE** in the next thrilling adventure of
THE GREY GHOST!!!

"HOLD YOUR BREATH GREY-GHOSTERS, THE MOST EXPLOSIVE CHAPTER IS STILL YET TO COME!!!"

The Great Grey-Ghost Art Contest

Dear Readers,

Between 2015 and 2016, the Nicholas Cara Facebook page ran what was dubbed 'The Great Grey Ghost Art Contest'. This contest gave readers the opportunity to express their vision artistically of what our hero the Grey Ghost looked like from their experience of reading 'The Shadow that Walks'. The winning pieces of art (orginally only two planned) received their own autographed copies and have their artwork featured in the numerous newpaper scenes in 'The Jeweled Kiss Mysteries'.

The contest was also used as a vessel to raise both awareness and funds for the pediatric charity 'Connor's Cure'. 'Connor's Cure', which provides funds for pediatric brain and spinal cancer research, and medical care for children and their families, was created by Paul "HHH" Levesque and Stephanie McMahon of the *WWE* after meeting Connor Mason Michalek as described on the charities website.

Connor was just 4 years old when he was diagnosed with Medulloblastoma, a rare tumor that affects the brain and spinal cord. Connor endured an 8 hour surgery, hospitalization for months where he had to relearn how to walk and talk, 8 weeks of radiation, and 4 years of chemotherapy. His parents were told he would most likely have trouble speaking, would be socially awkward, and would have very little hand and eye coordination. He was also told he would only have 1 year to live.

Through the love of his parents and Children's Hospital of Pittsburgh, Connor persevered over this affliction. In fact, Connor became so talkative and engaging that he became a local celebrity including superstar treatment by both the Pittsburgh Pirates and the WWE. Connor also played baseball for 3 years. He hit the ball every time he was at bat, and always scored a run. Connor did what so many of us don't do, he truly lived. He lived for every moment. He was always loving and compassionate. And he let everyone know that his dad and his little brother Jackson were his best friends. WWE Superstar Daniel Bryan said it best, "If you talked to Connor, you couldn't help but fall in love with him." And so many people continue to fall in love with Connor every day when they hear his story.

Connor lost his battle to cancer when he was just 8 years old, but his message of light and love continue to thrive.

Throughout the year of the contest with the help numerous celebrities through social media such AMC's Comic Book Men, Ming Chen and Mike Zapcic, MeTV's horror host Svengoolie, Mark Hamill as well as local institutions in the Huntsville area such as 'The Deep Comics and Games' and the Dr. Who convention team of 'Con Kasterborous' getting the word out, the contest was an amazing success. We were able to gather submissions from all across the country that in turn raised hundreds of dollars for the 'Connor's Cure' charity.

Out of the numerous submissions, the following four (I just couldn't stop at two) winners were chosen. Thank you everyone that participated and helped make this event such a success.

You can find out more about the 'Connor's Cure' charity and how you can donate as well at:

https://www.givetochildrens.org/CONNORSCURE

~Nicholas Cara

Rich Koz is the multiple Emmy award winning writer, producer and 'Man in the Black Hat' on the MeTV Saturday night staple show Svengoolie. Working under the original Svengoolie Jerry G. Bishop, Rich later took over the mantle of the premiere horror show icon of Chicago in the 1970's. Since then, with the use of his unique scary sense of horror and hilarity, Rich has taken the show from a local favorite in the Chicago area to a nationwide following on the MeTV network every Saturday night.

Even with all of that on his plate, Rich graciously took the time to submit this hilarious sketch into the Great Grey Ghost Art Contest when he heard that it would helping the Connor's Cure Charity. You can learn more about the talented Rich Koz and where you can find the Svengoolie show at Svengoolie.com. Just keep your eyes peeled for any flying rubber chickens!

The Grey Ghost: The Jeweled Kiss Mysteries

Bradley Beard has taken the pop art world by storm over the past few years completing his masterful "13 Months of Horror", a self-imposed challenge in which he created 421 horror-themed pop art portraits in a 396 day period and presented them consecutively each day on his Facebook page. Even with that kind of schedule, the amazing artist found time to help in the Great Grey Ghost Charity Art Contest with this original and horrifying take on the Ghostly Guardian. This marvelous piece of art actually inspired the interaction between Joe and Patsy at Martensii's in the Jeweled Kiss Mysteries story the moment I laid eyes on it.

You can see parts of the "13 Months of Horror" and other amazing pieces of Bradley's at BradleyBeard.com and find his new clothing line at fearwhatyouwear.com

James Bridgewater has always found the combination of his two loves (reading and artwork) in the world of comic books fascinating. An avid collector, James works as a graphic designer for Connect Advertising in Northern California where he lives with his wife Paula and their two dogs. James' knowledge of vintage graphic novels inspired his take of the classic Captain America #1 cover with respect to our ghostly hero.

James did not wish to be photographed near his winning artwork, however he wanted to use a photograph of his friend and fellow Grey-Ghoster, Ruby, who sadly passed away recently. Ruby was a true friend to all those that knew her and an avid reader. I had the privilege to speak to Ruby once during a signing event and I remember discussing her love of a few of the novel's characters but especially the events in the first novel that had surrounded a true historical event that happened very near to her hometown outside of Seattle, WA.

The Grey Ghost: The Jeweled Kiss Mysteries

Kathy Marson would like to credit her two children Benjamin and Mark for finding the Grey Ghost novels. Their love of building Lego sets first drew her to the novels when she investigated a photo she came across featuring our novel's mascot 'Little Grey' on Facebook. Because of that she wanted to incorporate not only her take on the Grey Ghost, but also her vision of what 'Little Grey' would look like in battle. Kathy has a bachelor's in art history and is working on a degree in computer aided graphics.
You might have noticed that even though Kathy's submission was picked as one of the winners it does not appear in the novel. This is because after discussing it with Kathy, she has graciously allowed us to purchase the rights to her artwork for use as the next Grey Ghost T-shirt Sale. This sale will take place in the next few months and once again benefit a pediatric cancer research organization (the same the Great Grey Ghost Art Contest did). Look for more information on the sale at NicholasCara.com in the upcoming weeks.

Nicholas Cara

ABOUT THE AUTHOR

Nicholas Cara is a story teller. He's someone who has flown across the grandest canyons in a single bound, if you count the distance between his couches when he was little. Later on he remembers once almost single handily taming the Wild West on a white stallion, if only his Mom had remembered to bring more quarters after they went grocery shopping. He's a man who last year traveled to the peaks of the world's tallest and snowiest heights only to find out when he was finished stringing them up, he had never tested the Christmas lights on his garage to see if any of the bulbs were bad, some were... He is a man who has been to the White House... on a visitor's tour. He's a man who has amazed crowds by hitting eight lifetime hole in ones... at Putt-Putt, and a man who... well he can go on and on... because like he said... Nicholas Cara is a story teller.

He IS though someone who honestly believes you can do anything if you put your mind to it and hopes you do too.

Working in Huntsville, Alabama as an Aerospace Engineer for NASA, Nick lives with his beautiful wife Kimberly, their son Thomas, their dog Jackson, and one very brave goldfish.

He can't thank his wife, son, parents, sister and grandparents enough for always believing in him. With their help, he is living an adventure better than any tale ever put to paper.

You can continue to follow the amazing adventures of Nicholas Cara and the Grey Ghost on Facebook and at www.NicholasCara.com.

Made in the USA
Columbia, SC
24 October 2024

64f82768-4cd7-4dfa-b16a-2f4fb4c6823fR01